KEITH FINNEY

A NORFOLK MYSTERY

THE LAVENDER KILLER

VINCI

BOOKS

KEITH
FINNEY

A NORFOLK MYSTERY

THE
LAVENDER
KILLER

VIRCI
BOOKS

By Keith Finney

For Joan

Vinci Books

vinci-books.com

Published by Vinci Books Ltd in 2025

1

Copyright © 2024 by Keith Finney

A CIP catalogue record for this book is available from the British Library.
Paperback ISBN: 9781036700980

Chapter One

A DISCOVERY

ANT STANTON and Lyn Blackthorn strolled through the sun-dappled lanes of Stanton Parva, arm in arm, as they made their way to the Wherry Inn. The village was a picture-perfect scene of English country life. Georgian red-brick houses stood proudly alongside thatched cottages and Victorian mews houses. The picturesque surroundings added to the excitement of celebrating Lyn's birthday at their favourite pub.

'Can you believe it? Another year older,' Lyn sighed, her eyes twinkling as she squeezed Ant's arm affectionately.

'Age is a number, don't you think?' Ant replied with a warm, playful smile, 'and besides, you're like a fine wine—only getting better with age.'

Lyn laughed; her cheeks flushed with a rosy hue. 'You can stop with the cliches.'

As they approached the Wherry Inn, the sounds of laughter and chatter spilled out onto the streets. A welcoming atmosphere enveloped the couple as they stepped inside and met by familiar faces who wished Lyn well on her special day.

'Happy birthday, Lyn,' called out the cheery Janice, polishing a pint glass behind the counter as others raised their drinks in unison.

'Thank you, everyone,' Lyn responded, beaming at the show of camaraderie. 'It's great to see you all.'

Ant led Lyn to a corner table, where he had secretly arranged for a bouquet of her favourite flowers to await her arrival. She gasped with delight, taking in the fragrant scent of roses and lilies. 'Oh, Ant! These are beautiful!'

'Only the best for you, love,' Ant replied, his dark eyes shining with adoration.

As they settled into their seats, the village came alive around them. Neighbours gossiped, friends shared stories, and laughter filled the air. An unmistakable sense of community wrapped itself around Ant and Lyn like a warm embrace. This was the Stanton Parva the couple loved.

'Here's to another wonderful year,' Ant said, raising his glass in toast. 'Happy birthday, Lyn.'

'Thank you, Ant,' she replied softly, her eyes glistening with emotion. 'I couldn't ask for a better way to celebrate.'

Ant glanced up from his drink, catching sight of the Wherry Inn's owner as he emerged from the kitchen. Jed, a stocky man with a salt-and-pepper beard, ran a tight ship while keeping his pub a welcoming place, making it the heart of the village.

'Evening, Ant, Lyn,' Jed greeted them gruffly, but not without a hint of a smile. 'Happy birthday, young lady. How is the school treating you?'

'Thank you, Jed,' Lyn replied warmly, sipping her lemonade. 'The school's been wonderful. The children are really responding to the new curriculum.'

'Ah, that's grand.' Jed nodded approvingly. 'Education is important. Don't you forget that.' He gave her a wink before turning his attention to Ant. 'And what about you, lad? Is that Morgan of yours holding up?'

'Still leaking water, as always,' Ant confessed with a chuckle. 'But it wouldn't be the same without its quirks, would it?'

'True enough,' Jed agreed, clapping Ant on the shoulder before excusing himself to serve other customers.

As they resumed their conversation, a diminutive, black-clad figure approached their table. Her hat perched precariously atop her silver hair. It was Phyllis, the village gossip, who could never resist the opportunity to spread her own unique brand of news.

'Ant! Lyn!' she exclaimed, her voice a blend of delight and conspiratorial intrigue. 'I simply must tell you the latest. You won't believe what happened to poor Mrs. Green at the post office!'

'Hello, Phyllis,' Lyn greeted politely, exchanging a knowing glance with Ant. 'What news do you have for us?'

She looked around as if scanning for spies, then leaned into Lyn, grunting as she did so and holding a hand to her left. 'I'm a martyr to my hip. I am. Isn't that right, Betty?'

Her best friend, who towered over her vocal companion, began to formulate a response. She knew Phyllis had no intention of listening, so gave up.

'Well,' began Phyllis, lowering her voice to a dramatic whisper. 'Mrs. Green went to collect her pension, as she does every week. But this time, there was a mix-up. They accused her of trying to claim someone else's money.' She paused for effect, eyes wide with theatrical horror.

'Goodness!' Lyn feigned surprise, playing along. 'What happened next?'

'Apparently,' Phyllis continued, relishing the attention, 'It turns out Mrs. Green had picked up Mr. Thompson's glasses by mistake. They look so similar, you see. So, she couldn't read the forms properly! The whole thing got resolved in moments, but not before Mr. Thompson had threatened to call the police!'

'Ah, well, misunderstandings happen,' Ant chimed in, hoping to defuse the situation. 'I'm sure everyone involved got a laugh out of it afterward.'

'Perhaps,' Phyllis conceded, although her expression suggested she would've preferred a more scandalous outcome. 'Well, I must be off. More stories to uncover. You know how it is.' She gave them a conspiratorial wink and bustled away, leaving Ant and Lyn to share an amused eyeroll.

'Never a dull moment with her around,' Ant mused, taking another sip of his drink.

'Indeed,' Lyn agreed, smiling. 'But it wouldn't be Stanton Parva without a bit of excitement, would it?'

'Speaking of excitement,' said Betty, sidling up to Ant and Lyn with a warm smile. 'I understand you two have been busy solving another one of Stanton Parva's little mysteries.'

'Ah, Betty, ever the voice of reason in this village,' Ant chuckled. 'We do what we can, but let's not give Phyllis any more fuel for the fire.'

'True enough,' Betty agreed, her eyes twinkling mischievously. 'Though it would be nice to learn of some genuine news instead of her... tall tales.'

'Genuine news?' Lyn asked with a light laugh. 'Well, I suppose our upcoming wedding may count as that.'

'Indeed!' Betty grinned. 'I'm sure Phyllis will spin it into a thrilling tale of intrigue and romance. But seriously, I'm so happy for you both.'

'Thank you, Betty,' Lyn replied warmly.

At that moment, Fitch, Ant, and Lyn's best friend, burst through the door of the Wherry Inn, grease-stained overalls and all. 'Sorry I'm late!' he exclaimed. 'Had to finish fixing Old Man Jenkins' tractor. The man never learns that duct tape isn't a permanent solution.'

'Ah, Fitch, our resident mechanical genius. How goes the world of engines and oil?' Ant enquired, shaking his hand.

'Busy as ever,' Fitch said, grinning. 'You wouldn't believe the number of people who come in with their cars held together by hope and prayers. Speaking of which, Ant, when are you bringing your Morgan in for a tune-up? She's been sounding a bit off lately.'

'Has she?' Ant frowned, concern for his beloved vintage sports car evident in his expression. 'I hadn't noticed. I'll bring her in tomorrow.'

'See that you do,' Fitch advised, wagging a finger. 'You don't want her breaking down on you during your honey-moon, do you?'

'Definitely not,' Lyn agreed, shuddering at the thought.

'Alright, Fitch, that's enough car talk for one evening,' Sophie interjected, looping an arm around his waist, and planting a kiss on his cheek. 'Let's not bore everyone with our 'Little Oily Rag's' endless knowledge of engines.'

'Fair enough,' Fitch conceded, allowing himself to be led away by his girlfriend. 'But remember Ant, tomorrow!'

'Tomorrow, I promise,' Ant replied, raising his pint in a mock toast.

Lyn smiled as she watched their friends move off,

leaving her and Ant to enjoy the cozy atmosphere of the Wherry Inn.

Detective Inspector Peter Riley entered the Wherry Inn, causing everyone to stop talking. The locals fell quiet when they saw his short grey hair and serious expression, but Lyn didn't want to assume his visit was anything other than social. She noticed her heart skip a beat.

'Evening, everyone,' Peter said, waving to the room at large, before fixing his gaze on Lyn with a mischievous glint in his eye. 'Don't worry, folks. I'm not here on official business. Just came to arrest Lyn for the heinous crime of getting older.'

The tension in the room dissipated as quickly as it had formed, and laughter bubbled up around them. Ant chuckled, wrapping an arm around Lyn's waist. 'Well, she'd best behave then, hadn't she?'

'Indeed,' agreed Lyn, smiling up at Peter as he approached the pair. 'Though it's rather generous of you to let me off the hook just this once.'

'Ah, well, I suppose I can make an exception for today,' Peter conceded, taking a seat at their table. 'But only because it's your birthday.'

Lyn was fascinated by the way the candlelight played on the tables and stained-glass windows. It cast a warm, golden glow that enveloped the inhabitants of the Wherry Inn like a comforting embrace.

As she gazed around the pub, she looked at the faces of her neighbours, each one a testament to the powerful sense of community that pervaded their village. Old Mr. Higgins propped up the bar with his customary tankard of ale. Young Rosie, who'd just turned eighteen, perched herself on a stool beside her young man, sipping a glass of white wine.

'Alright,' Peter said, clapping his hands together. 'Now

that we've established that I'm not here to rain on your parade, what say we raise a toast? To Lyn. May your day be filled with laughter and good company.'

'Thank you, Peter,' Lyn replied, touched by his sentiment. Raised glasses, and the sound of clinking glass filled the air as the gathered friends and neighbours celebrated the birthday girl.

'Cheers,' Ant whispered in her ear, squeezing her hand beneath the table. She returned the gesture, even though there was an undercurrent of tension in the air whenever Peter walked into a room. He was a police officer. Tonight was about friendship.

And as the evening wore on, laughter filled the pub. Music spilled out onto the cobblestone streets beyond. Lyn realised she wouldn't trade this moment for anything in the world.

Jed came out from behind the bar with a huge birthday buffet after the toasts to Lyn's birthday ended. The aroma of warm sausage rolls, cheese, and onion quiches, and a variety of sandwiches filled the air, mingling with the earthy scent of mudded field-boots.

'Jed, this looks fantastic!' Lyn exclaimed; her eyes were wide at the array of food that now adorned the long wooden table.

'Only the best for our birthday girl,' Jed replied gruffly, though his eyes twinkled with pride at her reaction.

Ant guided Lyn towards the buffet, where they both loaded their plates with the delicious offerings. He sneaked a few extra cocktail sausages onto Lyn's plate, knowing they were her favourite. While enjoying the sumptuous feast, Ant took a hearty swig of his beloved Fen-Bodger Ale, savouring the rich, malty flavour and smooth texture. Lyn, however, opted for lemonade, as she had a visit from the education department of the local authority scheduled for the following morning. She needed to be alert and at her best for their inspection of the village primary school.

'Have you tried these bread rolls yet?' Ant asked, picking one up and giving it a curious sniff. 'They've got something inside them, but I can't tell what it is.'

'Ooh, mystery rolls,' Lyn teased, playfully flicking a stray crumb at him. 'You'll have to try one and report back.'

Before Ant took a bite, Phyllis swooped in like a bird of prey, interrupting their light-hearted banter. 'My great-niece makes the most marvellous stuffed bread rolls,' she began, not waiting for an invitation to join their conversation. 'She once won a prize at the Norfolk Show Ground for her cheese and bacon filled ones. They were a tremendous hit!'

'Really, Phyllis? Ant responded with feigned enthusiasm, secretly sharing an amused look with Lyn.

'Of course, I taught her everything she knows about baking,' Phyllis continued, puffing out her chest with pride. 'I've always had a knack for it, you see. I dare say these rolls here are nothing compared to hers.'

Lyn bit back a smile as she watched Phyllis attempt to monopolise the conversation, steering it firmly towards her own interests. She knew to count on the village gossip to provide some entertainment at any gathering. It seemed that Phyllis's love of attention would never wane, especially when she believed herself to be particularly close to Ant.

'Phyllis, your great-niece's rolls sound absolutely delight-ful,' Lyn interjected, trying to steer the conversation back to a more inclusive topic. 'But I must admit, Jed's bread rolls here are delicious as well. Don't you think?'

'Indeed,' Ant agreed, finally taking a bite of the myste-rious roll. 'It appears we have sun-dried tomato and onions in this one. An interesting flavour combination.'

'Ah, sun-dried tomato and...did you say onions?' Betty exclaimed. 'I remember when Jed first introduced those rolls at the village fete last summer. Everyone was, er, curious about-.'

'Speaking of the village fete,' Phyllis interjected, cutting across Betty. 'Did I ever tell you about my award-winning marmalade? It's all about the oranges, you see. You simply must use the finest—'

'Phyllis,' Ant interrupted gently, 'We've all listened to the story of your marmalade more times than we can count. We should give someone else a chance to share an anecdote?'

Lyn smiled gratefully at Ant and agreed as they spent the next hour mingling with friends and sharing stories from their youth.

'It's almost nine-thirty and it'll be dark soon. We promised each other a quick stroll before turning in. Do you think they'd mind?' Lyn scanned the room anxiously.

'We'll soon find out.'

Before Lyn had caught her breath, Ant called for everyone's attention by tapping a fork on the side of his empty pint glass.

'Ladies, gentlemen...and Fitch. Your attention, please.'

What's he going to say? thought Lyn.

'Lyn has suggested she and I take a turn about the village to stretch her legs. Now, at her age, it's of the utmost importance to keep those muscles moving to stop 'em seizing up. So, without further ado, we shall take our leave of you, so that Lyn's new healthy life routine may commence.'

A friendly roar went up at Lyn's expense, who stared knowingly at her fiance.

'Thanks for nothing,' Lyn giggled as Ant held the pub

door open for her, stepping into the warm night air from the Wherry Inn. The setting sun seemed to rise and fall behind the higgledy-piggledy roofscape of the village. Each appearance led the pair on to the ultimate destination as they walked together down the High Street. Once past the buttercross and last of the cottages, they reached a flat landscape leading down to Stanton Broad.

'Let's walk past the lavender fields,' Lyn suggested. 'There's something magical about them of an evening.'

'Good idea,' Ant replied, squeezing her hand affectionately. They strolled on, leaving behind the soft laughter and chatter from the pub.

As they approached the Manningham's lavender field, the unmistakable scent of the purple blooms filled the air. The fragrant flowers swayed gently in the lightest of breezes, creating an almost hypnotic effect against a reddening sky.

'Isn't it beautiful?' Lyn whispered, pausing at the edge of the field to take in the sight. Ant nodded, equally captivated by the scene before them.

'Certainly,' he murmured. 'Do you remember us doing this as kids?'

'I remember us nicking the odd bunch like all the other kids, if that's what you mean.'

'Passion killer,' chuckled Ant.

Lyn smiled, but as her gaze swept across the field, something caught her eye in the near distance. A chill ran down her spine as she squinted to get a clearer view.

'Ant,' she whispered, her voice suddenly tense. 'Do you see that?'

'See what?' Ant asked, concern furrowing his brow as he followed her gaze.

'Over there,' she pointed. 'There's something...not right.'

'Over there. Do you see it?'

Ant squinted, trying to make out what Lyn had spotted. The failing light made it difficult to distinguish anything beyond a vague shape.

'Maybe it's just an animal,' he suggested, attempting to dismiss Lyn's unease with a light-hearted tone. 'A deer or a badger, perhaps?'

Lyn shook her head, her eyes never leaving the spot. 'No, it's not that... I can't explain it, but —'

'Let's look?' Ant suggested, his curiosity piqued by Lyn's concern.

'Alright,' Lyn agreed hesitantly. 'Be careful.'

They cautiously approached the spot where Lyn had noticed the disturbance in the lavender.

'Something's definitely been here,' Ant commented, crouching down to examine the crushed flowers. 'Or someone.'

'Look, over there,' Lyn whispered, her voice barely audible. She pointed towards a shadowy figure, partially obscured by the tall lavender stems. The figure was bent forward on its knees, as if about to pick a bunch of the fragrant crop.

'Who could that be?' Ant wondered aloud, his voice betraying a hint of concern.

'Shh,' Lyn hissed, grabbing onto Ant's arm. 'They've heard us.'

'I'm not leaving until I find out who it is and what they're doing here. He's no kid pinching flowers for his mum. You wait here while I see what he's up to.'

Lyn watched as Ant made swift progress towards the stranger.

'Be careful,' she whispered.

'Hey, what are you doing? Who are you?'

Ant's attempt to startle the man and gain an advantage failed. Instead, the stranger remained still.

'Watch out. He may have a knife,' shouted Lyn, all pretence at stealth now abandoned.

She watched as Ant continued his speedy progress, lavender parting in a rhythmic wave as he forced his way through the lush crop.

'I said, who are you? What are—

Chapter Two

UNSEEN EYES

ANT AND LYN stood over the body; their faces etched with disbelief. The man lay hunched over in the middle of the lavender field, his limbs arranged in an unnatural pose beneath him.

'Perhaps he had a heart attack and...Boom?' Ant suggested, scratching his head as he tried to make sense of the scene. 'Or a stroke?'

Lyn frowned, her keen blue eyes scanning the man's face for any signs of injury. ' There's a neat wound between his shoulders. It looks like a bullet entry point. But how and why did he end up here? We both know everyone in the village, and we've never seen him before.'

'True,' Ant conceded, rubbing his chin thoughtfully.'

Lyn stepped closer to the body and pointed at the small round tear in the man's jacket. 'Blood. We need to call Peter.'

Detective Inspector Peter Riley was not only their close friend but also an experienced detective. He'd be able to help them figure out what had happened to the stranger.

'I'll give Peter a ring. It won't be the first time he's come across this sort of thing.'

Lyn nodded. 'Of course,' she replied, her eyes never leaving the man's lifeless form. 'We owe it to him, whoever he is, to find out how this happened.'

As Ant pulled out his mobile and dialled Peter's number, Lyn continued to study the body, her mind racing with questions.

Who was this man, and how had he met such a tragic end? What secrets lay hidden beneath the fragrant lavender blooms? And what would they discover as they delved deeper into the mystery of the stranger's death?

'Peter,' Ant said, his voice serious as he relayed the situation to their friend. 'We need your help. There's a body in the lavender field—Yes, the one at the end of Cowgate Drove. We don't know who he is or how he got here. He's been shot by the looks of things.'

Minutes after Ant's call, the distant sound of police sirens grew louder. A brief time later, Detective Inspector Peter Riley's familiar car pulled up at the edge of the lavender field. The driver's door opened, and Riley stepped out. His tall frame and short-cropped grey hair were immediately recognisable even in the failing light.

'Thank you for coming so quickly,' Lyn said, relief clear in her voice.

'And so here we are again. And on your birthday, too!' Riley replied, scanning the scene with a keen eye. 'Now, what have we got here?'

'He's just as we found him about twenty minutes ago,' Ant explained, gesturing to the lifeless body. 'We were just discussing how he may have met his end.'

Lyn added, 'And neither of us thinks he's a local.'

'Interesting,' Riley mused, approaching the body with

caution. 'No doubt about it. That's a bullet wound. Not much blood. All the damage will be inside the body. Poor bloke.'

Ant nodded, watching as Riley crouched down beside the body, examining the man carefully. His professional demeanour put them both at ease.

I'm glad I don't have the responsibility of sorting this mess out, thought Lyn.

'Look at the way he's positioned,' Lyn whispered, as if in church, her eyes filled with concern. 'It's so unnatural.'

'Remember what Peter said—no jumping to conclusions,' replied Ant. 'Let him do his job and see what he discovers.'

As they watched Riley work, Ant admired his friend's methodical approach to the investigation. It reminded him of his time working for military intelligence. He was confident that, if anyone might uncover the truth behind this mysterious death, it was Detective Inspector Peter Riley.

'Alright,' said Riley, standing up and looking at his friends. 'It's murder alright.'

Lyn gasped, her hand covering her mouth in shock. 'Oh, no.'

'Poor man,' added Ant.

Peter agreed, his eyes narrowing. 'But that's not all. I've found something interesting.'

He held up a small slip of folded paper, which he had discovered in the deceased man's jacket pocket. Unfolding it, Peter read aloud:

'Meet me in the centre of the lavender field at 4.00 pm exactly. Don't be late this time.'

'I tell you what, though. Whoever wrote this has a flair for posh writing,' Peter added.

'Heavens,' Lyn murmured, her concern for the victim

intensifying. 'That sounds like an order, not a request. What say you?'

'It certainly does,' added Ant. 'It was a meeting of equals. What time do you reckon he met his end, Peter?'

The detective glanced down at the body. 'Most likely within minutes of his arrival,' answered Peter, tucking the note into an evidence bag. 'This poor soul expected trouble, but not to die. What made him show up, I wonder?'

'We need to find out who this man was and why someone wanted him dead.'

'Absolutely,' Lyn agreed, her voice filled with shock.'

'Well, we'll need to wait for the post-mortem to confirm the cause of death, no matter what my view is just now. In the meantime, I'll have my scene-of-crime team examine the vicinity and body, and get this place cordoned off. The station will also check the missing person reports for anyone matching this chap's description.'

'Is there anything we can do?' Lyn asked, eager to assist in the investigation.

'Actually, yes,' Riley said, eyeing Ant and Lyn thought-fully. 'First, I'd like you to speak with the landowner. I bet he's a friend of your family?'

Ant reflected for a moment. 'I hadn't considered that, but yes, that would be old Thomas Whitaker. He leased the land to one of the local farmers for years to grow lavender. We'll pay him a visit and see if he knows anything about our unfortunate victim here.'

'Excellent,' Peter nodded. 'And while you're at it, try to find out more about the people connected to this lavender crop. There might be someone who's seen or heard something.'

'Understood,' Lyn said, her eyes scanning the crime scene meticulously. She carefully stepped around the body, making sure not to disturb any potential evidence. Her keen gaze took in every detail, from the crushed lavender stalks beneath the man's lifeless form to the disturbed earth near the toes of his scuffed shoes.

'Be cautious when speaking with the locals, though,' Peter warned. 'We don't want to cause panic or give Phyllis reason to spread any gossip before we have all the facts.'

'Of course, Peter,' Ant assured him. 'We'll be discreet.'

Ant felt a pang of sadness as they left, seeing the trampled lavender flowers at the crime scene. He stooped and gently picked up a single intact blossom, inhaling its soothing scent. It was a poignant reminder of the beauty that persisted amid the darkness that had befallen their quiet village.

'Come on, Ant,' Lyn said softly, touching his arm. 'Let's go talk to Thomas and see what we can find out.'

'Right,' Ant agreed, pocketing the lavender blossom as a symbol of hope. Together, they walked back towards the village to pick up Ant's vintage sports car.

As they walked together, the sun dipped below the horizon, casting long shadows across the lavender, seeming to merge earth and sky into a purple haze. The crime scene, illuminated softly, stood as a testament to the mystery in Stanton Parva. A mystery that Ant, Lyn, and Detective Inspector Peter Riley were determined to solve, despite the challenges ahead.

Peter continued his meticulous examination of the crime scene. He knew that every detail could be crucial to solving the puzzle they now faced—and he wasn't about to let anything slip through the cracks. He took a deep breath, steadying himself for the task ahead.

'Right', he muttered, 'let's see what we can find.'

Riley meticulously inspected the tragic scene, navigating

through the rows of crushed lavender plants. His instincts, honed over years of police work, guided him as he searched for even the smallest detail that might prove significant.

Ant and Lyn turned to watch their friend from a distance.

'Peter will be out there a while yet,' Lyn observed, her gaze never leaving the detective. 'Do you think he'll find anything?'

'Hard to say,' Ant replied, his own eyes scrutinising Riley's movements. 'But knowing him, if there's something to be found, he'll discover it.'

As they watched the detective surveying the scene, Lyn noticed the sound of a distant rumble. She looked up at the darkening sky and felt drops of rain splatter against her cheeks. 'We'd better hurry before we get soaked.'

'Good Idea,' Ant agreed, pulling his coat collar up around his neck.

'I've got a class of six-year-olds waiting for me in the morning. They're a handful on the best of days, let alone when I'm sleep-deprived and soggy.'

'Ah, the joys of teaching,' Ant teased, winking at her as they quickened their pace.

Detective Inspector Riley caught up with them, having raced to beat the oncoming squall, breathing heavy from running.

'I suggest we all meet back at the station in a couple of hours to discuss our findings.'

'In a couple of hours? That'll be midnight. I've got to work tomorrow, unless you're volunteering to run my school for me?' Lyn said.

Peter thought for a moment. 'On second thoughts, perhaps we'll catch up over your lunch break?'

'A wise choice,' replied Lyn, wearing a wide smile.

At the edge of the field nearest the village, the trio passed a scene-of-crime team. Four soaking individuals gave an official acknowledgement to their superior.

'Good luck. We need all the evidence you can find,' said Peter in an authoritative tone. 'I know you won't let me down.'

The team continued to trudge forward carrying an array of heavy equipment to complete their investigation.

'Pulling rank Peter?'

The detective allowed a half-grin to form. 'I've done my fair share of getting soaked when I was a young Bobby. It's their turn now.'

As the trio approached the detective's police car, he offered his fellow investigators a lift.

'Thanks Peter,' said Lyn, 'But we'll call off on Whitaker and get back home to dry out. By the time we get in your car and soak your seats, we could be at my place. Listen, we'll see you tomorrow, yes?'

Peter smiled as he pulled his collar up against the driving rain before disappearing into the car.

'Why did you say that?' asked Ant, as he blew droplets of water from the tip of his nose.

'Don't be such a baby,' replied Lyn as she stepped up her pace, leaving Ant for dust.

Ant and Lyn, now drenched from the rain, approached the Old Schoolhouse to seek refuge and gather their thoughts. As they neared the Wherry Inn, Ant's resolve for a pint of Fen Bodger pale ale got the better of his desire to dry out. 'Shall we? Ant said as he opened the door to allow Lyn through.

'It doesn't look as though I've got a choice, does it? You are a daft lump. OK, but just a quick one, or it'll be you taking morning assembly tomorrow, not me.'

The door creaked open, revealing a cosy, dimly lit room filled with the familiar faces of villagers seeking solace from the storm.

'Ah, the birthday girl's back. I won't ask what you two have been up to. A pint of Fen-Bodger is it, Ant. And what about you, Lyn? You're not still on the lemonade?' Jed's enquiry met with a raucous reception from the locals, who had been busy demolishing Lyn's birthday buffet.

'Too right about my pint, Jed,' said Ant, acknowledging their friendly reception.

'I am, because the inspectors are still coming tomorrow,' lamented Lyn as she shrugged her shoulders at their host.

As they settled into a corner table, the weight of the day's events seemed to bear down on them. Their laughter subsided, replaced by contemplative silence.

'Ant,' Lyn began hesitantly, her gaze fixed on the dancing flames of the freshly lit wood fire in its huge dog-grate. 'Do you think one of the villagers could have killed that chap?'

'Let's not jump to conclusions,' Ant replied, rubbing his temples. 'What is Peter always saying? Follow the evidence? No matter where it takes us.'

'Right,' Lyn sighed, taking a sip of the lemonade the young bartender had slipped onto the small round table. 'It's just hard to take in that the village is about to discover its peace is about to be shattered by such a terrible crime.'

'We don't even know if that's the case yet,' said Ant as a reminder to his fiance.

An uninvited guest interrupted their conversation as he slid into the seat next to Lyn. 'Evening, folks,' he said with an inscrutable grin. 'I hear there's been a commotion this evening.'

'Has there? And you would be?' Ant replied cautiously, eyeing the newcomer with suspicion.

The short, stocky man grinned again. 'My name. Forgive me. What must you be thinking? It's Simon Broadbent. As for what I'm doing here. Well, it's to help you.'

Lyn eyed the man from tip to toe. 'Why us? The pub is full of people?'

'Indeed it is,' said the man with an enigmatic smile. 'But only one person around here is Lord Stanton, who is engaged to the local headteacher. Am I correct?'

Ant's temper got the better of him. 'That'll do, fella. Time you were on your way.'

The man didn't move a muscle. 'No need to be like that, Lord Stanton. Oh, I forgot, your PTSD gets the better of you sometimes, does it not?'

Lyn sensed the stranger knew how to trigger Ant's condition. Instinctively, she placed her hand on his thigh to reassure him, and not rise to the bait. Lyn's tactic worked as she noticed her fiance relax back into his chair.

'Time to leave, Mr Broadbent,' said Ant in a calm tone. 'I don't care what you think has happened, or that we may know about it. It's best you pop into the police station. They'll be happy to take a statement from you. At least that's what I'm told.'

'Of course,' said the stranger, raising his hands in mock surrender. 'I'm just a curious bystander, like everyone else. Well, I'll leave you to your evening. Oh, I almost forgot. Happy birthday, Miss Blackthorn.'

Broadbent's parting gift was a sickly smile to Lyn as he vanished into the crowd of the packed pub.

'What a horrible man,' began Lyn. 'And he knows a lot about us two. Creepy or what?'

'That stuff is simple to find out. All he had to do was

sweet-talk a couple of villagers or check us out on social media. You can't keep your life out of the public eye, even if you wanted to.'

Lyn finished her glass of lemonade and spent several seconds twirling its accompanying slice of lemon around the bottom of the glass.

'The question is, was that bloke trying to see what we knew, or just playing with us?'

'What do you reckon?'

Ant acknowledged Fitch, their closest friend, who had just entered the pub on the far side of the building. Lost in the loud hubbub, he couldn't hear what Fitch was trying to say.

'Are you listening to me?' said Lyn, unaware of the mechanic's arrival.

'Of course I am. All we can do is tell Peter Riley when we meet him tomorrow, because as sure as eggs are eggs, that bloke isn't going anywhere near a police station.'

As the night wore on, Ant and Lyn couldn't help but scrutinise the other patrons in the pub. A woman of around 28 years of age caught their attention. She continuously whispered to a man older than her while occasionally glancing at the pair.

'Something's off about her,' Ant whispered. 'I can't put my finger on it, but we should keep an eye on that.'

'Are you sure it's not that she's caught your eye?'

'Hilarious,' replied Ant, making sure his fiance hadn't meant the remark too seriously. 'Anyway, let's call it a night before we suspect everyone in the pub. Don't you?'

'Hang on a minute. Now you've drawn my attention to her, I want to check she's OK.'

'Eh? I'm confused.'

'It's the way she's looking at the bloke she's with. Perhaps she wants to leave, but he's keeping her here. Oh, hang on, it looks like she's off to the ladies. I'll be back in a minute,' said Lyn, getting up and following the young woman before Ant had a chance to comment.

Several minutes passed until the two women re-emerged into the bar. Shortly after, Lyn returned to Ant as the young women re-took her bar stool and smiled at her companion.

'Can't be much wrong between those two. They're all over one another,' offered Ant.

'Well, yes…and no'

'Priceless, Lyn. Do I get an explanation? '

'The good news is that you're right. Those two are madly in love. The downside is that her relative is dead set against the chap. That's why she's been looking around the pub. Her other half has said he's not bothered and is intent on sticking around the village.'

'Not bothered about what?'

'I couldn't get that out of her, Ant. All she said was her family is, how did she put it…snobbish. It seems she tried to reason with the relative, but to no avail.'

'Do we know who this mysterious person is?

'She wouldn't say, but it's clear him or her holds a lot of influence over her. I did well to get her first name out of her. It's Wendy.'

Ant turned to look at the couple at the bar. The woman still looked nervous. 'Well, listen. We've got enough on our plate without you turning into an agony aunt. Come on, let's be off.

Exiting the Wherry Arms, they missed saying goodbye to Fitch amid the chaos. As they stepped onto the pavement, a man rushing past caused Lyn to lose her balance. Only Ant's quick thinking avoided his fiance from slamming against the white lime-washed wall of the pub.

'Hey,' shouted Ant, to catch the hurried man's attention. Within seconds, the fellow rounded a sharp turn into an alleyway and was out of sight.

'What's wrong with the village tonight?' said Lyn as she smoothed down her still damp clothes from their earlier adventure. 'We find a dead man. Then we're harassed by a bloke who knows us inside out. Now we get poleaxed by a man who apologises, but who couldn't look me in the eye?'

'It means it's time for some rest,' replied Ant, trying to cheer Lyn up with an affectionate smile. 'We can start fresh tomorrow. We have a long day ahead of us.'

As the pair sauntered up the High Street and past the village church, a figure watched from the shadows as the duo disappeared into the darkness.

Chapter Three

THE GENTLEMAN FARMER

'THE OLD SCHOOLHOUSE', Lyn's home, exuded charm with the scent of potpourri and the soft glow of sunlight seeping through lace curtains. Ant sat across from Lyn at her knife-scored pine kitchen table, his fingers tapping rhythmically on the wood as if keeping time to their thoughts.

'Peter thinks we could help him again,' Ant said, his dark eyes glinting with curiosity. 'But I don't want us diving head-first into another investigation without considering what it might mean for us.'

Lyn glanced around the cosy room, her keen mind already mulling over the possibilities. 'We're the ones who have always pushed him to be involved. What's different this time? We're up for the challenge again...Aren't we?'

'Are we,' Ant replied, leaning back in his chair, and rubbing his chin thoughtfully. 'Remember when we discovered who murdered Bert Bampton, the Miller? Then the time we helped Peter deal with that horrible Chief

Inspector who attempted to frame him for a murder his son had committed. We didn't hesitate.'

Lyn couldn't help worrying about Ant's hesitancy this time. 'Our knack for solving village mysteries has brought us together, don't you think?'

Her fiance traced the same shape repeatedly on the knot-filled table.

'Is that meant to be an eight, or infinity?'

He smiled without looking at her. 'Either way, there's no way to break the cycle. It just goes on, and on.' Lyn gently laid her hand over his finger to stop the tracing. '

'Are you saying we're getting into a rut?'

Ant covered her hand with his free hand. 'No, no. What we've helped Peter with is far too serious for that, I just...I dunno. Perhaps…what I mean is we should...'

'Set a date for our wedding and prepare seriously for our new life together?' Lyn said in a tender voice.

The pair exchanged loving glances. The only thing that disrupted the silence was the rhythmic ticking of an old clock.

'Am I really that shallow?' said Ant.

'It's nothing to do with being shallow. It's not wrong to think about our future. Heavens, Ant, it was only a couple of months ago I was accusing you of not wanting to marry me.'

Both broke eye contact at the memory of the Reverend Morton's kidnap and the tragedy that followed.

'It's taken us a while to get over that. Then again, perhaps we haven't? Is that the cause of you wanting to get a move on with things? We could get a special licence and be married in a registry office in a couple of days. I don't need a big ceremony. I can hire a dress and we can ask Fitch and Sophie to act as witnesses?'

'Attractive though the idea sounds, you're aware my family would go nuts. I couldn't do that to them. Can you imagine all my relatives dusting off their coronets and whatever they've not worn since Queen Elizabeth's coronation in 1953?'

The pair broke into a raucous laughter at the mental picture Ant had painted.

'It'd be like a scene from, what was that Ealing Comedy called? Oh, yes. Kind Hearts and Coronets.'

The interlude pulled Ant out of his former mood as he got up to flick the coffee percolator on. 'On reflection, our wedding can wait a few more months. That should give us time to help Peter one more time.'

'And set a date for the wedding so a family of dusty aristocrats can locate their finery, without resorting to the darker plotline of that old film.'

As the percolator made its distinctive bubbling sound, Ant grabbed two mugs from a wall cupboard and selected a spoon from the cutlery drawer. 'Let's just hope we stay out of trouble this time. We've had close calls before, and I doubt mum and dad would be too pleased at having to postpone our nuptials for a second time.'

Lyn nodded thoughtfully, recalling how they'd faced danger and uncertainty during past investigations. But somehow, those experiences had only deepened their bond and heightened their desire to be together.

'Peter Riley trusts our instincts, and I trust him,' Lyn reasoned. 'I say we lend a hand. What about you?'

'I can't disagree,' said Ant as he passed his fiance a mug of freshly brewed coffee. 'Besides, how can we resist the allure of another puzzling case?'

With their decision made, Ant and Lyn exchanged a determined look and clasped hands, ready to approach the mystery with caution. Little did they know, their instincts and curiosity would take them down a treacherous path, but also strengthen their love.

The conversation dwindled as the pair enjoyed their steaming beverage. Lyn surprised Ant by producing a cake tin from an open shelf under the sizable kitchen table. 'It's not mum and dad's, is it? You know how much they enjoy your Saturday visits and weekly cake.'

Lyn smiled. 'Of course not. It's just that I've been more organised that usual... that was until yesterday evening, of course. I made two. You can have a piece of the spare one.'

'I'll not argue with that,' replied a smiling Ant as he grabbed a slice from an old Huntley and Palmer's biscuit tin.

'If your mum saw you eating cake without a plate, she'd have your old nanny box your ears.'

The memory of Nanny Jane filled Ant with nostalgic thoughts. 'Wow, that brings some memories back. Every time I visit her at Rose Cottage, it's like stepping back almost thirty-years. She still calls me Master Anthony. I've never had the courage to address her as anything other than Nanny. Isn't that incredible?'

'Oh, I don't know,' replied Lyn. 'I called my maternal grandma, Nain.'

'Nain?'

'Her family originated from the North of Wales. That's the traditional form of address over there.'

'What about grandad?'

'Taid', Lyn replied.

'Well blow me, I never knew that,' replied Ant as he took another bite of his Victoria Sponge, dropping an avalanche of crumbs as he did so.

'Ah, well, Rydych chi'n dysgu rhywbeth newydd bob dydd.'

'Who's Bob?' Asked Ant in a curious tone.

'Silly. It's Welsh for; "You learn something new every day."'

'Have you any more cake?'

'I give up.'

Just then, Ant's mobile rang. Torn between fishing another piece of cake out of the tin and answering the phone, Lyn's raised eyebrows convinced him to take the call.

'Oh, hello, Peter. No, we've not forgotten. Yes... yes. Well, Lyn's off to school so, no, I'll be going on my own.'

'He sounded in a rush?' said Lyn.

'I'll say. He cut me off. Just wait until I see him.'

Ant took an extra big bite of his second piece of cake.

'Judging by the mood he's put you in, we'd better get on with things. Then get on with our day.'

He licked his fingers as Lyn put a side plate on the table, not willing to see yet more of Ant's detritus over her table.

'I suppose so. Back to business, it is. Let's go over why we think the victim was in the lavender field in the first place?'

'Perhaps he was lured there by the promise of something valuable,' Lyn mused, her fingers tapping lightly on the surface of the wooden table. 'Or maybe it was a secret rendezvous gone wrong?'

'Could be,' Ant agreed, his eyes fixed on his Victoria Sponge. 'But we can't rule out the possibility that he met someone there by chance—and an argument escalated to violence.'

'True,' Lyn conceded, her gaze drifting towards the window where the freed sunlight shone a bright light into the kitchen. She imagined the lush lavender fields beyond, now tainted with tragedy. 'Regardless, we need more information if we're going to make any headway. And then there's the note Peter found. Not to mention the odd characters we met in the pub. That bloke wasn't half slimy.'

'I tell you what. Why don't I nip back down the pub when it opens?'

'Any excuse for a pint of Fen Bodger, eh? Or are you hoping to catch sight of that young blond again?'

Ant looked hurt. 'As if. You can come with me?'

'Er, no. If it's a toss-up between Jed's singing and being prepped for the school inspectors, I know which one I prefer.'

'I agree,' Ant said, which elicited a wry smile from his fiance.

'And don't forget to pay a visit to Thomas Whitaker.'

'Peter made it abundantly clear, I do that today. Right then. I'd better get going. I hope the kids are good for you at school this morning.'

As he crossed the front door threshold and stepped outside into the crisp air, he turned to give Lyn a peck on the cheek. 'I'll tell you as soon as I have anything. See you in a couple of hours.'

Ant contemplated the various scenarios that might explain the victim's death as he drove back to Stanton Hall. Each theory spun a new web of questions and intrigue. He realised the case was about to become more complicated before they found any answers.

———

FRIDAY LUNCHTIME SAW a deterioration in the weather, causing Ant to clip the Morgan's soft-top into position.

After a fifteen-minute journey, Ant stood on the pub's

doorstep. His breath formed small clouds as he hesitated for a moment, bracing himself for the task ahead.

Stepping inside the Wherry Arms, Ant became immediately enveloped by the warm atmosphere of the pub. A low-ceilinged room filled with a mix of locals nursing pints, and a small group of tourists enjoying one of Jed's culinary delights. The landlord was polishing pint glasses behind the bar with practiced efficiency.

'Afternoon, Jed,' said Ant, leaning casually against the bar. 'Been any more talk about what happened last night?'

'What do you mean?' said Jed with a half-smile.

'Don't give me that. I bet you know more about the bloke in the field than I do by now.'

Jed raised a bushy eyebrow, pausing his polishing. 'Well, you're aware what a rumour factory the village is.' He glanced around the room, lowering his voice. 'But now you mention it, I overheard a young couple talking about a meeting they were supposed to have down the lane. I thought it a bit odd. He looked shifty, but the woman, well, it didn't look as though butter would melt. Yet she was the one doing most of the yapping.'

'Really? But they didn't mention the lavender field?' Ant tried to appear nonchalant, but his curiosity piqued. 'Did you catch any details?'

'Can't say I did,' Jed replied, resuming his glass-polishing. 'They seemed keen to keep their voices down. But they didn't look like your usual village folk—more like city types.'

'Interesting,' Ant mused, playing with his mobile. 'Thanks, Jed. Let's see what this lot knows.'

As he wandered from table to table, chatting with the regulars, Ant couldn't help but feel a growing sense of unease. Whatever had transpired in the field was connected to the mysterious strangers. But how? And why might they be involved?

'Excuse me, Anthony,' a whispering voice interrupted his thoughts. He turned to see Phyllis. 'I couldn't help but over-hear your conversation with Jed just now.'

'Ah, Phyllis,' Ant sighed, attempting a smile. 'Always at the heart of things. What can I do for you?'

'Well,' she began, her eyes darting left and right as if she were sharing a state secret. 'I may have overheard those same gentlemen discussing their meeting. They mentioned something about an arrangement—a deal of some sort. Oh, and I heard them say it was the lavender field where they were supposed to meet.'

'Really?' Ant's heart quickened at this new piece of information. 'Thank you, Phyllis. That's extremely helpful.'

After he'd spoken to several other regulars to corrobo-rate what Phyllis had said, he slipped out of the pub. His mind raced with possibilities. Who were the two gossiping strangers? And what kind of deal had they been planning to make in that fateful field? He knew he needed to share the information with Lyn and Peter—but first, he would pay a visit to Thomas Whitaker, as Peter had requested.

As Ant strode purposefully up the High Street, he felt a growing sense of urgency to unravel the mystery. Whatever dark secrets lay hidden in the depths of the lavender field; he was determined to bring them to light.

———

ANT'S VINTAGE Morgan sports car, which always leaked water from the soft-top, pulled up outside the village primary school just as the lunch bell rang. He saw Lyn coming out of the main entrance, her blonde hair dancing in the breeze, and a look of relief on her face after dealing with the school inspectors. There you are,' Ant called out, waving her over. 'I have news!'

'News?' Lyn asked, raising an eyebrow as she first inspected the passenger seat for damp patches, then stepped into the Morgan. 'I hope it'll end up being more productive than my morning's been.'

'That bad?'

'Don't ask. Anyway, go on, tell me what you've been up to.'

'Remember that mysterious meeting I told you about earlier this morning? Well, I've got a lead. We need to pay a visit to Thomas Whitaker.'

'But you'd already planned to do that, so what's new?'

'Let me fill you in on the way,' Ant said, revving the engine and pulling away from the school.

As they neared Whitaker's Georgian House, Ant shared what he had learned at the pub. She listened intently, her mind racing with possibilities. The wealthy gentleman farmer who owned a large amount of land to the west of the village was an intriguing character. They both wondered if he held any secrets of his own.

'Good afternoon, Mr. Whitaker,' Ant greeted the older man as they stepped inside the grand foyer of the house. 'Thank you for agreeing to see us at such short notice.'

'Of course, my boy,' Whitaker replied warmly, extending a hand to shake Ant's hand with a firm grip. 'And Miss Blackthorn, always a pleasure. Now, Anthony, how are your parents doing? I haven't seen them for ages. We used to have great fun attending balls at each other's houses and suchlike.'

'They're fine, Mr Whitaker. I will remember you to them.'

'Good, good. That's the spirit. Now, to what do I owe the pleasure?'

Whitaker showed his guests into an elegant sitting room with an ornate Adams fireplace and floor to ceiling bay window. The furnishings matched the splendour of the decoration. The trio chatted for twenty minutes about agriculture and the challenges of working the land, while enjoying their coffee served by the house staff. 'And I know your father will think the same, Anthony,' concluded the host as he wandered over to the bay window to view his pristine lawn. 'Now enough of me prattling on. What can I do to help?'

Ant half-turned in his Chesterfield button-backed chair to address Mr Whitaker directly. 'We're helping Detective Riley in an investigation.'

Lyn chipped in and explained about finding the body. 'We're hoping you could tell us more about the tenant farmer leasing the lavender field from you.'

'Ah, yes. Terrible business, that.' Whitaker sighed. 'The tenant you're asking about is a man by the name of Gavin Holloway. Bit of a chancer if I'm honest. He's always looking for the next get-rich-quick scheme, rather than focusing on the demanding work required to maintain the land properly.'

'That's interesting,' Ant mused, making a mental note of the name. 'Has he held the lease for long?' Asked Ant.

'Him personally? No. His father—an honourable and hardworking man, leased the farm from my family for forty-years. Sadly, he's no longer with us. His son applied to take over the lease and, of course, I agreed.'

'Have there been problems then?' asked Lyn.

Whitaker turned away from the window. 'No. He's a keen young chap. About Anthony's age, I'd say. It's just, well, as I mentioned before, his head is filled with fanciful ideas that he never seems to see through. Meanwhile, the farm buildings are paying the price.'

After a short interval, when Ant and Lyn worked hard to dig into the working relationship between Whitaker and the leaseholder, Gavin Holloway, Ant drew the conversation to a close.

'Thank you for the information, Mr. Whitaker. We shall see what he has to say for himself.'

With that, Ant and Lyn excused themselves and made their way back to the lavender field, the sun now high in the sky, casting short shadows across the landscape. The scent of the flowers hung heavy in the air as they began combing through the rows of purple blooms. Their aim was to search for any additional clues or evidence that may have been overlooked.

'Ant!' Lyn suddenly exclaimed, pointing to something glinting in the sunlight. It was a small silver key.

'Here, take my handkerchief.' He held out a square of cotton fabric containing a monogram in one corner.

Lyn gave the item a sideways glance.

'It's clean, if that's what you're worried about.'

'Hmm, if you say so.'

Lyn crouched down and used the white fabric to rescue the shiny object.

'A key,' intoned Ant. 'It's pristine, and you found it on the surface. That means it can't have been here long.'

'Perhaps it belonged to the dead man?'

'Or whoever met him,' replied Ant. 'Either way, we need to show this to Peter right away.'

As the pair decamped the field, neither noticed the figure lurking at the edge of the treeline. He observed them intently. A shadowy presence who seemed deeply interested in what they were doing.

'Ah, there you are!' Riley called out as he opened the door to his small office at the police station. 'Have you anything for me?'

As they settled into their chairs, the pair briefed the detective on their meeting with Whitaker. Lyn then produced Ant's neatly folded handkerchief. 'We found something we think you should look at.'

'Really?' Riley raised an eyebrow, suddenly intrigued. 'Show me.'

'Here,' Lyn said, unwrapping the fabric to reveal the small silver key. 'We found this several yards from where the body was discovered.'

'Interesting,' Riley murmured, taking the swaddled key from Lyn. 'It's clean. Looks like a house key. I'll have my team examine it to see what this little gem can tell us.'

'I wonder if it might be connected to the meeting I heard about?' Ant wondered aloud, his eyes narrowing with thought. 'It's all feeling rather premeditated, wouldn't you say?'

'Meeting?'

As Ant briefed the detective about what he'd been told by Jed, owner of the Wherry Arms, he fixed his gaze on the silvery object.

'Oh, I see, you think they were discussing events leading to the man's death? We need to find out more about those two and the identity of the person our victim met.'

'We'll keep digging around. Gavin Holloway can hopefully fill a few gaps for us. We'll keep you informed of the outcome.'

'Good,' Riley said. 'I know I can count on the two of you.

Ant, Lyn, and Riley exchanged a determined look.

Back at the lavender field, a figure shuffled around the area where the body had been found. The man was tall and lean, with a weathered face that held secrets as old as the village itself. His eyes were dark and unreadable, betraying no hint of emotion as he scoured the area for something.

The air around the man crackled with tension, as though even nature itself sensed the brewing storm.

Chapter Four

A MISTAKE

ANT AND LYN sat on a wooden bench beneath an ancient oak tree in the village's heart. The leaves above them rustled gently in the breeze, casting dappled shadows onto the worn seat. They shared a packet of Sherbert Lemons Lyn had bought on a school trip she'd supervised to Sandringham, the King's Norfolk home.

'Ant, we can't do this on our own. It's too complicated,' Lyn said, her eyes earnest as she looked at him. 'We need help to crack this case.'

'Hmm,' Ant replied, as he fought to release a Sherbert Lemon from a gap in his teeth. 'What about Fitch and Sophie? We've roped them in before, even if Fitch moans like a bull with a sore head.'

'He does, but Sophie always brings him around. I tell you what, why don't I ask this time? He won't stand a chance. And will you stop pulling that silly face. How many times have I told you to get that loose filling fixed?'

The taste of citrus and sugar exploded on Ant's tongue as he finally freed the Sherbert Lemon from his teeth.

Lyn reached out to touch Ant's hand gently, her fingers brushing against his skin as she urged him to stop tugging at his cheek.

'I suppose you're right,' mumbled Ant as he looked with anticipation at the white paper bag Lyn held in her lap.

'You're agreeing with me about the dentist?'

'Not on your Nellie,' said Ant as he extended a hand towards the boiled sweets. 'I mean about Fitch and his better half. Why don't you have a chat to her while I nip to see Gavin Holloway?'

Lyn shook her head as she snatched the bag of sweets away from her fiance. 'Don't even think about it until you've got that tooth fixed. As for seeing Sophie, OK, that sounds like a plan.'

As she stood, Ant winced and let out a cry. 'By the...'

'No need to swear. Just get it fixed. The chemist will have something you can pack it with, but if you don't arrange an appointment with the dentist, I will.'

Ant allowed his puppy-dog eyes to do the talking for him.

'You are a baby. Come on, let's get on with things.'

Recognising his plea for sympathy had failed, he gave up. 'I tell you what, bring them to the lavender field in about an hour. Let's see what they come up with,' said Ant as he attempted to curry favour.

'That's better. Keep it up and the tooth fairy might pay you a visit after all.'

———

ANT KNOCKED FIRMLY on the door of Gavin Holloway's farmhouse, its dour brown paint chipping and peeling from the woodwork. He stood fidgeting nervously with the cuff of his jacket. Apart from an angry dog barking in the distance, no other signs of life stirred within the dilapidated dwelling.

'Who's there?' shouted a voice from inside, sounding as if it belonged to a man who enjoyed his own company. The door creaked open, revealing Gavin's scowling face. His untamed, mousy hair framed a pair of narrowed, suspicious eyes.

'Ah, Gavin, afternoon'. Ant greeted him with a warm smile that didn't reach his eyes. 'I wondered if I might have a quick word with you about the recent events in the village.'

'Events?' Gavin snorted, crossing his arms defensively. 'I know what you're on about, posh boy. You think I had something to do with that bloke you found in my field? You and the schoolteacher were trespassing. You know that don't you?'

'Not until we saw noticed a body we weren't. Anyway, what do you expect we should have done, leave him there?'

Gavin narrowed his eyes again, scrutinising his unwelcome visitor. 'Alright, fine,' he grumbled, opening the door wider and gesturing for Ant to enter. 'But make it quick.'

Ant stepped into the cottage. He surveyed the dimly lit room, cluttered with bric-a-brac, and which carried an underlying scent of damp. He looked up at a lone lightbulb illuminating an aged ceiling with bumps and flaking paint.

'Where were you on the night we found the body, Gavin?' Ant asked, trying to keep any accusation out of his tone.

'None of your business,' Gavin snapped, his face turning a shade of purple reminiscent of the crop he grew for a living. 'I don't see why I should tell you anything.'

'The fact is, you don't, Gavin. Would you rather the police came poking about and take a formal statement from you instead?'

'Fine,' he muttered, finally relenting. 'I was at home, alone, all night. Now, if you don't mind, I want you out.'

Ant engaged his host's eyeline. 'Do you get many visitors?'

'What do you think?' snorted Gavin. 'I don't need anyone. People mean trouble.'

'We all need other people, don't we? For example, you must sell your crop to someone?'

Gavin's scowl returned. 'What's that supposed to mean? That's my business, anyway.'

Ant smiled. 'For now, but don't you think the police will ask the same question? Look, I've not come to accuse you of anything. Let me help you. The murder investigation isn't going away, you know.'

Gavin's demeanour changed. 'Murder? Who mentioned murder?'

Ant watched as Gavin nervously played with the string bow holding his rough cotton trousers up. 'People never help. They just try to rip me off. I bet you're no different.'

The man's stare penetrated Ant's soul, as if wanting to see something different than he usually experienced.

'The truth is just now, people think you are a chancer, I—'

'Who says that?'

'It doesn't matter. The fact is that's what people say. That will get back to the police. Trust me and I'll make sure they hear about our meeting and get them to understand your circumstances. That's got to be better than them forming ideas about you from the rumour-mill, hasn't it?'

It didn't take long for Gavin to weigh his distrust of Ant against the alternative. 'All Right. I'm not convinced, but I'll give it a go. What do you want from me?'

Ant sensed the tension in the room abating. 'For now, nothing. I just want to be able to call on you and ask about this and that - and know you'll tell me the truth.'

Gavin looked at a crust of bread on the scruffy table next to him, picked up and sniffed the greyish food, then tossed it back onto the table where it landed like a stone on concrete. 'I suppose so,' he mumbled.

'Then we have a deal. I'll be off now. Look, here's my mobile number if you need to get in touch. Otherwise, I'll see you around when I've anything to share with you, OK?'

Ant handed over a scrap of paper he'd found in his pocket, in which he'd jotted his mobile number. 'Thank you for your time, Gavin. I'll be on my way.'

As he exited the cottage and drove the short distance from the farmhouse to the lavender field, he mulled over what had just happened.

Well, that went far better than I expected. Let's hope he keeps his word.

As he pulled onto the verge just short of a muddy layby at the bottom of the lavender field, he noticed a vehicle in his rear-view mirror.

That's good timing.

Nudging the Morgan sports car further onto the verge, Ant took care to stay clear of the deep drainage ditch that skirted the field.

Within seconds, Fitch's clattering Land Rover pulled up behind the Morgan, and rattled to a stop.

'Perfect timing, eh?' Ant said as he slid out of his car and approach the Land Rover. Inside sat Fitch behind the wheel, with Lyn and Sophie scrunched together on a narrow bench seat to his left side.

The four friends stood at the edge of the field, taking in the scene before them. The vibrant purple blooms stretched out endlessly, swaying gently in the breeze and filling the air with their soothing fragrance. It was a stark contrast to the muddy layby just beyond them.

'I thought we might start with the layby,' Ant said as he encouraged the others to walk the few yards to the rutted surface of widening in the narrow road.

'Why here?' asked Fitch, straightening up his tall frame from being hunched in the Land Rover.

'Remember I told you we think the dead man arranged to meet someone in the field? Well, it looks like he came on foot, or at least the police haven't found his car, but that the other person parked here.'

'Any reason for thinking that?' asked Sophie.

'To be honest, no,' replied Lyn. 'It's just that nothing else occurred to us and we thought it worth looking into.'

Fitch fixated on something to his front. 'Fair enough. What about those tyre marks?'

He walked a few feet and crouched down to examine the tracks more closely without stepping into the caked mud or touching anything.

'Any idea what kind of car might have made these tracks?' Lyn asked, her eyes following her friend's every move.

Fitch knelt beside the marks, his eyes narrowing as he meticulously examined every detail. Ant and Lyn watched intently, trying to gauge their friend's thoughts, while Sophie snapped images from various angles on her mobile.

'Interesting,' Fitch mused aloud, tracing a finger just

above the grooves. 'These tracks have a unique pattern-almost like a fingerprint.'

'Can you tell what kind of car made them?' Ant asked, his curiosity piqued.

Fitch shook his head slowly. 'Not yet. But the depth suggests it was a heavy vehicle, possibly a four-wheel drive.' He glanced up at the others.

'Really?' Lyn's heart raced at the prospect. 'You think these tracks might belong to the murderer's car?'

'Perhaps,' Fitch replied cautiously, not wanting to get their hopes up.

As they traced the path of the tyre marks, Fitch continued to share his observations. 'Notice how the spacing between the tracks is consistent? The driver must have maintained a fixed line. If they were in a hurry or trying to escape, I'd expect a more erratic pattern.'

'True,' Lyn thought aloud, her mind racing with possibilities. 'Could that mean the murderer wasn't worried about being caught?'

'Or perhaps they were just careful not to make a noise by roaring away from the scene.'

'Either way,' Fitch said, examining a deep imprint, 'they didn't think we'd be checking.'

The camaraderie between the four friends was palpable as they continued their investigation.

'Hang on,' Fitch said, crouching down again. 'To misquote The Spice Girls song, Two Becomes Four.'

'Spice Girls? What are you talking about?' Ant said in a confused tone.

Fitch looked up at his friend, 'You remember... Oh, you don't, of course. If I remember correctly, Vaughn Williams is more to your taste, isn't it?'

'I like the Spice Girls,' said Sophie, doing an imitation of one of the bands dance routines.

'Yes, yes,' Ant said. 'The tracks?'

'I was wrong, they don't belong to a modern car at all.'

'What do you mean?' Lyn asked, puzzled.

'The pattern is distinct. Just like the old Jaguar cars used.

'Go on,' Lyn urged, her heart pounding with anticipation.

'Late '60s, I'd say. That would make it a Series 1 Jag,' Fitch said, running his fingers along the indentations.

'Really?' Sophie chimed in, trying to hide her amusement. 'I knew my little oily rag was an expert.'

'Never mind that now,' Ant said, patting his friend on the back.

Fitch rubbed his chin. 'They're big old cars, that's for sure.'

'Big enough to transport something,' Sophie added, a note of unease creeping into her voice.

'Like a body?' Lyn whispered, shuddering involuntarily.

'Let's not jump to conclusions,' Ant cautioned. 'We need to gather more evidence before we can let Peter Riley in on what we think, or he'll think we've all gone daft.'

'Right,' Ant declared, 'We should investigate recent vehicle thefts or sales. If the car's stolen, it could give us a lead on the culprit.'

'Or if it was sold, perhaps the seller knows something about the buyer,' Fitch chimed in, rubbing his chin thoughtfully.

'Good idea,' Sophie agreed. 'But don't forget about checking nearby garages or repair shops – they might have seen it recently.'

Fitch looked uncomfortable, concerned that in their enthusiasm they'd gone too far. 'Hang on a minute, think about how long it would take even four of us to check up on that lot. You two are going to have to tell Peter Riley what we've found and let his team do the leg work. Besides, if we get even more heavy rain, those tracks are going to vanish.'

Fitch's assessment brought the group back to the realities of the case as they exchanged deflated looks.

'Fitch is right,' declared Lyn. 'This is police work. But I tell you what we can check out, there's a garage type thing near what's left of Legget piggery. It's hidden away, so it could be an ideal place for someone trying to avoid attention.'

'Hilltop Garage? The one run by old Bert?' Fitch asked, suddenly grinning. 'He's a bit of a character, isn't he? The last time I spoke to him, he spent half an hour telling me about his pet chicken, Gregory. He even showed me a photo of them together at his workbench.'

The group laughed, the moment of levity providing a welcome break from the seriousness of their work.

'Alright,' Ant said, wiping a tear of laughter from his eye. 'We've got some solid leads to follow up on. Let's split up and cover more ground. Lyn and I will head to the garage and chat with Bert. Then we'll let Peter know what we've discovered. I suggest you two ask around the local garage trade about any strangers they've had in enquiring about van or van repairs.'

'I'm up for that,' Lyn agreed, giving Ant's hand a supportive squeeze.

'We'll start fresh tomorrow. Let's meet at the tea shop at what, mid-day to catch up on things,' Lyn suggested. 'And don't forget, whoever arrives last has to treat the rest of us.'

———

THE FOLLOWING MORNING, Ant awoke to the sound of birdsong filtering through the gap in the bedroom curtains. He stretched lazily and glanced over at the clock, reasoning since it was Saturday, he could have a lie in. That was until he remembered it wasn't a normal weekend at all and that a busy day lay ahead.

Let's hope we get to the truth, Ant thought as he made his way down to the breakfast room of Stanton Hall.

'Morning, Son. I thought you might miss breakfast. David was about to clear the buffet table.'

The young butler busied himself tossing the kedgeree between two silver forks.

After winking at David, the butler, and filling his plate, Ant strode over to a large mahogany dining table, one end of which had been laid for three breakfast places.

'Mum's not come down yet, then?' Ant said as he looked at an unused table setting.

'Your Mum is having a lie in,' said the Earl of Stanton as he gathered the last of his sausage, ready to finish his meal.

'Is she OK?'

'Just sleepy, that's all. And what about you? What have you been up to?'

Ant spent the next ten minutes telling his father all about the investigation.

'No wonder we've not seen so much of you these last few days. Talking of which, I'd better get on. I've a meeting with our Land Agent. I'm sure it's nothing, but he says we've had someone lurking about Lark Wood. Some of the staff says he just stands there, watching them.'

'That's a bit odd, don't you think?' Ant said.

'As I say, it may all be quite innocent, but I'll do the rounds and see what's going on. Remember me to Lyn, won't you. Will we see your young lady today?'

Ant smiled at his father. 'If you mean is the cake baked. Yes, it is. She'll be over later. Anyway, have a good morning. I won't be far behind you. Lyn and I have an appointment with old Bert at his garage.'

The earl wore a surprised expression. 'Bert? So, he's still alive! Well, what do you know, he was tinkering with old bangers when I was a young man. Heaven knows how he's kept going all these years, he was hopeless when it came to remembering to charge his customers. He didn't seem the slightest bit interested in money.'

Ant smiled at his father. 'Well, it doesn't seem to have done him any harm, does it?'

With that, the earl waved at his son and disappeared through an open doorway.

A CRISP BREEZE swept through Stanton Parva as Ant and Lyn made their way to Bert's garage. Although sunny, there was an edge to the crisp air, so much so that the soft top of the Morgan remained firmly in place.

As they pulled up outside the part-hidden garage, the smell of bacon, mixed with engine oil filled the air, mingling with the earthy scent of the surrounding countryside. Ant sauntered through the open workshop door to see Bert frying bacon in a black-stained frying pan on top of a pot-belly stove.

'Hello, you two, what can I do for you? Fancy a bit of back-bacon, I've plenty?' He asked in a grandfatherly way, his bushy eyebrows stressing his weather-worn cheeks and cheery face.

'Morning, Bert,' Ant greeted him. 'That look so good, but no thanks, we've eaten.'

'Speak for yourself,' Lyn said. 'I haven't got a cook to prepare breakfast and a butler to serve it. Yes, please, Bert, I'll have a couple of rashers.'

Bert's smile widened. 'Good, let's get some local goodness into you, and help yourself to bread and dripping.'

'Dripping? I haven't had that since I was a little girl,' Lyn said as she coated two pieces of bread with the thick substance.

As the pair tucked into their snack, Ant admired the range of old tools lining Bert's workspace. 'I bet some of these could tell a few stories.'

Bert laughed, spitting bits of bread and bacon over his bushy grey beard. 'Some of those are my father's and still do the job. I'm eighty-two now, so they'll see me out. With no kids to leave 'em to, I suppose they'll end up in a skip, or at some car boot sale being flogged for fifty-pence a time.'

Ant shook his head. 'That's an awful thought, Bert. I tell you what, whenever you decide to retire, I'll buy the lot. I'll give you a fair price. We can't let this sort of history scatter to the four winds. There's local history on those walls.'

Bert let out a belly laugh at the thought of retiring. 'The only way I'm going out of here is feet first, young Anthony. I tell you what though. If you're serious, I'll make sure the lot come to you when I pop-me-clogs. What about that? Just one condition.'

'That's enormously generous. Thank you so much. But what's the condition?'

Bert bellowed again, this time sharing even more of food debris with his visitors. 'You tell me why the two of you have come all this way to watch a doddery old bloke eating bacon?'

'That's put you in your place,' Lyn said. 'The thing is, Bert, we're trying to find someone who might have brought a van in for repair or tried to buy one from a local garage. I don't suppose——.'

'Not me, lass. I've done all the buying, repairing, and selling I'm going to do. It's too much bother. All I do now is tinker with my own stuff, sorry. It's sounds serious. Anything to do with that scallywag, Gavin's place?'

Lyn nodded, her disappointment plain to see. 'Ah well, it was worth a try, and the bacon made the trip worth it, anyway.'

Bert gave Lyn a sympathetic smile. 'Is that the only thing you've got to follow up on?'

Lyn felt for her mobile. Well, there's this, but Fitch has already cracked which vehicle made the tyre marks.'

Bert craned his neck to get a better view of the photo.

'Ah, well, I can certainly look,' the elderly man replied, curiosity piqued.

Bert scrutinised the photos before commenting. 'Fitch has done well. I agree with the lad, they're from a series one Jaguar XJ6, late sixties or early seventies. Funnily enough, I saw one the other day. There aren't many left. They're collector's items now.'

Ant and Lyn exchanged excited looks. 'Are you sure? said Ant.'

Bert nodded. 'Dunlop made a special tyre for the Series One. If you know what you're looking for, you can't mistake them.'

'Thank you, Bert. You've given us a lot to think about.'

'Happy to help,' Bert said as he turned back to his workbench and offered Gregory, his pet chicken, a titbit of bacon.

'Amazing,' commented Lyn.

'He's not fussy. If it's food, he'll have it.'

After a light-hearted chat about how to keep chickens

happy, the pair said their goodbyes and climbed back into the Morgan.

As they left the garage, Ant felt the weight of expectation settling on his shoulders. The investigation was proving to be far more complex than they'd initially expected, and they couldn't afford any more mistakes. They needed to find the Jaguar and its driver.

Chapter Five

AN UNFRIENDLY WELCOME

THE SUN CAST short mid-day shadows on the ancient village of Stanton Parva as Ant and Lyn sat outside Sandra's tearoom. They sipped coffee while discussing their plan with tea-drinking Detective Inspector Peter Riley.

'Right,' Ant began. 'We were supposed to meet up with Fitch and Sophie, but he's been called to a recovery job on the A47, and she's gone with him.'

'Not to worry,' Riley replied, swirling the leaf-tea in his half-filled China cup. 'They can update us later. What have you two unearthed so far?'

Lyn leaned forward, eager to brief their close friend. 'Well, we've identified a couple of villagers who might know something about the murder. We thought we'd split up and talk to them, get a feel for what was going on around here before... well, you know. Also, Fitch thinks he's identified the type of car we think parked in the layby by the lavender field on the day of the murder.'

'Hang on,' Peter said, looking uneasy. 'How can you be

sure how old the tyre marks are, or the make of car? Be careful you don't get too carried away with apparent clues.'

'I know what you mean,' Ant replied. 'But Old Bert agrees with Fitch that the tracks belong to an ancient Jaguar. As for the age of the tracks, well, we don't know how old they are, but—.'

'But nothing,' interjected Peter. 'You can't make assumptions like that about in a murder investigation. Think of the resources we could waste following up a guess.' He could see his response had deflated his two friends. 'I tell you what, I'll get a forensic team out there. They'll work their magic cross-referencing the weather over the last few days with the condition of the tracks. I suspect they will also compare the depth of the pattern with the soil conditions to work out the approximate weight of the vehicle that made them.'

Riley's comments did the trick in raising Ant and Lyn's mood.

'You're a corker,' Lyn said.

'Aren't I?' Peter replied with a huge smile.

'Thanks, Peter,' Lyn said in a cheerful tone.

Several moments of amiable chat passed as the trio emptied their drinks and finished off a selection of pastries.

As Peter sat his cup back into its saucer, the detective returned to business. 'And what about the villagers you mentioned?'

'Most of it came from Phyillis.' Lyn watched as the detective shifted uncomfortably in his chair.

'I know, I know. She can be, er, eccentric. But she's always got her antennae out for the strange, the unusual, or outright salacious.'

'And as for our intelligence,' added Ant. 'You know what the Wherry Arms is like. Most of the lads will sell their favourite aunt for a free pint. Fermented hops loosen the tongue, don't they?'

'Well, yes. I suppose so, but—' Peter started.

'Come on, you old cynic. What's to lose by us having a quick word? We'll soon pick up if there's any substance to what they have to say for themselves. Then we'll update you. You can then decide what comes next.'

'Hmm, you'd be good at selling cars, or double glazing, or anything else I don't think I need.'

Peter picked up the last fragment of his pastry between a finger and thumb. 'Go on, then. And don't go too far. I know you two.'

'If we didn't know you better, I'd swear that was a rebuke,' Lyn said with a mischievous smile.

Peter narrowed his eyes in mock-scrutiny. 'I'd love to come with you, but I've got the head of forensics coming over to brief me from Wymondham. Their report into the death is ready. Let's hope they've identified additional evidence we can use. And yes. Before you ask, I'll brief him on the tyre marks Fitch identified.'

The detective watched as the couple made their way down the cobblestone high street. After checking the time on his mobile, he settled the bill and sauntered up a gentle incline back to the police station.

'Alright,' Ant said, pulling a small notepad from his pocket. 'I'll talk to Bryony Jenkins at the florist's shop. She might have seen something unusual.'

'That's a good idea,' Lyn said. 'I'll head over to the bakery. Kevin always has his ear to the ground and might have heard something on his delivery rounds.'

'Perfect,' Ant nodded, looking over his shoulder as he crossed the narrow street. 'We'll meet at the buttercross in an hour.'

Ant entered the small, fragrant florist's shop, the scent of roses and lilies enveloping him as he approached the counter. Bryony Jenkins, a petite woman in her sixties with a talent for all things green, greeted him with a warm smile.

'Hello, Anthony! What can I do for you today? Need a spray of flowers for your lovely fiancé?'

'Hello, Bryony,' Ant replied, his dark eyes twinkling mischievously. 'Sorry, I'm here to ask you about something. We're trying to find out if anyone saw a stranger lurking about on either Wednesday or Thursday?'

'Ah, you're working with Peter Riley again, are you? The police should pay you two, don't you think? You put a lot of time in to help them.'

'Oh, dear. That makes the village sound like a crime hot spot, doesn't it?' Ant replied with a friendly grin.

Bryony busied herself making up a spray of blooms on the countertop as she chatted away. A thought suddenly entered her head. Stopping mid-stream as she began cutting a piece of floral wire, she gave her visitor a serious glance.

'Well, now that you mention it, I saw someone near the lavender field the other day.'

'Really?' Ant leaned in. 'Can you recall which day?'

Bryony looked to the low ceiling as if seeking inspiration. 'Wednesday. No, wait. Now was it Wednesday, I wonder?'

Ant hung on to every word, hoping the florist might remember which day she meant.

'Now I remember, because Mrs Fletcher came in to complain about some flowers she bought from me had wilted. Some people are silly, you know. Well, I told her that—'

'The day, Bryony. It is important.'

Bryony momentarily closed her eyes, as if resetting her

thoughts. 'Listen to me. What an old gossip I am. Now, let me think. Yes. It was Thursday. About four o'clock. 'I remember the time because,' The woman paused. 'Oh, there I go again.'

This time, Ant became eager to hear more. 'Go on, Bryony. Why do you remember the time so clearly?'

The florist unexpectedly vanished from sight as she ducked under the counter. Just as quickly, she popped up again, placed a large green planting sponge on the counter, and pointed to it.

Ant gave the misshapen object a perplexed glance, which he then transferred to Bryony.

'Do you not see?' Bryony said in an exasperated tone. 'He ran over it.'

'Who did?'

'The man in the field, I mean.'

'Which man? Sorry. I'm a little confused.'

'He knocked me off my bike. He did. Good job it's one of those old Co-op delivery bikes with the metal basket frame on the front. The only thing was, it was full of flowers for a customer, so I had to carry the sponge under my arm. And that's when it happened.'

'When what happened?'

Bryony returned Ant's confused stare. 'I've told you. A great lump of a man appeared from the lavender field and knocked me off my bike. It all happened so fast. Just look at the bruise on my shin. Well, a woman of my age, that'll take ages to go down.'

The florist rolled up a wide fitting trouser leg. Ant feigned glancing at the injury. Ant averted his gaze.

'What a dreadful experience for you. Have you seen Doctor Thorndike about it?'

'Doctors? Haven't been to one for twenty-five years, so I'm not going to start now. Anyway, butter is the best thing.'

'Butter?'

'For bumps and bruises. That's what my mother always said.'

'Does it work?'

'To be truthful, it's a bit sticky. My stockings make it smear. Never mind, mum swore by it and that's good enough for me.'

Ant thought for a moment. That's a mental picture that'll take some shifting.

'Did you get a look at the ruffian?'

'Of course,' she said, recalling the details. 'A small, chubby man with scruffy brown hair and unkempt clothing. I only glimpsed him, but it was enough.'

Ant scratched the centre of his forehead while he formed his last question. 'Why didn't you go to the police once you heard what happened the next day?'

Bryony shrugged her shoulders as she picked up the thin wire again and recommenced work on her latest order. 'I visited my sister in Lowestoft on Thursday evening and stayed overnight. When I got back, I had some orders to get out. When Phyllis came in and told me, I thought it was another of her tall tales.'

'So,' Ant said, prompting Bryony to continue.

'So, I assumed the police would do the rounds to see if anyone heard or saw anything. Except you came first.'

'Sort of makes sense, I suppose', Ant thought.

'Well, thank you, Bryony. You've been incredibly helpful,' Ant said, scribbling notes on his pad. 'If you remember anything else, please let me, or Peter Riley, know.'

'Will do,' she replied, patting his hand gently. 'You two be careful now. We want no more tragedy in the village.'

As he left the sweet-smelling premises, a thought stopped him in his tracks. Bryony has just described the victim. Was he trying to flee his attacker when he knocked her off her bike? Ant thought.

Meanwhile, Lyn stepped into the warmth of Kevin Thompson's bakery, the smell of fresh bread and pastries filling her senses. The baker, a slightly built, short man in his mid-fifties and always covered in a fine layer of flour, greeted her with a hearty smile.

'Hello, Lyn! Here for a tasty treat or two, I hope?'

Lyn surveyed the fayre, selecting a wholemeal loaf and a baker's dozen of seeded buns. 'Can you put them aside for me? I'll pick them up later.'

The baker smiled, pleased to make a sale, no matter what the value. 'Of course. I'll make sure they stay nice and fresh for you.'

He gave Lyn a sideways glance. 'Something tells me the bread and buns were not your reason for calling in today. Am I correct?'

Lyn offered Kevin a weak smile. 'To be truthful, I want to ask you about recent events in the lavender field,' Lyn replied, her voice soft and engaging.

Kevin smiled and raised his eyebrows. 'She will be the undoing of me. I told her in the strictest of confidence.'

'Who?'

His smile broadened. 'I suppose I should have known, but she bought an extra loaf and half-a-dozen iced fancies.'

Lyn shook her head in a light-hearted response. 'Ah, I guess you mean—'

'No need for a name, is there? I was doing my deliveries and overheard an argument between two men near the bottom of the field on the day it happened. You know, in the layby.'

'An argument?' Lyn asked, her heart racing. 'Could you make out what they were saying?'

'Not much, I'm afraid,' he admitted. 'But it wasn't just banter. Raised voices, pointing of fingers. That sort of thing.'

Just then, her mobile rang. She saw from the display that Ant's name illuminated. Deciding to reject the call, she pressed the red button and turned back to the baker.

'Is that Anthony checking up on you?'

She could feel her cheeks reddening.

'Something like that. Anyway, what time was it you came across the two men?' Lyn said, relieved to have moved the conversation on.

Kevin took out a small notebook from the chest pocket of his pristine white work-coat. 'Now, let me see,' He flicked from page to page until he came across one entry in particular. 'I thought so. Yes.'

The baker thought for a moment. 'Funnily enough, it was the afternoon. You see, I always do my deliveries first thing in the morning. Well, you know that, don't you? Anyway, the day before yesterday, I had a special order for a customer, so I closed up for half an hour and took it over. It must have been about 3.30 when I drove past the layby.'

Lyn's face lit up. 'That could be so helpful to the police. You might just have seen the murderer.'

'Oh, don't say that, Lyn. I'd hate to think I could have stopped what happened later that day.'

Lyn shook her head. 'Not at all, Kevin. You may have just helped the police get closer to whoever did that horrible thing. By the way, did you get a look at the car?'

Kevin shook his head. 'No, other than it was an old one, you know, a sort of vintage. You see, I was too busy watching the two blokes. They were a bit like Laural and

Hardy, except the other way around. I don't mean funny. Hmm, I'm not explaining this very well. It's just that one was small, chubby, and needed a new suit, while the other was tall and dapper, if you know what I mean? but...'

'But what, Kevin?'

The baker looked anywhere but at Lyn. 'Well, perhaps I'm going bonkers, but the tall one looked a bit like Ian Williams.'

Lyn sidled up to Kevin and gave him a friendly peck on the cheek.

'What is that for?' said the baker in a surprised tone as his cheeks flushed.

'Kevin, you do not know how useful that is...but why haven't you told the police?'

The baker became suddenly serious. 'Am I in trouble, then? You see, I get up so early in the mornings to bake the day's stock. Then I'm in the shop all day. When I'm finished, all I want to do is go home to bed.'

Lyn offered a comforting smile. 'No, you're not. I'll let Inspector Riley know what you've said. I suppose we all take you for granted, don't we? We just expect our bread to turn up, without making the connection that you've been up since who knows what time baking.'

Her thoughtfulness only made Kevin blush even more. 'I don't mind. It's been a good little business and I'm lucky I still have enough loyal customers to keep me going. Most villages have lost their baker, as you know.'

'And we'll keep supporting you, so you've no worries on that score. That said, I'd better be off. I'm meeting Ant soon, and I don't want to be late. He'll never let me hear the last of it if I am.'

'Give my regards to Anthony, will you?'

'I will, and thanks again for the info. Kevin.'

As the church clock struck noon, Ant and Lyn arrived at the buttercross within two minutes of each other. As the pair exchanged findings, they found it hard to contain their excitement. The information gleaned from their interviews pointed to a clear timeline. And information about the physical characteristics of the two men involved.

As their animated discussion continued, a familiar figure approached.

'I thought I'd find you two here,' Fitch said.

'That didn't take you long. I thought the recovery job would keep you out of trouble for hours. More to the point, was is the Jaguar we're looking for?' Ant said in jest.

'May be. A Jaguar, yes, but is it the one we want? I don't know yet. The traffic police wanted it shifting quickly. It was a straight breakdown, no casualties, but you know how quickly traffic backs up on that stretch of the '47. To save time, I just winched it on the back of the truck and brought it back to the garage. Sophie's in the office, so it'll be safe until we can take a proper look at it.'

'I was joking,' said Ant, with his eyes wide open. 'You don't mean to tell me you picked up a Jag.?'

'Coincidence, or what?' replied Fitch with a wry smile.

'What about the driver?' Lyn said.

'That's the strange thing. They'd vanished, leaving the car unlocked. The police said they'd check out who owned the car, so I guess Peter can tell you the results of the search.'

Ant nodded. 'Strange about the driver. If we can confirm the car's tyres match the tracks you discovered in the layby, it's game on. We also unearthed some intriguing information. Bryony Jenkins noticed a suspicious man near the lavender fields, and Kevin Thompson heard an argument between two men close by. He thinks he recognised one of them as Ian Williams.'

'Seems like we have our work cut out for us,' Lyn remarked, her brow furrowing as she considered their next steps.

'It certainly does,' agreed Fitch. 'But where do we start?'

The trio stared at each other before Ant thought of an idea. 'We've got to talk with Ian Williams.'

'He's a right hothead. Do you think we can manage him?' Lyn said.

'Well, we all know he likes to put himself about, so the chances are he might know something of interest. That's if he's prepared to behave and talk without hitting out,' said Ant. 'I'll give Peter a ring to brief him and see if he wants to join us.'

———

'HERE WE ARE,' Ant whispered as they neared Ian Williams' messy thatched cottage. The ivy-covered walls and an overgrown garden made the plot look out of place in the beautiful countryside. The air was heavy with tension as Detective Riley led the way up a brick-weave path covered in a thick, velvety moss that made walking hazardous.

As he knocked firmly on the door, Ant couldn't help but notice Lyn's hand resting reassuringly on his arm. Her concern for the potentially volatile situation was all too apparent. 'Remember,' she whispered, 'we're just here to do some research. Don't let him get under your skin.'

The door creaked open, revealing a tall, clean-shaven man with a wild look in his eyes. 'A copper, eh? What do you want?' Ian growled, his voice low and menacing.

'Good afternoon, Mr. Williams,' Peter began, his tone professional yet friendly. 'My name is—'

'I know who you are. I see you've brought protection with you. Much good they'll do you; a schoolteacher and a toff.' Ian Williams sniffed the air exaggeratedly to show disdain towards his uninvited guests.

Peter ignored the homeowner's taunts. 'We were hoping to have a chat with you about the unfortunate incident in the lavender fields earlier this week.'

Ian's eyes narrowed, his gaze darting back and forth between the trio. 'Always use ten words when one does the job, you lot. Murder is what you mean, so say it. Anyway, I know nothing about that,' he spat, attempting to close the door.

'Wait!' Ant interjected, holding out a hand. 'We've heard some rumours about arguments taking place near the crime scene, and we thought you might shed some light on the subject.'

'Rumours? Is that what I am now, gossip fodder for the village busybodies?' Williams huffed, crossing his arms defensively. 'Fine, have it your way. Come in and make it quick. I've got stuff to do.'

Lyn observed clues to Ian's tumultuous past in the cluttered living room. She felt a shiver run down her spine as she imagined the rage that must have caused such destruction.

'Mr. Williams,' Peter began, 'Can you please tell us where you were on the day of the murder?'

'I'm a suspect now, am I?'

'Not at all.'

'Then it's none of your business,' Williams snapped, his face reddening with rage.

'Let me rephrase that for you, Mr Willimas. As you

eloquently opined earlier, the police must say what they mean.'

'What you on about copper?' Can't even use plain English. You've been around that toff for too long.'

Lyn sensed Ant tense. She leaned into him and cupped his fisted hand with her own.

'Please, Ian,' Lyn implored, her voice gentle but firm. 'We're only trying to help. If you could just provide a clear alibi, we'll be able to rule you out of the investigation.'

'Alibi?' Williams scoffed, his agitation growing. 'Why should I have to prove anything to you meddling busybodies?'

'Look,' Ant said, trying to maintain a level tone. 'We understand you must be fed up with getting the blame for things you haven't done. Well, why not put a stop to the same thing happening now?'

Peter butted in. 'Is there anything you can tell us about an argument near the lavender fields? It might help us find the real perpetrator.'

'Get out!' Williams roared, his patience finally snapping. 'I've had enough of you lot. If you haven't got a warrant, get out of my house before I throw you out.'

Peter remained calm throughout the altercation. 'Very well, Mr. Williams,' nodding to Ant and Lyn as they made their way back towards the door. 'Thank you for your time. I'm sure that if you don't visit the police station when you've calmed down, we'll pay you the courtesy of paying you another call. Do I make myself clear?'

Williams said nothing. Instead, he held the front door wide open and emitted a throaty growl as his three guests stepped back onto the moss-covered path.

Ant couldn't shake the feeling that Williams' tantrum

had cost them an opportunity. What secrets was he hiding, and how far would he go to protect them?

'Come on,' Lyn murmured, squeezing Ant's hand as they followed Detective Riley back to his car. 'We'll find another way to sort this out. We always do.'

'Right,' sighed Peter as they reached the police car. 'It's clear that Williams isn't interested in cooperating. His behaviour was certainly... well, odd.'

'Odd indeed,' Lyn agreed. 'He practically chased us out of his house. He must be hiding something.' She glanced at Ant, who seemed lost in thought. His eyes focused on the distant lavender fields.

'Ant?' she prompted gently, squeezing his hand.

'Sorry, I was just thinking about what we've learned so far,' he said, shaking himself back to the present. 'Bryony's sighting of the suspicious man and Kevin overhearing an argument. Peter, why didn't you tell Ian we have a sighting in the field that day?'

The detective smiled. 'It doesn't do to lay all your cards on the table at once. I know that's a terrible cliché, but it'll do him no harm to sweat a little. If he was the man seen arguing, he'll make a move eventually, now that he knows the police are interested in him. I'll be watching and waiting.'

'What now, then?' said Lyn.

'Well,' Peter said, drumming his fingers against the steering wheel as he slipped the car into first gear and gently let the clutch out. 'Let's revisit the crime scene and see if we've missed anything.'

'Let's do it,' Lyn agreed, brushing a stray lock of her blonde hair behind her ear.

As they neared the lavender field, the lingering scent of the flowers permeated the still air transfixed them.

Within minutes, they stood knee deep in a sea of purple. A menagerie of wildlife buzzed about the blooms, each taking only what it needed from the crop of dazzling flowers.

Suddenly, Lyn froze.

'What's the matter?' Asked Ant.

Lyn felt a shiver run down her spine. 'Have you ever felt as if you're being watched?'

She looked around. Silence, other than the sound of the field gate slamming shut.

'Have you seen something?' Ant said as Peter ran towards the field entrance to see if he could discover why the spring-loaded gate slammed shut.

'What is it, Lyn?' asked Ant, concerned for his fiance.

She gave him a hug. 'Oh, I'm being daft, but I'm sure I saw Broadbent, you know, the one who—'

'Yes, I know who you mean. The question is, what's he doing here, and why was he watching us?

Chapter Six

QUESTIONS, QUESTIONS

AS ANT PULLED up to Stanton Hall, the gravel crunched beneath the wheels of his sports car. Lyn glanced at him and smiled.

'I'm glad you've put seeing that Broadbent fella behind you. We'll catch up with him, don't you worry. One thing's for sure. Let's not let him spoil a cracking meal with mum and dad.'

Lyn nodded, 'Absolutely.'

As they passed through the ornate entrance doors to the great house, the grand hall shimmered under the dancing crystals of an elegant chandelier.

Lyn carefully balanced her weekly confection, a delicious combination of frosting, sponge, and filling.

'Another successful cake delivery,' she said cheerfully, as they entered the morning room carrying Lyn's weekly confection.

'They'll love it, as usual,' agreed Ant. 'And just in time for dinner. Let's go and find them. I expect they're in the drawing room having pre-dinner drinks.'

'Ah, there you are, my dears,' the countess said with a warm expression.

The banter continued for several minutes while they moved through to the Jacobean dining room and took their assigned seats. Meanwhile, David, the butler, fussed around making sure everything was at hand.

While enjoying a delicious meal, Ant's parents eagerly asked about their son and his fiance's latest case.

'Any leads on why this poor soul met his tragic end?' asked the Earl.

'Let them get their feet under the table. As always, you are too forward.'

The earl took the gentle reprimand in good spirits, born out of a lifetime loving partnership with his wife. 'My bad...er, isn't that what the young ones say these days?'

His three companions shared a look of amusement.

'It's not an expression we use, but well done for trying to move with the times, Dad,' Ant said as he winked at his mother.

'To answer your question, we're still following up leads. It seems like it could be one of three motives: a settling of scores, a business deal gone wrong-perhaps over land, or some kind of unpaid debt.'

'Then there's the matter of the key,' Lyn responded.

'Key? a key to what?' asked the countess.

Ant and Lyn exchanged earnest looks.

'Actually, you've touched on an excellent point. You see, we found a pristine key next to the site of the attack. It strikes me that the murderer may have set the police a riddle?'

'Ah, I see,' said the earl. 'You mean the reprobate is suggesting both individuals are linked in some way, and that if you can find that link, the riddle of why they did it in the first place will be solved?'

As David served the first course of liver pate served with French bread and onion bacon jam, the conversation continued.

'The rascal sounds a little too confident for my liking,' said the countess.

'I've come across such types during my time in the army. Such people are clever, intelligent. Eventually, however, they all make a silly mistake and pay the price.'

'Do you miss it at all, son?'

The earl's reference to a career that led to Ant suffering with PTSD brought the conversation to a halt. The countess, and Lyn played aimlessly with their food, not wanting to catch Ant's eye.

'That's a strange thing to ask, Dad?'

His father attempted to brush the issue aside. 'No reason, Anthony. Simply the ramblings of an old man. It's just that you mentioned the army. I assumed you'd been thinking about your service.'

Ant took the time to spread a knife tip of pate onto a piece of French bread, which gave him time to think of a response.

'If you're asking why the army keep me on leave of absence, rather than discharging me on medical grounds, yes, I do. But you know as well as I do that because of the intelligence work I undertook they'll never let go of me completely.'

A loud clinking sound rang out as Lyn dropped her cutlery onto her bone China dining plate. 'You don't seriously mean you'd consider another tour, do you? Remember what it's done to you. We all live with the consequences, Ant. It's not just about you.'

All conversation ceased as the tension within the room reached a crescendo.

The earl placed his napkin on the table and stood. He looked each of his companions in turn before speaking. 'I want to apologise to you all. I did not intend that my enquiry should cause pain or discomfort to anyone, not least to the three closest and most dearly loved people I have in the world. Anthony, please forgive me for my impertinence.'

Lyn remained tense as she waited for her fiance to respond.

At length, Ant placed his uneaten bred onto his plate. 'There's nothing to forgive, Dad. I know you always mean well and haven't an impertinent bone in your body. You're correct in one sense. Of course, I think about my service sometimes. The thing is, I try to remember the good bits, not that other stuff that drags me down.' He turned to Lyn. 'I'm all too aware of the effect my illness has on you all. All I can do is to promise you I'll keep working at getting better, so no, my darling, I have no intention of becoming operational again. If the army are content to keep paying me for doing nothing, I'll take the money. At some point they'll realise I'm of no further use to them, and I can be trusted to keep my word as far the Official Secrets Act is concerned.'

'Bravo,' said the countess. 'I expect no less from you. Now, shall we finish our first course before David and Chef resign for us ruining their carefully laid plans for the evening?'

The intervention broke the tension as gossip became the order of the day as the butler waiting patiently by the dumb waiter, having given the signal to chef to send up the mains.

'You mentioned a deal gone wrong as a plausible reason for the unpleasantness that's gone on in the village,' said the earl. 'I bet you didn't know we owned land around that lavender field for hundreds of years. If I remember correctly, your grandfather told me once that we sold it to Thomas Whitaker's family.'

Lyn smiled, which countered Ant's surprised expression. 'I should have known the family owned the land at some point. Is there anything in and around Stanton Parva your ancestors haven't owned around here?'

The earl looked to his wife. 'Not much, now you come to mention it.'

In fact,' added the earl, 'I've one of the old ledgers in the library. I'll just—'

'You'll do no such thing, husband. David, please serve the next course while the Earl of Stanton still has the means to eat, for if he makes a move towards that door, you have my permission to throw your largest silver platter at him.'

It was a close-run thing as to who looked most shocked, Ant's father, or the butler.

As the earl resumed his seat, the countess looked at her husband. 'That's better. Now, shall we eat?'

———

THE LIBRARY always had a settling effect on Ant. It was a place to lose himself among rows of books, ancient and modern, all to be enjoyed in a cascade of natural daylight that in the daytime, flooded in from a magnificent floor to ceiling bay window.

'Ah, here it is,' said the earl as he retrieved a huge, leather-bound ledger. The title, deeply embossed in gold lettering announced, 'Land transactions: 1765 to 1899.'

'Here, let me help you with that,' said Ant as he lifted the heavy tome onto the large, oblong reading table that dominated the centre of the large room.

Lyn joined Ant as he opened the great book, while the earl, pleased to be free of the weight, took a seat that gave him the best view of a full moon that bathed him in a soft light.

The contrast between the directed light fittings illuminating the reading table, and cool luminescent of the moon, gave the room a startling array of light and soft shade that blended seamlessly into each other to create an intoxicating atmosphere.

As Ant turned the vellum pages of the historical record, he marvelled at the number of transactions the family had conducted over the centuries. He flicked through each entry, noting its date, until he reached the period in history most likely to cover his interest. Before he had chance to examine a page, Lyn broke the silence. 'Look, here,' she exclaimed, drawing his attention to a tattered map of the village.

'What?' Ant replied, studying the detail. 'Heavens, it shows who owned what in... what's the date again?'

Lyn took her time to decipher the old-fashioned numerals in one corner of the map. '1891.'

'We still owned the lavender field at that point,' Ant announced.

'We're getting close. Let's look what's on the next page,' said Lyn.

Turning to the next entry, Ant scrolled down the entries until he came upon a name he recognised. 'There it is. We sold what is now the lavender field, together with other land. I reckon about five hundred acres in all. It includes the farm buildings Gavin Holloway occupies and the manor house Thomas Whitaker owns.'

'I'm not sure this moves us on much, but at least we know a little about who owns what. We need to be careful we don't get sidetracked chasing dead ends, instead of concentrating on finding our killer,' Lyn said.

Ant nodded. 'I guess you're right, but it's fascinating all the same.' As Ant closed the leather-bound leviathan, a monochrome photograph fell to the floor.

Lyn stooped to recover the image. 'It's a group of farm hands. Looks like they're either building or demolishing a building. I wonder what life was like back then. It must have been hard,' Lyn said.

'I should think you're right,' Ant replied, aware that the life his ancestors led couldn't have been more different to the people they employed. He looked at the image again. It was as if the weight of generations rested on his shoulders – a responsibility he took seriously. 'You know,' he said, turning to Lyn, 'Imagine how many generations of the family have poured over these documents.'

'And I'm ashamed to say they probably didn't look after their staff and tenant farmers as well as they might,' the earl said from his seat in the bay window. 'Times change though and I want to believe we do things correctly these days.'

Ant and Lyn reflected on the earl's thoughts. Soon it would be their responsibility to not only abide by the law but go beyond legal requirements to give all their staff a decent living. But for now, they had more pressing matters to deal with.

'Do you want me to put the ledger back, Dad?'

'Oh, would you, son. It'll save me asking poor David to do it, he's only a whisp of a fellow.'

As Ant lifted the weighty item, he was almost sorry he'd volunteered for the task.'

'See you, Dad,' he said, trying not to sound too out of breath.

'Look after yourselves, you two,' the earl replied, winking

at Lyn as he spoke. She responded by placing a hand over her mouth to stop herself laughing.

Once in the archive, Ant felt immediate relief as he dropped the file onto a dusty table, causing a fine mist to fill the air within the small room.

'Well, that's sorted your exercise requirements out for the day. Come on, we'd better say goodnight to your mum before you drop me off at home.' Lyn said.

Ant was about to follow when another ledger caught his eye. Lyn sensed his hesitation. 'Come on, Ant. It's getting late.'

'I know,' Ant said, 'But look at this.' He held up the narrow, long ancient book. He read aloud the words written on the front. 'Liber de Wintonia.'

'Listen, posh boy, we didn't all study Latin at high school... or public school in your case. What does it translate as? and does it have anything to do with our investigations?'

'Not unless our suspects had a land dispute going on in 1086.

'1086? What are you talking about?'

Ant smiled. 'It translates as, 'Book of Winchester.'

'Wait a minute. Wasn't that where—.'

'The Doomsday Book resided? Yes, except they called it 'the Great Survey', Ant replied.

'Ah, now I remember. The reference to 'Doomsday' is because its entries couldn't be altered, and the scholars likened it to the last judgement,' Lyn said.

'Got it in one,' Ant said. 'Although this parchment in this book is only about Stanton Parva. I've no idea how it comes to be here. I suppose Uncle Percival might know. Anyway, it's not getting us any nearer to what we came in here for, is it?'

'No,' Lyn began. 'Except several families in the village go back hundreds and hundreds of years. What if—'

'That would be crazy, are you really saying there might be something in here that links to modern times?' Ant said. 'Anyway, it will only list the place, landowner and number of free men and villains, plus buildings and livestock. Then they estimated a total value so the king could levy the correct taxes.'

'You've got me interested now. There must be something in here about local families down the centuries?'

'I thought you said we needed to go?'

'Ten minutes max, now get looking,' Lyn said pointing to a dusty shelf.

'This looks interesting.'

'What is it?'

'A list.' Lyn replied. 'Were the Stanton family involved in politics at all?'

Ant scratched his head,' I'm sure Dad told me about one of the family being an MP at one time. Why do you ask?'

Lyn pointed to three or four familiar names on the handwritten list. 'Someone drew this list up to make sure they were contacted and told to vote the right way, if you know what I mean.'

'But only property owing men had the vote during the 19th century?'

'Precisely,' Lyn replied.

Soon, Ant began to smile. 'You clever so-and-so. I get what you're saying. OK, who's on the list whose family still live in the village?'

Lyn interrogated the list again. 'Prichard, Owens, oh, and look, the Longmans.'

'Anyone else you recognise?' Ant enquired.

'Let's see. Ah, Butcher, but I suppose every village had

one of those? Here we go, Whitaker, er,' Lyn struggled to decipher the quill-written handwriting. 'I think it says, yes, Fletcher. The others are too far gone for me to read.'

Ant took his mobile from his jacket pocket. 'Lyn, it's almost eleven. Time for me to get you home.'

Lyn gave a sigh and reluctantly folded the parchment. 'I suppose you're right, but one thing. What if the dead man had something to do with a land deal? Let's say he was a descendent of the Pritchard's, or Longman's and believed the land was his?'

'What, and tried to sell land he didn't own to Jaguar, man? Far-fetched, don't you think? There's nothing linking our victim to anything, never mind land fraud.'

'But we don't know that do we? A lingering bitterness from past grievances could still fester beneath the surface. And if someone were to reopen old wounds—'

Just then David, the butler, appeared before, his face expressionless and his posture rigid. 'Sir, there is a telephone call for you.'

'Thank you, David,' Ant replied, trying to hide his surprise at the unexpected interruption. 'I'll take it in the morning room.'

'Who could that be at this time of night? 'Ant mused. 'Listen, take the Morgan and get a good night's sleep. Something tells me tomorrow will be busy.

After seeing Lyn off, Ant made for the morning room and picked up an old-fashioned, heavy, black telephone handset. 'Anthony Stanton speaking.'

'Ah, Viscount Stanton,' the voice on the other end purred, sounding both suave and somehow sinister. 'I was hoping we could meet to discuss a matter of mutual interest.'

'Who is this?' Ant demanded, his instincts on high alert.

'Names can wait, Viscount Stanton,' the man oozed. 'Tell me, how did your visit to Mr. Holloway go? He is a wild one, isn't he?'

Ant's heart hammered as icy tendrils of dread coiled around him. 'How did he know about my meeting with Holloway?' His mind raced, trying to make sense of the call and any connection between the victim and the mysterious caller?

'Very well,' Ant said, his voice steady despite the turmoil churning within him. 'When and where?'

'Tomorrow evening, at the Black Swan Inn,' the man replied. 'Nine o'clock sharp. And come alone, Viscount Stanton. I trust you will keep our conversation... discreet.'

'Of course,' Ant said tightly, his mind racing with questions and possibilities. 'I'll be there.'

'Excellent.'

The line went dead, leaving Ant clutching the phone, his heart pounding like a distant drum—a harbinger of secrets and imminent danger.

Chapter Seven

DANGER EVERYWHERE

SUNLIGHT STREAMED through the stained-glass windows, painting St Peter's church floor with vibrant colours. Anthony 'Ant' Stanton and Lynda 'Lyn' Blackthorn sat side by side in an oak pew, waiting for the service to begin.

Around them, the church brimmed with the low hum of villagers exchanging pleasantries. The air was rich with the scent of polished wood and the faintest hint of candle smoke. Phyllis, small and dressed in black with a net hat, moved quietly between pews. She gathered whispers like treasures, then spread them with added embellishments, her voice a soft rustle in the sacred hush.

The Reverand Morton welcomed his flock at the end of the chancel as the church bells rang their last peels.

Behind him, a large crucifix hung on the ancient stone wall, casting a shadow that seemed to reach out and embrace the congregation.

'Isn't it wonderful to see him back on form?' whispered Lyn, her eyes reflecting the glow of splintered colours filling the air.

'So good,' Ant replied, his lips curving into a warm smile. 'His words resonate more deeply today, somehow. You know, I thought we'd lost him when that Alison King woman almost killed him. I'm glad she got a life sentence for her crimes. It's only been six months, but it seems a lifetime ago.'

The church organ came to life forty-five minutes later, playing a triumphant piece as the congregation departed.

'I bet you don't know what that form of music is called?' Ant asked as he stood back to allow Lyn to exit by the east door.

'What are you on about?' Lyn replied as she smiled at villagers crowding the narrow gravel walkway.

'It's called a Voluntary,' Peter chipped in.

'Oh,' muttered Ant, disappointed his attempt to impress Lyn failed at the first hurdle.

'Honestly, Ant,' Lyn said. 'That head of yours is so full of useless trivia. It's a wonder you've space for anything else up there.'

Peter and Lyn swapped amused glances as Ant lifted his chin to appear unfazed by the rebuke.

The trio stood amid tombstones and yew trees, reaching towards the sky with outstretched branches. Ant's gaze drifted towards the village green where children played, their laughter carrying lightly on the breeze. He turned to Detective Inspector Peter Riley and his face grew serious as he told him about the mysterious phone call from the previous night.

'We need to decide how to handle this,' Ant said, his fingers absently tracing the outline of the remembrance cross pinned to his blazer.

'An ambush might be too risky,' Lyn interjected. 'But

ignoring it could mean missing a crucial piece of the puzzle.'

Peter rubbed his chin, his grey eyes sharp beneath a creased brow. 'You're not seriously considering going alone, are you?'

'Perhaps,' Ant mused, though his internal dialogue wrestled with the potential dangers.

'And don't forget the documents we discovered just before that call,' Lyn added.

'Another layer to the investigation?' Peter's irritation became palpable as Lyn briefed him on the document search related to a land dispute. 'We can't chase shadows without evidence, Lyn.'

'Understood, Peter,' Lyn conceded with a soft sigh, not fully masking her disappointment. 'But we can't ignore any avenues, however unlikely they may seem.'

'Look, let's agree to disagree then,' Peter stated flatly, folding his arms. 'Police resources are overstretched as it is; land disputes are not my priority. Anyway, they're classed as civil disputes, and therefore none of the police's business.'

Peter redirected the conversation between him and Lyn to the paper found in the victim's pocket to ease the tension. They meticulously examined its details for any potential significance. As they continued investigating, Ant's attention shifted towards his brother's grave in the distance.

Lyn noticed the shift in her fiance's demeanour and turned to the detective.

'Let's give Ant a moment, shall we?' Lyn said, touching Peter's arm.

With a nod of understanding, the detective stepped away, allowing Ant the solitude he needed. He moved with muted reverence among the graves, pausing at his brother's headstone. Placing one hand on the cold granite, Ant spoke words meant only for the departed.

'Clues are surfacing, but everything's tangled together. We don't really have a clue what we should concentrate on,' he confided softly, his heart heavy with the weight of responsibility. 'I miss you so much, brother.'

Behind him, the world continued to turn; villagers passed by, life went on. Yet in this hallowed space, time seemed to stand still. It offered Ant a momentary respite from the burdens he carried. With a final, lingering touch on the headstone, Ant straightened, his resolve returning to the job in hand.

―――――

LYN AND ANT ambled along a winding country road, the chatter of their morning at church dissipating into a comfortable silence. The sun cast a benevolent glow over Stanton Parva, dappling the path before them with patches of light that filtered through the lush canopy overhead. It was a perfect English summer day, with a gentle breeze and the sweet smell of flowers.

'Perfect weather for a stroll, isn't it?' Lyn remarked, her voice laced with contentment as she looked up at the clear blue sky.

'Yes,' Ant replied, looking at the hawthorn hedgerows with poppies in the fields. 'And no better company,' he added with a smile, squeezing her hand gently.

'Right answer,' Lyn responded with a loving smile.

Ant couldn't stop thinking about the strange call from the previous evening, and whether it was safe to go to the meet the stranger.

'What could be so important that it demands secrecy?'

he mused internally, trying to piece together the puzzle that grew more complex by the hour.

'Ant,' Lyn said, breaking into his thoughts, 'do you really think going alone is wise? There's something unsettling about this whole affair.'

'Perhaps,' Ant conceded, his thoughts racing as he considered her words. 'But if it leads us to the truth behind the murder, I'll take my chances. Besides, I won't truly be alone if Peter has his way with that listening device.'

The tranquillity of the moment exploded as the growing roar of an engine in the distance neared. Lyn's expression tightened as the sound of the approaching car intensified, its presence out of place in the usually serene country lane.

'Seems someone's in a hurry,' she observed, a hint of apprehension creeping into her tone.

'Indeed,' Ant agreed, a tinge of unease seeping into his thoughts. He glanced over his shoulder, noting the speed at which the vehicle approached. 'This is no leisurely Sunday driver,' he thought, his instincts prickling with warning.

'Doesn't sound like Fitch's recovery truck, that's for sure,' Lyn quipped, though her attempt at humour crackled with concern.

'Nor my Morgan,' Ant added dryly. 'It would've coughed and spluttered long before reaching that velocity.'

Their banter did little to mask the building tension as the sound grew louder, the car's rapid approach casting a shadow over the sunny afternoon. Ant's protective nature surged to the forefront; despite his penchant for unravelling mysteries, the safety of his fiancée held paramount importance.

'Let's step aside, shall we?' he suggested, steering Lyn towards the grassy verge. 'Let's not make it two days in a row that we almost get ourselves run over.'

'Not likely,' Lyn agreed, her senses now on high alert.

The car's engine note reached fever pitch, the vehicle itself still hidden by a bend in the road. It was a dissonant symphony against the peaceful backdrop, a reminder that even in the most idyllic settings, danger could strike out of nowhere. Ant's heart raced, not with fear, but with the adrenaline of the unknown. Was this mere coincidence, or a sign that their investigation had rattled someone's cage?

'Stay close,' Ant said quietly, his hand instinctively moving to protect his fiance. The calm shattered as the car approached, leaving him to wonder if this was just the beginning of a bigger storm.

The car's engine howled like a banshee, shattering the tranquillity of the countryside. Ant glanced back, his eyes widening as he saw the vehicle careering around the bend, its tyres screeching in protest.

'Lyn!' he shouted, the urgency in his voice slicing through the still air like a blade.

'Heavens!' Lyn gasped, her words a mere whisper lost to the roar of the engine. The car was not veering; it was targeting them, a deadly missile locked onto its course.

'Jump!' Ant cried out as he grasped Lyn's arm, propelling them both towards the safety of the ditch. They tumbled into the undergrowth, the world tilting wildly as brambles and nettles clawed at their clothes.

The car blasted past, mere inches from where they'd stood moments before. A surge of wind followed, violent enough to send detritus skyward into a disorganised frenzy. The unpleasant scent of burnt rubber lingered in the air, an acrid reminder of the danger that had just screamed by.

'Are you alright?' Ant's voice trembled slightly as he helped Lyn to her feet, his hands checking her over with hurried concern.

'Y-yes,' she stammered, still trying to catch her breath, her pulse erratic and loud in her ears. She brushed away leaves and twigs, her mind reeling from the shock.

'Blimey, that was too close for comfort,' Ant said, his usual warm smile replaced with a tight-lipped grimace. He could feel the rapid drumming of his own heart, an echo of the fear that had gripped him when he realised the car would not stop.

'Someone's playing a very dangerous game,' Lyn muttered, her blue eyes dark with the reflection of their shared thought. They clung to each other for a moment longer, grounding themselves in the wake of the adrenaline that coursed through their veins.

Ant felt the protective instinct that always lurked beneath his affable exterior harden into resolve. As much as he cherished the quiet life in Stanton Parva, he couldn't ignore the shadows that crept along its edges. Whoever had tried to run them down had just escalated the stakes of their strange mystery. He had no intention of backing off from a challenge.

Ant and Lyn stood motionless in the roadside ditch. The damp soil underfoot ignored in the stillness that followed the car's reckless departure. The vehicle's noise disappeared, leaving only their heavy breathing and occasional bird sounds in the summer air.

They exchanged a look, the sort of mute communication known only to the two of them.

'Was that the same car Fitch mentioned?' Her own expression mirroring the concern etched into Ant's features.

'It can't be,' he replied. 'That one is still at his garage.'

'Is it?' Lyn asked.

He thought for a few seconds. 'Only one way to settle it.' Ant retrieved his mobile and pressed the quick-dial key.

Within seconds, Fitch's cheery voice vied with birdsong for Ant's attention.

'Are you sure?' he said in response to his question to Fitch. Slowly, he ended the call and slipped the mobile back into his trouser pocket.

'What's up?'

'It's gone.'

Lyn frowned. 'What, you mean the owner has collected it?'

'Someone took the car. Fitch was out and Sophie had gone home. He just said when he got back, the Jaguar wasn't there. Fitch reckoned unless someone broke into it, they came ready with a set of keys to make a quick getaway.'

'Has he told Peter?'

'He's left a message at the police station for him.'

Ant's thoughts swirled with implications. The enigmatic caller, a possible land dispute, and now this—a brazen attempt to run them over that could have ended in injury, or worse. It wasn't only about solving a mystery anymore. This was personal. The peaceful façade of Stanton Parva was cracking, revealing a hidden layer of malice that seemed intent on ensnaring them both.

'Let's not jump to conclusions,' Lyn cautioned, her rational side surfacing despite the jolt of adrenaline. 'But we can't ignore the timing. It's too much of a coincidence, and you know what Peter always says about that.'

'Hmm,' Ant responded, his mind a dance of strategy and suspicion. He took another steadying breath, the scent of wildflowers and freshly cut grass a stark contrast to the danger they'd narrowly escaped. 'We'll have to tread carefully, Lyn. Whoever's behind this, they're serious about warning us off.'

———

THE WHERRY ARMS was a hum of activity, the clinking of cutlery and glasses creating a melody that was as much a part of Sunday lunch as the roast itself. Ant and Lyn squeezed through the throng of villagers, nodding, and exchanging pleasantries with familiar faces.

'Nearly missed you both today,' Jed called out from behind the bar, his voice rising above the din as they reached him. 'Heard there was a bit of excitement on Church Lane.'

Ant chuckled, leaning on the polished wood of the counter. 'If by 'excitement' you mean an attempt on our lives, then yes, utterly thrilling. Anyway, who told you about it?'

Jed's eyes widened for a moment before he let out a hearty laugh, mirth crinkling the corners of his eyes. 'Who do you think? Fitch can't hold his beer any better than his tongue. You do know I'll have to insist on payment upfront, just in case they get you next time.'

'Ah, always down to brass tacks with you, isn't it?' Ant ribbed back, his grin not wavering. 'How about we put this round on the house, for old times' sake?'

'Only interested in money, am I?' Jed winked and tapped the side of his nose, sliding over a pint of Fen Bodger pale ale and a lemonade. 'For you two, I'll make an exception. Just this once.'

'Generous to a fault,' Ant said, lifting his glass in a toast before taking a sip.

As they settled into a corner table, Lyn's laughter mingled with the surrounding chatter. She told Mrs. Waverly about her recent classroom adventure while Ant listened, finding comfort in her soft voice.

'Another oddity to add to our collection,' Lyn murmured between sips of her drink, bringing up the mysterious call again. 'It seems someone is very determined to have your attention, Ant.'

'Too determined,' Ant replied, looking deep into the amber of his pale ale.

'Sorry to interrupt,' came Peter's muffled voice as he joined them, almost unnoticed amid the lively atmosphere. 'Can't stay long, but what's this I hear about a near-miss?'

'Ah, Peter,' Ant greeted, inclining his head slightly. 'Yes, someone fancied using us for target practice—'

'Deliberate, you think?'

'Seems rather coincidental otherwise,' Lyn added.

'Is it connected to the murder?' Ant ventured; his voice tinged with the gravity of the situation. 'The same make of car seen at the scene, now nearly running us over.'

'Could be,' Peter conceded, tapping his fingers on the wooden table. 'Someone's trying to send a message. Or silence potential threats.'

'Which means we're getting closer,' Lyn said, her determination clear despite the softness of her tone.

'Perhaps,' Peter mused, 'but we can't jump to conclusions. We need to focus on the tangible leads. And no, that doesn't include land disputes, Lyn.'

She nodded, though her mind still flickered to the folded paper. The edges of the mystery creased within. But she knew better than to push her theories on rigid police protocols—at least for now.

'Listen, before I go, here's the tech. I mentioned when you told me about your madcap idea. Make sure you're wearing this tonight.'

He handed Ant a tiny microphone receiver and radio transmitter no larger than a needle thimble. 'I want to hear everything that happens. Keep your wits about you,' Peter finished, standing to leave. 'And tread carefully. Whoever's behind this is a serious player.'

'Always do,' Ant assured him as he hurried the electronics out of sight. A smile played at the edges of his lips, though his heart hammered with the weight of unsaid fears.

With that, Peter navigated through the throng of patrons and out the pub door, leaving Ant and Lyn amid the clatter of dishes and a loud hubbub of conversation.

After Peter's departure, the couple ate in companionable silence. Afterwards, even as Ant joked with Jed about adding the meal to the free drinks, a shadow of unease lingered, like the stillness before a storm.

'Put it on my tab, will you, Jed?' Ant called out, wiping his mouth with a napkin.

Jed, polishing a glass behind the bar, chuckled. 'There he goes again! Lord Stanton's heir, always the aristocrat in settling his debts.'

'Ah, but that's how we Stanton's got our estate in the first place,' Ant retorted with a grin, playing along with the banter. 'Old-fashioned cunning, a dash of charm, and a dose of luck.'

'Ha! Well, watch out, or you'll find yourself washing dishes in the back!' Jed waved them off with a good-natured smile.

Lyn smiled, taking Ant's arm as they stood to leave, her laughter mingling with the cozy cacophony of the Wherry Arms regulars. The tension of the afternoon had dissipated like mist over the fields at dawn. However, the threat still hung in the air, unspoken but ever present.

As they left the happy surroundings of the village pub, they failed to notice the shadowy figure who slipped out just after them. Draped in loose clothing and topped with a wide-brimmed hat, their attire obscured any discernible features.

'Quite the day, eh?' Ant remarked, his voice betraying a hint of the fatigue he felt.

'I'm shattered, to be honest,' Lyn replied, linking her arm through his. 'How are you feeling about tonight?'

Still, the clandestine follower tracked them. Their steps were careful, calculated, keeping a discreet but constant distance.

———

NIGHT HAD CREPT over the countryside by the time Ant arrived at the anonymous pub, thirty miles from the comforting familiarity of Stanton Parva. The narrow-wooded road leading to it was barely more than a track, hemmed in by encroaching trees that whispered secrets in the wind.

Inside the almost deserted pub, the few patrons huddled over their pints paid him no attention. Ant's gaze darted around the dimly lit space, seeking faces, gestures—anything amiss. It was impossible not to feel watched, though no eyes seemed to linger on him. His stomach churned with a mix of apprehension and defiance.

Remember why you're here, he muttered under his breath, his fingers tapping rhythmically against the side of his leg.

He settled at the bar, ordered a pint of the local ale, and pretended to be engrossed by the worn wood grain of the countertop. The pungent aroma of stale beer hung in the stale, threatening air. An undercurrent that reminded Ant of Peter's warnings.

'Your presence is welcome, Viscount Stanton,' came a

whisper, so close it sent a shiver down Ant's spine. He stiffened; the icy breath on his neck felt like the touch of a ghost. 'Don't turn around.'

Ant obliged, noting that the barman had disappeared.

'Who are you?' Ant asked, his voice steady despite the adrenaline coursing through his veins.

'Instructions first. Leave the building and walk to the hut around the back,' the voice continued, its menace thinly veiled.

Ant's hand clenched around his glass, knuckles whitening. He contemplated the risk, the potential trap awaiting him, but the mention of Lyn would make him walk through fire if need be.

'Listen carefully,' the voice was low but clear. 'An associate of mine is watching over Lyn. It's important we take care of those we love, isn't it, Viscount Stanton?'

'Threaten me, not her,' Ant shot back, turning his head slightly only to glimpse the brimmed hat before it disappeared.

'Move now,' the voice commanded.

Ant stood and made his way to the door, his pulse thumping in his ears. As he stepped outside to be met by a thunderstorm, his thoughts raced. Is this how it's to end, after all the dangers I faced in the army? Not with a bang, but a whisper? Be smart, Ant, he admonished himself, stepping off the well-trodden path and into the embrace of the dark woods. Each crunch of leaves underfoot echoed ominously, the shadows of the trees casting long fingers across his path.

Is that the place, I wonder?

'Patience,' the night responded. Ant knew he was walking deeper into uncertainty, each step taking him further from safety to a truth that might shatter his world.

Chapter Eight

EAVESDROPPING

THE MORNING mist clung to the cobblestones of Stanton Parva like a shroud, seeping into the crevices and casting the quaint village in a spectral pallor. Lyn stood at her front door, worry creasing her kind face as she peered down the lane.

'Nothing?' she asked, her voice betraying a tremble as Detective Inspector Peter Riley approached, his own expression grim.

'Dead silence after he left the Fox and Whistle,' Riley confirmed, referring to the listening device Ant wore. 'We sent a squad to interview the barman, but the place was deserted.'

'What, empty?'

'No, I mean deserted—literally. The place was boarded up and looked like it'd been that way for years.'

'It doesn't make sense, and Ant's never just vanished before.' Lyn wrapped her arms around herself for reassurance. 'He knows I worry.'

'Which is exactly why we're not sitting on our hands,'

Riley replied, his usual stoicism giving way to a sense of urgency. 'The last thing we caught on his microphone was a man telling Ant to walk out of the pub. I've got officers combing the surrounding area for clues. We'll find him.'

Lyn nodded uncertainly at Peter. 'I wish I could stay, but I need to get to work. You will keep me updated, won't you? If I need to, I can leave my deputy to manage things.'

'To be honest, it's probably better you do your head-teacher stuff, rather than sit at home worrying, don't you think?'

She shrugged her shoulders. 'I suppose so.'

As Lyn turned back to enter the house, she sensed Peter hesitating. 'Is anything else worrying you? You not sleeping either?'

The detective looked pensively at the stone pavement.

'Peter, what is it? Is there something you're not telling me?'

'No... no. It's just. Heck, there's no way I can keep this from you. There's been a second incident.'

'What?' Lyn gasped, shocked out of her personal concerns for Ant.

'Mrs Henderson found a young woman in a bad way not an hour ago in her herb garden. The woman thought her dead at first' Peter explained, his voice tinged with disbelief.

Lyn's mind raced. 'What's happening to our village? It's as if someone has a vendetta against us.' Lyn thought. Her mind resembled a tangled maze, desperately searching for answers, but finding only more questions and uncertainty.

'That's that, then. Even with Ant missing, I can't ignore this.' Her mind raced, grappling with the dual crises. 'I'll ring my deputy and take a day's leave so I can help.'

'Are you sure? ' Riley questioned with an uncertain

smile. 'I need to get back to Mrs Henderson's cottage. Do you want to come?'

'Try stopping me,' Lyn said, stepping out with a newfound purpose.

As they moved towards the heart of the village, Lyn couldn't shake Ant from her thoughts. She clung to the hope that he was out there somewhere, following a lead about the murder. The idea offered a sliver of comfort, but the uncertainty gnawed at her.

The village green, usually a tableau of rural tranquillity, was marred by the sight of a scenes of crime unit and ambulance parked next to Mrs Henderson picturesque cottage.

'A murder and near fatal attack in one week,' Peter murmured, his grey eyes scanning the scene as he led Lyn to the rear garden.

Lyn approached the scene with trepidation.

'Are you OK?' Peter said.

Lyn stood in astonished silence before finally turning to the detective. 'Lavender. She's in a bed of lavender.'

'Didn't Mrs Henderson see or hear anything?'

'Afraid not,' Peter replied. 'She was at her daughter's place for the night. She arrived back here early this morning. Pegging some washing out she... '

'That must have been awful for her.' Lyn continued to survey the sad scene as the paramedics worked on the victim with quiet determination. Then, a terrible truth began to dawn. 'Peter, I know... I mean, recognise her?'

The detective looked stunned. 'What makes you say that?'

Lyn moved to her left to take another look at the victim's face as the paramedics frantically checked for signs of life. 'Her name is Wendy. We saw her in the pub. You know, the one staring around looking anxious. She was with that chap around her age. At first, Ant and I thought she was looking at us in the Wherry arms at my birthday bash. I had a word with her. She said something about a relative not liking her boyfriend, but the lad was determined to stick around. I think she wanted to get out of the village as soon as she could.'

'If you're right that it was the woman you saw, it gives us a solid lead. We just need to be careful you want it to be who you saw, you know, clutching at—'

'I know what you mean. But I'm certain it's her. Now all we need to do is find the man she was with—and who the mysterious relative is.'

Peter looked down at the victim. 'Is she still alive?' he asked a member of the paramedic team.

'Barely,' replied the clinician, her face etched with concern. 'We've called for the air—'

Before the medic could finish her sentence, the sound of a helicopter shattered the strange silence that had settled over the village.

Within seconds, what had been a distant dot in a cloudless sky, morphed into a metallic saviour as the machine slowly landed on the green.

Within two minutes, the emergency team took charge of the victim. Satisfied she remained in a stable condition; they began their evacuation procedure.

'Norfolk and Norwich hospital?' the detective asked.

'Yes, they're the nearest designated trauma centre to us,' responded the team leader without taking his eyes off the unconscious patient.

Ten minutes passed before the thumping power of the helicopter rotors filled the still air, signally the unwieldy machine was about to lift off. Soon it became a dot in the sky again, before disappearing into the distance.

While everyone had been watching the helicopter, Lyn kept herself busy surveying the herb garden. Suddenly, she shouted for Peter.

'Look to your right, about six feet in front of you.'

Peter narrowed his eyes as he attempted to see what Lyn appeared so excited about. A Key.

The detective scratched his forehead. 'There's no doubt the two incidents are linked. Hardly a mark on the poor woman, yet critically injured, the lavender, and a key. We must assume whoever did this thought they'd killed her. Are they deliberately sending a message. Baiting us? Having a laugh at everyone else, including the victims' expense?'

'Why a key?' Lyn said in a bewildered tone.

Peter stepped onto the side-path, stooped, and picked up the shiny stainless-steel object with a gloved hand. 'A key can convey many meanings. A locked container in which something valuable is kept. However, in this case, I suspect our dangerous friend is taunting us by hinting that every-thing he or she does acts as a clue to some much larger end game.'

'It sounds bonkers, but what's happened is beyond a coincidence. You've said loads of times you don't believe in them. And as for lavender, it's not just a flower. It's been used for thousands of years for its healing properties. On the other hand, drink enough pure lavender oil and it can kill.'

'I didn't know that,' Peter responded. 'One thing I can say is no toxins were found in our first victim. If you're right, lavender toxin won't be present in this young lady's toxicology report either. All we can hope is that she survives and can tell us what happened, and if she recognised her attacker.'

'Perhaps the perpetrator is playing with us again. You know, leading us to assume the placement of the bodies among lavender signals a peaceful sleep, if you get my meaning?'

'I do,' Peter replied. 'they're using the lavender as a metaphor for danger. You know, too much of a good thing and all that?'

Lyn picked a tall stem from the scented flower and squeezed the head between a finger and thumb to release its fragrant aroma. 'Another metaphor? What if they're telling us not to look at the obvious?'

Peter picked his own stem and placed it under his nose. The effect was immediate, and the sneezing fit took time to abate.'

'See what I mean,' Lyn said.

'What, that I'm allergic to the stuff?' replied Peter as he broke out in a fit of sneezing.

'No, silly. More like, 'Look at me from a distance and you'll be fine. Get too close and you'll pay the price.'

'To the lavender?' Peter said.

'To whoever has an interest in that field.'

THE PEACEFUL COTTAGE of Nancy Fairfield blended seamlessly into the village with its thatched roof and ivy-covered walls. With a nod from Peter, Lyn rapped on the door, the sound crisp in the morning air.

Nancy opened the door with a smile that didn't reach her eyes. She wore a light jacket, chequered shirt, trousers, and stout boots. 'Detective Riley, Miss Blackthorn. Not a visit I was expecting. I'm just leaving. What can I do for you?'

'Anywhere interesting?'

'Not really, just some friends down Lane End.'

'May we come in?' Peter asked, his voice cordial yet authoritative.'

'Of course,' Nancy replied, stepping aside to grant them entry.

The interior of the cottage was as charming as its exterior, with floral patterns and porcelain figurines adorning every surface. Yet, as they took their seats in the petite living room, the air between them crackled with tension.

'We're here about the unfortunate incident across the road,' Peter started, his gaze never leaving Nancy's face. 'I'm sure you've heard.'

'Such a dreadful thing,' she said, clasping her hands together. 'Poor Mrs Henderson must be beside herself.'

'Indeed,' Lyn chimed in, observing Nancy's reaction closely. 'We were hoping you might shed some light on what happened.'

'Me? Oh, I hardly think I could be of help...' Nancy trailed off, her fingers fidgeting with the hem of her skirt.

'Any detail, no matter how small, could be important,' Peter pressed the matter and pointed to the front window. 'You have a line of sight to the house.'

'Where you at home last night?' Lyn asked gently, her mind racing with the alternative scenarios. 'We understand these questions can unsettle, but we must ask.'

'I understand. In fact, I was at home all night. Alone, as usual. Nothing exciting, I'm afraid.'

'Can anyone corroborate that?' Peter asked, his eyes narrowing ever so slightly.

'Corroborate?' Nancy echoed, a hint of nervousness

creeping into her voice. 'No, I don't suppose they can. It was just me and my books.'

Peter and Lyn exchanged a glance, unspoken thoughts passing between them. They had reached an impasse—the same frustrating dead end that haunted the cases at every turn.

Nancy Fairfield sat primly on a chintz-patterned armchair; her fingers laced neatly in her lap. The morning light suffused the cottage, dust motes dancing like tiny spectres around her. Her smile was warm, yet her eyes didn't meet theirs, giving Lyn an uneasy feeling.

'I see,' Peter said in a reassuring tone, 'Might I ask what you were reading?' His dark eyes scanned Nancy's face for any trace of deceit.

'Oh, just some Agatha Christie,' Nancy chirped. 'Nothing like a murder mystery to pass the evening, don't you think?'

'Quite fitting,' Peter remarked dryly, taking salient points down in a small leather-bound notebook. 'And during the period engrossed in your novel, did you see or hear anything unusual?'

'Unusual?' She tilted her head slightly, as though the thought had never occurred to her. 'No. It was an ordinary night.'

'Must've been riveting to keep you from noticing the storm,' Lyn said.

Nancy's laugh tinkled through the room like fragile bells. 'I suppose I was lost in the world of whodunit. You know what Agatha Christie books are like.'

'Forgive me for pressing,' Peter said, his interest piqued by Nancy's over casual demeanour. 'Your solitude doesn't offer much in the way of an alibi, and given the circumstances.'

'Are you suggesting I had something to do with this awful business?' Nancy's tone was light, but her knuckles whitened where they gripped each other.

'Just doing my job,' Peter interjected.

'Of course,' Nancy replied, finally locking gazes with the detective. 'Is there anything else I can help you with?'

'Perhaps later,' Lyn said, her intuition whispering that Nancy Fairfield was not as transparent as she seemed. 'We appreciate your time.'

'Think nothing of it,' Nancy said, standing up to show them out. 'Let me know if there's more I can do.'

As they stepped outside, the sun dipped behind a cloud, casting a shadow over the garden. Lyn paused, looking back at the cottage. 'What are you hiding behind those cheerful curtains, Nancy Fairfield?' she mused softly.

'Whatever it is, we'll uncover it,' Peter assured her, his voice steady despite the gnawing uncertainty that plagued them both.

'Let's hope so,' Lyn replied, glancing at the sky as if expecting the heavens to reveal the answers they sought.

———

LYN'S FINGERS curled tightly around a steaming mug of coffee in the modernised kitchen of the Old School House. Detective Inspector Peter Riley tapped his fingers on the table, his eyes clouded like the sky outside.

'Something doesn't sit right with me,' Lyn confessed, breaking the silence that had settled between them. Her voice was steady, but her mind raced with concern for Ant and the vexing puzzle Nancy Fairfield presented.

'Her alibi is watertight, on paper at least,' Peter replied, the furrows in his brow deepening. 'But that saccharine smile... It's as if she's performing.'

'I agree,' Lyn replied, setting down her coffee with more force than intended. She stood abruptly, pacing the length of the rug, her footsteps muffled by its thick weave. 'But we've nothing to connect her to either murder. No motive, no opportunity?'

'Perhaps there's something we're missing, some thread we've yet to pull,' Peter suggested, following her movement with his gaze. His own frustration mirrored hers.

As Lyn paused by window, she watched a robin flit from branch to branch in the garden, its red breast a dash of colour against the darkening day.

'Sometimes I wonder if we're doing any good at all,' Lyn said, her reflection in the window glass, staring back at her with questioning eyes. 'We try to instil honesty in the children at school, yet here we are, adults mired in deceit.'

Peter rose to join her. 'You do better than you know, Lyn. Both in the classroom and out here helping the police.' He placed a reassuring hand on her shoulder. 'This village needs people like you and Ant. People who care enough to make a difference.'

The warmth of his words did little to dislodge the rock of worry weighing on her chest. Was Ant chasing leads or had he become one himself? The mere thought pricked her heart with sharp barbs of fear.

'Speaking of Ant,' Peter said, reading her expression, 'Remember, Fitch and Sophie are helping, too. They'll find him.'

'Of course,' she replied, though the assurance sounded hollow even to her own ears.

'Let's go over the meeting with Nancy again before I get

the statement typed for her to sign,' Peter proposed. 'There might be a detail we've overlooked.'

They sat once more and went through what she'd said. Two words whirled inside Lyn's head: Lane End. 'Did you notice the mudded garden fork standing on a folded newspaper in her kitchen?'

'In the living room, no,' Peter responded.

'No. As we arrived, the door between the living room and kitchen was fully open. I thought nothing of it.'

'Sorry, Lyn, it's been a long day. Have I missed something?'

'As we left, I noticed the closed door. I couldn't work out what was different about the room at first, but now I do. The door,' Lyn said, her voice tinged with excitement.

'Nope, still not with you.'

'Let me ask you a question. Did you see any footprints near the body at Mrs Henderson's, because I didn't?'

Peter's face lightened. 'I get it, the fork. Something to turn over any compacted soil. You are a bright one. I'll get one of my officers to bring it, and the newspaper, to the police station.'

'I tell you what. Why don't we pay Vera Ellersly a visit? If I remember correctly, she's the Chair of the Gardening Club. Has been for years. She might give us some information about Nancy?'

'What's all this talk about, a gardening club? Nancy didn't mention one?' Peter said.

'No, she didn't. But she mentioned Lane End. That track leads only to the allotments. The Gardening Club has a big shed down there. And that's where they hold their meetings.'

A slow grin spread across Peter's face, the first genuine smile she'd seen from him all day. 'Now that's something we can work with,' he declared, a spark of hope igniting between them.

The wind tousled Lyn's hair as they walked to Mrs Ellersly's cottage. The sun was dipping low as it dodged the clouds.

'Remember, play it casual,' Peter murmured, his eyes scanning the surroundings with practiced caution.

'Of course,' Lyn replied, though her heart drummed a rapid beat against her ribcage. With every step, the weight of urgency pressed upon her; Ant's absence had become a dull ache, a worry that refused to be sidelined even by the gravity of the situation.

They approached the door, its paint flaking gently under the assault of time. Peter rapped sharply, twice. A moment passed before the door creaked open to reveal its jaunty owner, her silver hair wound into a tight bun.

'Good evening, Mrs Ellersly,' Lyn began, mustering a smile that felt like a mask. 'I apologise for calling of an evening, but may we have a word?'

'Of course, my dears. Do come in,' the woman beckoned, her voice sweet as treacle but with an undertone of steel. Lyn knew that as chair of the gardening club, she had a well-earned reputation as being ruthless when the need arose.

Inside, the air was thick with the scent of lavender and beeswax. They settled into overstuffed armchairs that attempted to swallow them whole as Mrs Ellersly perched on the rounded arm of a sofa.

'Are the allotments open each day Mrs Ellersly?'

The petite lady offered a smile. 'Please, do call me Vera. As for the allotments, yes, every day of the year. You try to keep them away and a riot would ensue.'

'Thank you, er, Vera. And yesterday?'

'Of course. Weekends are the busiest. It's funny, really. Most of our members are retired, so one day is much the same as any other, but for some reason the weekends are the most popular.'

Lyn took up the questioning. 'Was there anything different about yesterday?'

'I see, you've heard, have you. I'm surprised you think it worth a visit by the police, though?'

'Well, you know how these things work. Why don't you tell us all about it so we can clear things up?' said Peter, playing along with Vera's surprising news.

Vera stroked the material of her dress again, only this time with greater vigour. 'We never meet of a Sunday, the vicar would not be best pleased if we missed his evening service to talk about vegetables, not even at harvest time.' She giggled at her own joke.

'No, no, of course not. So, what was different about last night?' Peter asked.

Vera stiffened her gate. 'Sabotage and subterfuge.'

'What?' exclaimed Lyn, 'In a gardening club?'

Vera gave her guests an imperious look. 'It's rife between Association members, and I'm afraid to say, within individual clubs. So, I called a special meeting last night to stamp it out. To call a spade a spade.'

This time Vera made no attempt to smile at the use of a cliche.

'What happened?' Lyn asked, keen to hear more.

'I chucked Evelyn Huckaby out of the club. Undeniable evidence of her tinkering with Albert Laymen's gooseberries. Also, a rival club chair made the mistake of sending me a blind copy of an email to the interloper, asking what our club was going to put up for the next grower's competition.'

The room fell into silence at the grave revelation before Lyn ventured a question.

'Vera, did you keep an attendance sheet? Do members sign in or anything?'

They certainly do sign in. I insist upon it so no one can say they missed club announcements and blame it on me.'

'And for last night?' Peter asked.

'Absolutely. Would you like to see the attendance sheet, Inspector Riley?'

'If I may.'

Vera busied herself checking which of the five ring-binder folders that sat neatly on a shelf she needed to consult. 'Ah, here it is.' She opened the folder at the most recent entry and passed it to Peter. Lyn moved position so she could also scan the list.

Seconds passed as Peter interrogated the document. His fore finger rested on one name in particular, Nancy Fair-field. Neither Peter nor Lyn let on they'd found what they came to discover. However, Nancy's presence complicated, rather than clarified their investigation.

'Well, Vera. You've been most helpful,' Peter said as he closed the file and handed it back to its owner.

'Was it of use?' Vera said, wearing an expression that expected a detailed response.

'It was,' Peter responded in a tone that made clear no further information would be forthcoming.

As they rose to leave, Vera followed them to the door, her movements stiff. 'If I can be of any further help, you will let me know, won't you?' Vera said, her voice tinged with the hope that Peter might tell her more about the reason for his call.

'Thanks' for that,' Peter said, offering Vera a smile.

'And for your time,' Lyn added, stepping out into the

twilight, where the scent of the impending night mingled with the fading day.

'Anytime, dear,' Vera's voice called from the doorway. 'Do take care.'

The walk back was muted, each lost in their thoughts. As they reached the crossroads, Peter stopped abruptly, causing Lyn to bump into him.

'She knew after I asked for the file that we weren't there because of the inter-club rivalry.'

'Yes, I picked up on that, too.'

'The question is, Lyn, why did Nancy Fairfield lie to us?'

Their conversation ended sharply as Peter took hold of Lyn.

'What are you doing? Peter, let go of me.'

'Shush,' Peter replied, stepping in front of his companion. 'There's someone coming at us.'

Ahead, a figure emerged from the shadows, bounding forward. Were they about to meet the man responsible for killing one man and maiming a second victim. Was it their turn next?

Chapter Nine

FIRE AND WATER

LYN'S EMOTIONS exploded as the figure drew close. The dim light revealed not a killer, but Ant's father, the Earl of Stanton. His face strained with lines of worry that deepened with each step he took.

'What's wrong?' Lyn asked, her voice trembling as she braced herself for the worst.

'Anthony...' the Earl began, clutching his chest and catching his breath. 'They've found him.'

The news stunned Lyn as she attempted to process the joyful news. 'Is he alright?' Her heart pounded furiously, the mix of fear and relief tangled like an animal trying to break free of a thorn hedge.

'He's alive, but—'

'But what?' Peter pressed; his expression taut.

'Someone set fire to Field Surfer—with him on it. She's half-submerged at Stanton Staithe.'

A chill descended, colder than any winter breeze. The revelation hung between them, heavy with implications. Someone had wanted Ant silenced, but why?

'You go ahead,' Peter said. 'I'll ring the station to get my officers and scenes of crime team sorted. I'll follow in a couple of minutes.'

'I'll take you straight to him,' said the earl in an urgent tone. 'Come with me, I'll tell you as much as I know on the way.'

Lyn followed, her legs shaky with a mixture of dread and relief. Fifteen minutes later, Lyn caught her first glimpse of the smouldering wreck of the Earl's beloved Norfolk Wherry.

Field Surfer, lay at an odd angle in the staithe.

Ant lay on the damp grass, wrapped in an emergency foil blanket, his complexion pale, but at least he was alive.

'Ant!' Lyn cried out, rushing to his side. 'Are you alright?'

He managed a weak smile as he reached up to greet his fiance. 'I've had better days.'

'Who did this?' Lyn asked urgently, kneeling beside him, her protective instincts coming to the fore.

'I wish I knew,' Ant replied, his voice hoarse from the smoke. 'He came at me from behind once I left that pub. He told me what to do. Didn't Peter pick it all up on the radio link? Anyway, I didn't see his face.'

A familiar voice spoke from behind the pair. 'No, we lost the link after he told you to go into the woods. I've got our experts trying to analyse the recording, but I hold little hope of getting anything from it.'

'What else can you remember?' asked Lyn.

'He told me to head for a building just inside the woods. After that, nothing.'

'Yet you ended up on your father's boat, which was then set on fire. Whoever it was didn't intend only to rough you up, they—.'

'Don't say it, Peter' interjected Lyn. 'We all know what they intended to do. But why? What has Ant got to do with anything?'

'Well, at least we know he had an accomplice. There's no way he'd have got you into a vehicle and placed you on the boat without help. Was he on deck, or in the cabin?' Peter asked as he turned to Fitch.

'Below deck,' confirmed Fitch. 'We only just got him out. Have you any idea what a dead weight an unconscious bloke is to shift?'

The moment of levity helped the group lighten the mood on a sombre evening. However, Ant remained distracted.

'It can't be just about the murder, otherwise we'd all be targets.' Ant coughed as he surveyed to the smouldering hull

The detective, Lyn, and Fitch exchanged an uncomfortable glance.

Ant's gaze dropped to the closely cropped grass as he pulled the foil blanket up around his neckline. 'I'm sorry, Dad.'

The earl stepped forward to put a reassuring hand on his son's shoulder. 'Sorry? What is there to be sorry about?'

'Field Surfer. I know how much she meant to you. To us all. But especially you.'

Ant's father squeezed his son's shoulder. 'It was a wreck when I bought her all those years ago. And in worse shape than we see her now. She'll soon be better than before. You'll see.'

'Did you notice anything? Any detail?' Lyn probed gently.

'Only this,' Ant said, and from his pocket, he produced a small, sodden piece of paper. Unfolding it revealed half of a photograph—a woman smiling, cut off just as it reached whatever stood next to her.

'What does it mean do you think?' Lyn asked.

'That's the thing,' Ant said, rolling onto his side and coughing. 'They expected me to find it, like a message.'

'Or a warning,' Peter added, studying the torn edges. 'Do you recognise her?'

'Never seen the woman before,' Ant admitted. 'But whoever did this wanted me to find it.'

'Find what, though? What does it mean?' Lyn's mind raced with questions, each one more troubling than the last.

Lyn strained to see the tattered photograph. 'Let me look at that.'

Peter handed the small image over. 'Have you seen her before?'

Lyn scrutinised the artifact. Eventually she spoke. 'Yes, and so have you.'

'What do you mean?' Peter said wearing a confused expression.

'Look again.'

The detective complied. Slowly something dawned on him. 'Good grief, it's her, isn't it?'

Lyn nodded excitedly.

'Will someone tell me what's going on before we all freeze, particularly your fiance, Lyn?'

Instead, Peter spent the next few minutes bringing them all up to date with the day's events.

'Blimy,' Fitch said. 'And I thought we'd been busy.'

'Time to get you in the warm,' the Earl of Stanton suggested, his protective instincts taking over. 'We can puzzle this out once you're settled.'

'Right,' Peter agreed. 'We'll need to comb the area for evidence. Whoever did this might still be out there. Criminal profiling tells me our man likes to lay clues, which means he needs to watch us to get some kind of twisted kick out of other people's misery.'

Lyn helped Ant to his feet, supporting him as they made their way back to Stanton Hall. Her thoughts were a whirlwind of concern for Ant and the mystery of the half-photograph. Who was the woman? And how did she fit into the tangled web of secrets that enveloped Stanton Parva?

As they approached the grand façade of the hall, a light flickered at the impressive entrance door. Countess Stanton appeared, her silver hair a beacon of warmth in the dark.

'Thank goodness you're safe,' she murmured, embracing her son.

'Thanks to Fitch and Sophie here,' Ant said, offering a grateful nod.

Once inside, they settled Ant by the fireplace, the crackling flames casting dancing shadows across his drawn features.

'It may be June, but it's a cool evening and we need to get you dry,' the countess said.

The remark made her son smile, reminding him when he was sick as a child and his mother would insist on him sleeping by a comforting fireside. 'Thank you, Mum.'

Lyn couldn't shake the feeling that the photo was a key piece in a larger puzzle. A puzzle that at least one disturbed individual expected the police to solve, and in so doing expose the woman to more harm.

But why plant the photo on Ant if whoever did this already thought he'd killed her? Unless it's the person we don't see in the picture they're after? Lyn thought.

'Tomorrow,' Peter said, breaking the silence, 'we start fresh. We'll unravel this, piece by piece.'

'Starting with Nancy Fairfield,' Lyn added. 'We know she lied, and I intend to find out about what, and why.'

'Be careful, both of you,' the earl warned. 'This isn't a game. Field Surfer proves that.'

Lyn squeezed Ant's hand, her gaze meeting his. There was a unspoken promise there—a vow to see justice done and to protect one another.

As Lyn headed back to the village. What might the morning bring?

In the night's quiet, the pieces were moving, unseen, and the game was far from over.

THE MORNING LIGHT filtered through the curtains of Lyn's Victorian home, casting a warm glow across the embroidered duvet. She awoke with a start, a dream of shadowy figures still clinging to the edges of her consciousness.

She lay still for a moment, allowing the remnants of sleep to dissipate and the reality of the situation to settle in.

The village came alive, with the scent of bread and the sounds of chatter and milk bottles marking the start of a new day.

No sooner had Lyn boiled a kettle on her aging AGA oven than the doorbell rang. Peter greeted her still-groggy demeanour with a hearty smile.

'Tea?'

'You need coffee,' Peter said as he accepted his host's invitation to enter.

'Hmm, you're right. Do you know how to use the percolator?'

Peter smiled. 'It's me you're talking to, not Anthony. Is he up and about yet?'

Lyn gazed at her surrounding as if expecting her fiance to appear from thin air. 'Er... no, he stayed up at the Hall last night. His mother wouldn't let him out of her sight.'

The detective busied himself fiddling with the percolator, eager not to reveal his weakness with technology. 'I guess you can't blame her, you know, in the circumstances?'

Lyn gave Peter a contemplative look. 'They'll never get over losing their eldest. Sometimes they're over-protective of Ant, but he understands. 'You press that button, you know, to switch the thingy on.'

'Yes, yes. About to do so,' Peter responded, none too convincingly.

Lyn's consciousness returned as she observed Peter making coffee and handing her a hot mug.

'You know,' Lyn began. 'I reckon this is the most complicated case we've worked on together by far. The sheer number of witnesses and suspects for a murder and one attempted murder makes my head spin.'

'You have a point. It always helps to group events together where there seems to be a link. That way you avoid getting lost in the detail and shooting off at a tangent.' Peter blew across the rim of his coffee mug. The steam caused him to half-close his eyes as he took a sip.

'I wish I had your sense of order,' Lyn said as she mirrored her guest's actions. 'So, what do we go at first today?'

'One thing is for sure. We can forget Anthony for now. I imagine the family will have called Dr Thorndike in to give him the once over. As for searching Field Surfer for clues, I'm happy for the boatyard to lift her out of the water and transport her back to their workshops. Once the fire investigators determine the accelerants used and the seat of the fire, my boys and girls can thoroughly inspect the entire boat.'

'How do you reckon they got Ant onto Field Surfer?'

'That's for my lot to look at. In the meantime, as we agreed last night, we should pay Nancy Fairfield a visit. We now know she was lying to us yesterday. Let's push a little harder this time, shall we?'

'Ah, sorry, I forgot you saying that' Lyn said. 'Don't worry, I'll be awake by the time we get there.

After ten minutes, they left the old School House and walked through the cobblestoned high street.

'Phyllis is already at it,' Lyn observed with a wry smile, spotting the compact figure in black, her ever-present hat perched atop her head like a raven.

'Two murders in as many weeks,' Phyllis declared to her mute companion, Betty, who nodded along. 'Mark my words, something wicked this way comes.'

'Indeed,' Lyn murmured under her breath, even when you get your facts wrong. She exchanged a knowing glance with Peter.

Their arrival at Nancy Fairfield's cottage offered a picturesque scene: roses climbing the trellis and the hum of bees busy at work. Yet, beneath the veneer of tranquillity, unease lurked, the spectre of suspicion casting long shadows over the garden's vibrant hues.

'Lyn, Inspector Riley. Two visits in as many days. I am popular. What can I do for you this time?' Nancy greeted them, her friendly demeanour tinged with the slightest edge of nervousness.

Lyn noted Nancy's appearance, the way her hands fidgeted with the hem of her apron, and the subtle shift in her stance as they entered. It was a dance of apprehension and forced pleasantry, performed under the watchful eyes of the village's most curious residents.

'Morning, Nancy,' Lyn greeted in return, her voice light but her gaze sharp. 'We're just following up on a few details.'

'Of course,' Nancy replied, ushering them into her living room.

'Let's start with where you were on the evening of the second murder,' Peter began, his tone gentle yet firm.

'Oh dear, straight into things, I see. Wouldn't you like a nice cup of tea first?'

'I'm afraid not. We have a busy day ahead, so may we continue?'

'Er...yes, of course.'

Nancy repeated her alibi, speaking of a quiet evening spent with her knitting and reading. Still, her words seemed to float in the space between truth and fabrication, leaving Lyn and Peter to sift through her words in search of inconsistencies.

'Did anyone see you that evening? You know, to corroborate your story?' Lyn prodded, watching Nancy's reaction closely.

'Only Alfred, I'm afraid,' Nancy said with a nervous laugh.

'Alfred? then where might we find him?'

Nancy giggled nervously and pointed to an old sideboard decorating one wall of the small room. 'He's hiding under there. He doesn't like strangers. Still, he's better than Peggy Lowther's cat. She hisses and scratches anyone that comes within striking distance.'

Peter's moment of hope faded in an instant as he glowered at the cat, who returned the favour with a yawn.

Lyn shared a look with Peter. 'And you're sure you didn't meet anyone, or, oh, I don't know, go anywhere?'

Nancy gave her a quizzical glance. 'Forgive me, Lyn. We've known each other for many years, and I'd like to think we respect and like each other?'

'Of course, Nancy.'

'Then please accept what I have already told Inspector Riley and you.'

It was as if the air froze in the small living room. Even the sounds of village life seemed to evaporate, leaving just the three of them as if suspended in time.

'No offence intended,' Peter said in a calm tone. 'Let's call it a day, shall we? I'm sure you'll let us know if you hear anything that might help our investigations, right?'

The detective's levity allowed the two women to disengage without either losing face.

'Yes, of course I will. Now, let me show you both out.'

'Where do we go from here? That was uncomfortable,' Lyn mused, her forehead creased with a thousand thoughts.

'Keep digging. The truth is there, somewhere. We just need to find it.'

As they walked back towards the heart of the village, the church bell rang out, its sombre notes resonating with the gravity of their task.

THE SOFT PATTER of rain on the orangery roof of Stanton Hall provided a soothing backdrop to the tense gathering within. With a clean bill of health, Antony Stanton sat at a wrought-iron table, tracing the intricate design in search of truth. Lyn perched beside him, her blonde hair catching the faint light that seeped through the grey clouds overhead.

Lyn had briefed on the morning's events. Now he wished to open a fresh line of investigation.

'The Spindler family name keeps popping up in our record archive as people who were fond of land disputes in the past.'

'As in, Kevin Spindler's family?' Fitch asked.

'The same. And like his fore bares, he's at odds with half the village.'

Lyn nodded. 'You think he had something to gain from both incidents.'

Fitch, a man whose sharp eyes missed little, leaned forward, resting his elbows on the table. 'It's funny you should mention him. When I picked the Jaguar up, I got chatting to one bystander who said he saw the man running from the car. He didn't see his face, but he said the fella had a long ponytail. I dismissed it until you mention his name.'

Sophie clasped her teacup, the floral pattern almost lost in the tight grip of her hands. 'But suspicions aren't enough, are they? We need more than a hippy hairstyle to go on.'

'Which is precisely why we should confront him.' Ant's declaration hung between the group like a challenge.

'A visit might just shake loose the truth,' Lyn replied, her gaze flickering towards the window.

'Agreed,' Ant said, rising from his chair, before wishing he hadn't moved. 'Ug, that hurt.'

Lyn rushed to settling her fiance back into the chair. 'Silly man. What do expect after being knocked out and almost burnt to death? You're not going anywhere, at least for today'.

Ant, resigned to his fate, slumped into his chair.

'Let's get ready, then. Time to pay Mr. Spindler a neighbourly call,' said Fitch.

'I'll follow you in the MINI,' Lyn announced.

'Don't you want to come with us?' asked Fitch as Sophie smiled in the background.

'You must be joking. Ant's Morgan is bad enough without me getting into your clapped-out recovery truck. Mind you, at least you'll never get lost.'

'What do you mean? Fitch asked.

'The trail of engine oil you leave behind you.'

'Very funny, not.' Fitch replied, feigning a hurt look.

The air buzzed with a mix of anticipation and trepidation, each individual grappling with the consequences that lay ahead.

Stepping out from their vehicles, the trio took in the crisp scent of the early evening air; the rural landscape a sombre backdrop to their mission. Lyn felt the weight of responsibility tighten around her chest as she led the way, the gravel crunching underfoot marking their every step.

Sophie hesitated.

'What's up?' Lyn asked.

'Three's a crowd.'

'Eh?'

'We're going in mob handed. Why don't you two go? I'll wait in the truck. What do you say?'

Lyn thought for a moment. 'I get what you mean. OK, it's decided.'

'Remember, we're just here for a chat,' Lyn whispered, her eyes scanning the windows for any sign of movement in Kevin Spindler's majestic home.

'Of course,' Fitch replied, though his voice betrayed a hint of the nervous energy that buzzed beneath his calm exterior. With a deep breath, he rapped sharply on the wood, the sound echoing in the stillness of the country lane.

They waited, the silence stretching between them, filled only by the distant cawing of a rook perched atop the nearby church spire. Fitch felt his heart drumming a staccato rhythm against his ribs, each beat a reminder of what was at stake.

The door swung open abruptly, revealing Kevin Spindler in the flesh. His eyebrows lifted in genuine surprise, a smile playing at the corners of his mouth. 'Fitch, Lynda, what a...pleasant surprise. To what do I owe the pleasure?'

'Hello, Kevin,' Fitch said, matching his host's polite tone while inwardly steeling himself for the conversation ahead. 'We were hoping to have a word, if you've got a moment?'

'Of course, come in,' Kevin said, stepping aside with a gracious sweep of his arm. 'I was just enjoying a spot of tea. Would you care to join me?'

Lyn exchanged a quick, almost imperceptible glance with Fitch before crossing the threshold. 'That would be lovely, thank you,' Lyn said.

Fitch observed the worn carpets and beeswax scent in the hallway, evidence of Kevin's reverence for tradition. It was hard to reconcile this image with the man who might be capable of such dark deeds as the village had witnessed recently.

'Please, sit down,' Kevin gestured towards the sitting room, where a fire crackled merrily in the hearth despite the mild weather outside.

'Thank you,' Lyn said, smoothing out her skirt as she took a seat on the edge of a floral-patterned armchair. Her mind raced as it sifted through the evidence they had collected, searching for the most delicate way to broach the subject.

Fitch sat down beside her and looked at a framed photograph on the mantelpiece. It showed Kevin with a woman they were younger and carefree. He wondered what secrets lay hidden behind those smiling faces.

'Kevin, we...' Lyn began, only to be interrupted by the man himself.

'Ah, I'm forgetting my manners. I'll get that tea first, then discuss why you're here.'

'Right, tea, yes,' Fitch echoed, feeling the weight of suspicion like a stone in his stomach. They needed answers, but how to extract answers without showing their hand?

As Kevin disappeared into the kitchen, Fitch leaned over to Lyn, his voice barely above a whisper. 'We tread carefully. Remember, we're just two concerned villagers seeking the truth.'

'Got it,' Lyn murmured. 'But which truth will he offer us?'

The kettle whistled a tune of domestic normality as Kevin Spindler busied himself with the teapot, his back to Fitch and Lyn. The quaintness of the kitchen, with its hand-painted tiles and copper pots hanging from a rack, stood in stark contrast to the unease that knotted in Fitch's gut. He caught Lyn's eye, offering her an encouraging nod. Their communication perfected over years of partnership.

'Kevin,' Lyn said, her voice steady but warm, 'we've come across something rather troubling.'

Kevin turned, teapot in hand. 'Oh?' he asked, arching an eyebrow as he poured the amber liquid into fine China cups, the floral pattern matching the curtains.

Fitch cleared his throat and leaned forward. 'It's about the, er, incidents.' His fingers traced the armrest of the chair, feeling the texture of the fabric. 'We wanted to know if you had any information you might share with us?'

'Me?' Kevin chuckled, though it lacked mirth. 'I'm as baffled as everyone else by everything that's happened.'

'Ant and I dug a couple of things up from the Stanton Archives,' Lyn continued, her gaze locked onto Kevin's face, searching for a flicker of recognition or guilt. 'The odd thing is your family name keeps cropping up.'

'Is that so?' Kevin's expression hardened, the jovial neighbour facade slipping away. 'And what exactly does your 'evidence' suggest?' He took a sip of tea, his hand steady, his eyes never leaving theirs.

'Conflicts, Kevin,' Lyn replied, her tone gentle yet unyielding. 'Old grudges. Motives that one could not easily dismiss, even today.'

'Motives?' Kevin's laugh was bitter now, his shock morphing into indignation. 'You think I had a motive to harm anyone here? I've lived in this village my entire life! My family longer than Anthony's. What is it you're trying to say?'

'We hoped you might help us understand,' Lyn said softly, her hands folded in her lap. 'Perhaps clear things up?'

'Clear things up?' Kevin's voice rose an octave. 'You barge into my home, disrupt my afternoon with accusations, and expect me to be forthcoming?' He shook his head, a lock of hair falling over his forehead. 'I assure you; I have nothing to do with these... incidents. I have all the land, and money, I need.'

'Who mentioned anything about land or money, Kevin?' Fitch said, in the style of an afterthought.

Fitch and Lyn, both sensing the delicate balance of their enquiry tipping dangerously into violence, knew they needed to tread lightly, yet the urgency of their quest pressed upon them like the encroaching shadows of the evening.

'Of course, we believe you, Kevin,' Lyn said. 'It's just that—'

'Enough!' Kevin interrupted, standing abruptly, his chair

scraping against the tiled floor. 'I won't entertain this ludicrous interrogation any further.'

Lyn reached out, her touch light on Kevin's arm. 'We're only seeking the truth,' she implored, her blue eyes reflecting a sincerity that often disarmed even the most guarded souls.

'Truth...' Kevin muttered, his stance softening under Lyn's earnest gaze. 'Well then, you've wasted your time. I don't know what you want me to say.'

'Anything that could explain—' Fitch began, only to halt as Kevin raised a hand.

'Nothing to explain,' Kevin insisted. 'That is the end of it.'

Their hearts sank with the weight of disappointment, yet the seeds of doubt had been sown. As they sat in Kevin's cozy home, tension filled the air with unanswered questions and the fear of unjustly accusing the innocent.

'Kevin,' Fitch began, with a measured calmness that belied the tempest of thoughts within, 'it's essential for your own sake. If there's any alibi you can provide, any sliver of evidence that could distance you from these heinous acts...'

His words hung unfinished in the air, a bridge half-built between accusation and understanding.

Kevin, his back ramrod straight, interrogated them with eyes that seemed to harden by the second. 'You think I have an alibi just tucked up my sleeve, do you?' The veneer of civility cracked, revealing a flash of indignation. 'Inconvenient, it might be for you. I was alone at home on those nights.'

'Not for us, Kevin.' Fitch responded. 'The next people to ask you that question will be the police. We hoped to have been able to head that off by coming to see you first. But...'

Lyn leaned forward, her hands clasped tightly in her lap,

the gold band on her finger catching the light from the antique lamp.

'Perhaps someone saw you earlier in the evening? Or later? Any minor detail could help clear this up.'

'Later?' Kevin scoffed, his voice rising to a crescendo of frustration. 'What do you want from me? No one tracks my comings and goings!'

Fitch studied him, noting the rigidity of Kevin's posture, the way his hands clenched, then unclenched. He realised then the sheer absurdity of their position—a schoolteacher and Fitch playing detective. But the stakes were too high to abandon their pursuit, even as doubt nipped at the edges of their resolve.

'Accusing a man without proof—it's a dangerous game you're playing,' Kevin said, his tone sharpened to a honed knife. 'A very dangerous game indeed.'

'Nobody is accusing you, Kevin,' Lyn soothed, her voice a soft counterpoint to the tension in the room. 'We're simply trying to piece together a puzzle that's missing far too many pieces.'

'By assuming I'm the one hiding them!' Kevin's face reddened, a bloom of anger against the pallor of his cheeks. 'I've been nothing but cooperative, and yet here you are, ready to pin dreadful crimes on me based on what? Village gossip?'

'Kevin, we—'

'No!' His outburst sliced through Fitch's placating gesture. 'Get out of my house. Now.' His voice brooked no argument.

Fitch stood, the leg of his chair scraping across the floor announcing an echo of finality. They moved towards the door, casting one last look over their shoulders at the man, whose anger was about to erupt.

Chapter Ten

A TEMPORARY PAUSE

THE SHRILL RING of a mobile telephone pierced the quiet of the night, jolting Ant awake. His heart pounded as he fumbled for the receiver in the darkness. 'Hello?'

'Anthony, it's Ann Jones from the village,' came the breathless voice on the other end. 'Tom rang me saying there's trouble up on Ten Acres. He said someone's trying to steal the sheep. I didn't know what to do, so I rang the police, then you.'

Ant's pulse quickened at the thought of his staff in danger and livestock being stolen. He threw off the covers and rolled out of bed, adrenaline coursing through his veins causing his injuries to temporarily fade into the background. 'Thanks Ann, I'll get there straight away. And don't worry. I'll make sure Tom's OK,' he said, his voice urgent.

Hanging up the call. He dressed hastily, grabbing a torch, and slipping into his boots. As he headed for the door.

As he raced towards the field, his thoughts swirled like a storm. It wasn't the first time the Stanton Estate had been

targeted. He hated rustlers; it was an affront to everything he held dear – his family, the village, and the people within it.

Ant's heart pounded as he brought the buggy to a stop at the field entrance. The sound of barking sheep dogs and a panicked bleating filled his ears.

'Tom! Where are you?' Ant shouted, his voice tense with concern.

'Over here, Ant!' came Tom's strained reply from some-where within the chaos.

The dim beam of Ant's torch flickered over the scene, revealing sheep scattering in all directions as two snarling dogs darted through the flock. In the chaotic melee, Ant spotted Tom, his loyal shepherd grappling with an intruder.

'Get off him!' Ant roared, his fists flying as he tried to fend off the attacker. But the raider landed a solid blow, sending Tom staggering back with a cry of pain.

'Tom!' Ant yelled, fear gripping his chest like a vice. He sprinted towards his friend, dodging panicked sheep and snapping dogs as he went.

As Ant drew near, he noticed Tom had landed a few hits on the rustler, who was sporting a rapidly swelling eye. Despite the pain etched across Tom's face, he stubbornly refused to back down.

'Leave our sheep alone, you coward!' Tom spat, lunging forward again. But this time, the raider was ready for him, sidestepping Tom's charge and delivering a punch to his ribs.

'Enough!' Ant roared, fury surging through him as he reached the pair. He swung his torch at the assailant, connecting with a satisfying thud. The man howled in pain and stumbled away, clutching his head.

'Are you alright, Tom?' Ant asked urgently, kneeling

beside his injured employee as the rustler retreated into the night.

'Could be better,' Tom wheezed, wincing as he clutched his side. 'But I'll live.'

'Thank heavens for that,' Ant breathed, relief washing over him. But as the chaos of the disrupted flock continued to swirl around them, he knew they couldn't let their guard down just yet.

'Stay put, Tom. I want to make sure no one else is lurking about,' Ant said determination hardening his resolve.

Tom lay in the damp grass, his breath coming in shallow rasps. With each laboured inhale, Ant could see the pain that gripped his friend. The way he cradled his arm suggested it was broken.

'Can you move?' Ant asked, concern lacing his voice as he surveyed the damage.

'Reckon so,' Tom replied through gritted teeth. 'Just give me a hand.'

As Ant helped Tom to his feet, he caught sight of the bruising that had already begun to bloom on Tom's side. It served as a stark reminder of just how close they'd come to losing more than just their sheep.

'Let's get you back to the hall,' Ant said firmly, supporting Tom's weight as best he could. 'I'll call Dr Thorndike and have him look at you.'

'Ant, the sheep...' Tom protested weakly, but Ant shook his head.

'Your health is more important right now, Tom,' Ant insisted. 'I'll deal with the rustlers, I promise.'

With Tom safely settled into a chair at the estate, Ant wasted no time in making the calls. Thorndike was on his way, and the local constabulary had been updated about the rustling incident.

'We'll do everything we can to apprehend these criminals,' Constable Jenkins assured him over the phone.

'Thank you, Constable,' Ant replied, determination lining his words. 'I won't let them terrorise our village any longer.'

He hung up the phone and glanced out the window, his gaze falling on the still-scattered flock in the distance. These weren't just animals to Ant; they were an integral part of the estate, of the community that he had sworn to protect. He would not stand idly by while outsiders threatened their livelihoods.

'Tom,' Ant said, turning back to his injured friend. 'I need your help.'

'Anything, Ant,' Tom replied, wincing as he shifted in the chair.

'Once Dr Thorndike has patched you up, I want you to help me track these rustlers down,' Ant declared, his eyes alight with determination. 'We'll work with the authorities, but we know our land better than anyone. We can put an end to this.'

Tom nodded, a grim smile on his lips. 'You can count on me and the rest of the lads and lasses.'

As the two men shared a moment of muted resolve, the bright moon cast its soft shadow across the estate. The challenges of the night were far from over. Both men knew the rustlers would be back.

'We'll be ready for them next time, I promise you, Ant said, his voice edged with steely determination.

———

IN THE WARM living room of Lyn's snug home, she stared blankly at the stack of school reports she was supposed to be reviewing. Her divorced parents' raised voices seeped through the closed door, making it impossible for her to concentrate. She rubbed her temples, struggling to keep her composure as she listened to their never-ending bickering.

'Janet, I've told you a thousand times, I didn't forget your birthday on purpose!' her father exclaimed defensively.

'Of course not, Philip,' her mother snapped sarcastically. 'You were too busy with that wretched golf tournament to remember your own wife's birthday!'

'Ex-wife,' her father corrected her, his tone dripping with resentment.

Lyn sighed heavily, feeling as if she were being torn in two by their constant feuding.

I knew inviting them both over for dinner was a bad idea. Divorced for twenty years and still they miss each other enough to enjoy arguing.

The pressure from the local authority on her school was already weighing heavily on her shoulders. Now she had to play referee between her parents, who couldn't seem to spend five minutes in each other's company without biting lumps from each other.

'Please, can we all just try to get along, just for once?' Lyn implored, opening the door to confront her parents. Her eyes welled up with tears, betraying her emotional turmoil. 'I'm under enough stress as it is, without having to deal with this as well. You both agreed before I asked you over that you wouldn't argue. If you still can't stand to be in the same room after all this time, let's stop for the day, shall we?'

Her mother looked taken aback, while her father shifted

uncomfortably. 'We're sorry, darling,' he said sheepishly. 'We don't mean to upset you.'

'Then please,' Lyn pleaded, 'try to find common ground. If not for yourselves, then for me. You're both adults. Surely you can manage that for a couple of hours?'

Her mother sighed, nodding reluctantly. 'Alright, Lyn. We promise.'

'Thank you,' Lyn murmured, retreating to the living room. She closed the door behind her, hoping that their truce would last.

As she tried to re-focus on the school reports, Lyn thought about Ant and the dangers he faced on the estate. His earlier call about Tom's injuries had deeply affected her. She knew Ant would risk everything to protect the flock and maintain order. She hoped fervently that he would be safe, even as she braced herself for the challenge her parents posed.

A few minutes later, Lyn heard a gentle tap on the door between her room and the hallway. 'Are we all alright in here?' her mother asked cautiously, peeking through the living room door.

Lyn looked up, offering a tight-lipped smile. 'Yes, Mum, everything's fine.'

'Good,' her mother replied, hesitating for a moment before adding softly, 'I'm sorry about earlier, Lyn. Your father and I will try harder to get along.'

'Thank you, Mum,' Lyn said. There was hope for her parents yet – and, by extension, for her own frayed nerves.

But as she turned her attention back to the stack of papers, an uneasy feeling settled in the pit of her stomach. As much as she longed for peace, she knew that the imme-diate path ahead would be anything but smooth. And as the day wore on, the tension in the air seemed to thicken, hinting at a storm yet to come.

Her thoughts kept drifting back to Ant, worry gnawing at her heart. She couldn't help but feel guilty for not being there to support him. Their crime-solving partnership had always been a strength for them, but now she was stuck in the village when he needed her most.

'Here you are, love,' her mother said softly, placing a steaming cup of tea beside Lyn's papers. She glanced at her daughter with concern, the lines on her face deepening. 'You look exhausted, dear. You should take a break.'

'Can't afford to, Mum,' Lyn muttered, taking a sip of the tea and wincing at the scalding heat. 'These reports need to be done pronto, and I still have to prepare for my meeting with the local authority.' She couldn't help but feel resentful. If only her parents could behave like grown-ups, she might have been able to concentrate on her work.

'Your father and I will keep it down,' her mother promised again, patting Lyn's hand gently before retreating to the kitchen.

But even in the fleeting moments of silence, Lyn struggled to focus on her professional duties. Her parents' relentless arguing had taken a toll on her mental and emotional well-being, and the strain was showing in her relationship with Ant. He had always been her rock, but now he was grappling with his own problems. The weight of it all threatened to crush her.

'Ant,' she whispered to herself, her eyes misting over as she stared at the empty chair beside her. She imagined him there, offering words of comfort and support. She longed for his powerful arms around her, his warmth chasing away the icy knot in her chest.

'Please be safe, my love,' she murmured, her voice barely audible. 'I need you.'

Lyn stared at the chipped floral teacup in her hands, the hot liquid inside doing little to soothe her frayed nerves. Determination flared within her as she set the cup down with a decisive clink and stood up. She refused to let her parents' tumultuous relationship continue to wreak havoc on her own life.

As she stepped into the kitchen, Lyn challenged her parents. 'Right,' she announced, her voice firm despite her inner turmoil. 'This has gone on long enough.'

Her parents exchanged uneasy glances, understanding the gravity of the situation but unsure how to proceed. Lyn braced herself for the inevitable resistance, but she had to try, for all their sakes.

'Mother, Father, please,' she implored, her voice softening. 'Is there any way you two can sit down and truly discuss your differences? Perhaps find some common ground or compromise—at least when you're with me?'

Her father sighed, running a hand through his greying hair. 'I suppose we could... try.'

'Good,' Lyn said firmly. 'Let's sit down together in the living room. No raised voices, no accusations. '

Lyn couldn't help but feel a wave of helplessness wash over her. Despite the long separation, she held onto hope that something might yet be salvaged in her parents' broken relationship. If only Ant was here, he would know what to do.

Ant, she thought, a pang of worry tightening her chest. Please come back safely.

Teapot in hand, Lyn returned to the living room, where her parents sat stiffly perched on opposite ends of the floral-patterned sofa. The tension in the air was palpable, yet they both seemed willing to try for their daughter's sake.

'Right,' Lyn said, taking a deep breath. 'Let's make a start.'

As they tentatively embarked on the difficult conversation, Lyn couldn't shake the feeling that things were far from resolved. Her parents' attempts to understand each other were just the start of an arduous journey, and Ant's absence weighed heavily on her. She hoped, with every fibre of her being, that they would find their way back to each other soon, so they could face the challenges ahead together.

The weather outside matched the tension inside the old schoolhouse. The future remained uncertain for her parents and Lyn's relationship with Ant. Only time would tell whether they could navigate these trials and emerge stronger.

Chapter Eleven

A SURPRISE VISITOR

THE MORNING SUN cast a gentle glow over the cobblestone path as Ant reached Lyn's home, 'the Old Schoolhouse'.

'Heavens!' Lyn gasped, her hands flying to her mouth as she took in the sight of him. His dark hair tousled, a purple-tinged bruise blossoming under his left eye, and various scrapes marking his powerful arms. 'I didn't think it was that bad?'

'Let's just say those rustlers weren't too keen on an audience,' Ant replied with a half-grin.

In the comforting confines of her sitting room, Lyn dabbed at Ant's grazes with antiseptic. Her touch was as tender as if she were handling delicate porcelain instead of flesh and blood. The remedy's smell mixed with the lavender outside, creating a peaceful moment interrupted by Lyn's worried gaze.

Ant tried to reassure his fiance, but the lingering fear of what could have happened remained.

Desperate to change the subject, Ant tilted his head,

studying Lyn's face, which carried its own tale of a sleepless night. 'How was dinner with your parents? Peaceful, I hope?'

Lyn's lips pressed into a thin line, and she set the cotton ball aside with more force than necessary. 'I'd rather not talk about it,' she said, the shadows beneath her eyes betraying the strain of the evening's familial tempest.

'Understood.' Ant's voice was soft, laced with empathy. He knew all too well the echoes of arguments that had filled Lyn's childhood home. Echoes that refused to be silenced even by divorce and divided households.

A clock ticked somewhere in the background, marking the passage of time. It reminded them of the present threats lurking beyond Lyn's flower-filled haven. Yet there remained an undercurrent of resolve between Ant and Lyn. A shared determination to face whatever dangers lay ahead, together.

'Right then,' Ant said with a renewed sense of purpose, offering Lyn a smile that promised adventure mixed with the ordinary. 'Shall we tackle today's mysteries?'

'Let's do it,' Lyn said, her response immediate and accompanied by a nod that sent her blonde hair glinting in the sunlight. 'Where do you suggest we start?'

'Sheep,' Ant replied.

'Sheep?'

'You know, fluffy, awkward, always eating and—'

'Yes, I get the picture. Thank you very much. I presume you mean we go back to the field in which you picked up that black eye?'

Ant laughed as he opened the front door to allow Lyn to pass. 'Er, we'll take the MINI if you don't mind,' Lyn remarked.

'Coward. The Morgan is in fine fettle.'

'That's what you say, but if you think I'm going to risk

another soaking from its leaking roof, you've another think coming.'

'But it might not rain?'

'And pigs can fly,' retorted Lyn as she slammed the door shut, then rattled it with the cast-iron door knocker to make sure.

'On one condition, then,' Ant remarked.

Lyn turned to give her fiance a curious glance. 'And?'

'I drive.' Before Lyn could react, he'd relieved her of the car key and claimed the driver's seat.

Will he ever grow up? Lyn thought with an inward smile.

The landscape stretched before them, a quilt of green dotted with the gentle white fluff of sheep grazing. As the sun cast a golden glow over the flat landscape, the air was alive with the bucolic symphony of bleating lambs and birdsong. All appeared calm and picturesque, but it concealed the violent events of the previous night.

'Beautiful, isn't it?' Lyn remarked, her words floating away on the breeze.

'It is,' Ant agreed, his eyes scanning the idyllic terrain that acted as an unwitting backdrop to danger. 'Hard to imagine anything untoward happening in such a place.'

They reached the spot where the rustlers had ambushed Ant. The tranquillity of the location made the memory of last night's scuffle even more jarring. The ground bore the scars of the commotion: trampled grass, scattered wool fibres, and hoof prints etched into the soft pasture like a chaotic dance.

'Look there,' Ant pointed to a thorny hedgerow, where a piece of fabric fluttered in the wind, snagged on a branch as if waving an unspoken clue. It was a stark reminder that beauty often harbours unseen threats.

'Careful,' Lyn cautioned as Ant approached, his hand encased in the protective shield of a handkerchief as he disentangled the shred of evidence.

'Got it.' He held the torn fabric up to the light, examining its texture and colour. 'This could belong to anyone, but it might just lead us to our midnight marauder.'

'You don't think this has anything to do with...' Lyn left the question hanging.

Ant shook his head. 'I doubt it. This feels more like greed than malice. Our killer is cunning, calculating—this is too... mundane for their style.'

'Still,' Lyn mused, 'every clue is a step closer to understanding what's been going on.'

'Yes,' Ant replied, pocketing the fabric with care. The sun was climbing higher now, its rays warming the skin, but unable to dispel the chill of what lay hidden among the beauty of their surroundings. They turned back towards the village, their minds pooling with thoughts of the night's events, each step taking them deeper into the heart of the mystery.

Ant guided the MINI down the narrow lane, its engine purring with a comforting reliability. The lush green fields of the Stanton Estate enveloped them as they approached Ant's home, a majestic manor house. One that had guarded the village for centuries.

The Earl, his features drawn tighter than the strings of an English longbow, paced the gravel drive as they arrived. His stoic demeanour betrayed by the concern etched into his furrowed brow. 'Dreadful business, this rustling,' he muttered upon seeing Ant, the sight of his son's bruised visage causing a momentary falter in his voice.

'Father, it's only a scratch,' Ant assured him, though the

protective glint in the Earl's eyes suggested he found little comfort in the dismissal.

Countess Stanton emerged from the grand entrance, her silver hair catching the mid-morning sun like a halo. Her gaze hovered over Ant's injuries, a mother's worry making her otherwise serene face tense. 'Anthony, my dear, come inside. We'll have something to take your mind off last night's events.'

In the dining room, the conversation wavered between the fragrant aroma of baked scones and the less palatable topics of theft and murder. Lyn noted the way the countess steered their conversation towards the upcoming village fete, even as the rustling attack lingered like an uninvited guest at the table.

'Mother, we're being careful,' Ant said, intercepting the concerns that danced behind her eyes. 'Our amateur sleuthing is just a way to help the police and have a bit of fun, nothing more.'

'Anthony, I just—' the countess started, only to be reassured by Lyn's gentle smile.

'We look out for each other,' Lyn added, placing a reassuring hand on the countess's shoulder.

After an hour of strained conversation, their departure from Stanton Hall brought a reaffirmation from Ant that they'd be careful. The lingering embrace from Ant's mother conveyed more than words could. As they left the safety of the estate and drove back into the village, Lyn felt a prickling sensation at the back of her neck.

After parking the MINI at Lyn's house, the pair strolled into the village centre. They passed by the quaint row of shops; their windows displaying an array of local crafts and produce. The villagers went about their day with cheerful nods and waves, yet Lyn couldn't shake the unsettling sense of eyes following their every move.

'Are you alright?' Ant asked.

'Just a feeling,' she murmured, casting a glance over her shoulder where shadows played between the buildings. 'It's nothing.'

'Trust your instincts,' Ant advised in a soft tone, his own gaze taking in the peaceful façade of the village with a renewed wariness.

As they continued their walk, Lyn's alertness did not wane. It hung between them, as if whispering caution with every step they took towards the heart of the village.

With the unsettling feeling of unseen eyes upon them, Ant and Lyn made a taciturn agreement. Their next stop would be the police station to see Detective Inspector Peter Riley. Though the villagers were familiar faces, recent events had cast a shadow over even the friendliest of smiles.

'Peter's experience will be useful now,' Anthony commented as they approached the police station. Lyn nodded, her mind already racing with what they might learn from the seasoned inspector.

They stepped inside to be met by the friendly face of the desk sergeant. This was a man who'd known the pair since they were children and he a beat bobby. As they shared past adventures and laughed about the sergeant catching them scrumping, an office door opened.

'Ah, the amateur detectives return.' Riley greeted them with a wry smile. He ushered them into his cluttered office, where papers lay in organised chaos across his desk.

'Rough night, I hear,' Riley said, gesturing for them to sit as he studied Ant's bruised features. 'Tell me everything.'

Ant recounted the previous evening's events, his voice

steady despite the memory of hands grappling in the darkness and the bleating panic of sheep. Lyn watched Riley, noting the furrow between his brows deepen with each detail.

'Can't say I'm not worried about you both,' Riley admitted after a thoughtful silence. 'I'll have some of my lads do extra rounds near Stanton Hall. Just until we've got this sorted.'

'Thank you, Peter,' Lyn said, relieved yet still feeling the weight of unease settle in her stomach. 'We just want to sort this out without more trouble finding us first.'

'Trouble finds those who go looking for it,' Riley remarked, but his tone was devoid of judgement. 'But I know you two won't just sit by. Just promise me you'll be careful.'

'We will,' Ant assured him, standing up to leave. 'And if there's anything we can do to assist...'

'Keep your eyes open and stay out of harm's way,' Riley replied, escorting them to the door. 'That's help enough for now.'

The warm sun greeted them as they stepped back outside, the police station's door closing behind them with a definitive click. They shared a look, the kind that spoke volumes without a word needing to be uttered.

'Let's head home,' Lyn suggested, though the notion of home brought little comfort when shadows could lurk around any corner.

'Your place it is,' Ant agreed, offering her a small, determined smile as they walked side by side, each lost in thoughts of what lay ahead.

They had taken a dozen steps from the police station when Riley's voice called them back. 'One more thing,' he said, his expression as serious as the matter at hand. Ant and Lyn turned, watching as Riley gestured to a man standing to attention at a nearby lamppost.

'Constable Finch will keep an eye out for you, Lyn,' Riley explained. 'Plain clothes, of course.'

'I appreciate that, Peter,' Ant said in a muted voice, while squeezing Lyn's hand.

As they walked back to Lyn's home, the quaint charm of Stanton Parva unfolded around them. The village green looking inviting under the comforting afternoon sun. But beneath the idyllic surface, unease gnawed at Lyn's mind, her senses heightened to where the sight of a stranger, or banging shop door, made her heart skip a beat.

'Murder has no place here,' Ant said, as if by stating it, he could make it true.

'Nor anywhere,' Lyn agreed, her voice carrying her unwavering commitment to justice.

'Let's go over everything once we get home,' Ant suggested. 'Perhaps we missed something yesterday.'

'Lead the way, Sherlock,' Lyn teased, taking solace in the light banter that always seemed to bubble between them, even in the darkest of times.

'Home again, then,' Lyn said, though the word felt hollow when safety was such a fragile thing.

'Home it is,' Ant echoed, his tone resolute as they approached the old schoolhouse. The sun rode high in the sky and a slight breeze caused flowering baskets to rotate and sway, as if to show off their dazzling arrangements.

In contrast, as they reached the door, a sudden prickle of awareness ran down Lyn's spine. She paused. Her gaze drawn to the growing gloom behind them. There was nothing to see, and yet...

'Imagination,' she chided herself, but as Ant locked the door behind them, the sense of someone watching lingered.

Ant picked up the antique phone, its Bakelite casing cool to his touch, and dialled Fitch's number with a practiced hand. He glanced at Lyn, perched on the edge of the kitchen table, offering him a half-smile.

'Hello, Fitch? It's Ant,' he said, his voice low but clear. 'We've had a bit of excitement at Stanton Hall last night.'

Lyn watched as Ant filled in their friend on the rustling incident, his dark brows knitting together as he spoke.

'Can you keep your ear to the ground for us?' Ant asked, his tone serious. 'Anything unusual could be a lead.'

'Of course,' Lyn heard Fitch's voice crackle over the line. 'I'll let you know if I hear anything amiss.'

'Thanks, Fitch. We're counting on you,' Ant replied before hanging up. He turned back to Lyn, and she read the resolve in his eyes. They were in this together.

Ant said, 'Alright, let's get to work,' as he rolled up his sleeves. 'Let's get down to business.'

The old schoolhouse, once filled with the laughter of children, now held an air of quiet determination. Papers lay scattered on the immense table, with Lyn's tidy handwriting next to Ant's messy script. They examined alibis, timelines, and Peter's interviews. Each piece offering a clue to solve the puzzle.

'Could it be...?' Lyn murmured, tapping a finger against the timeline she'd drawn.

'Perhaps,' Ant mused, leaning in to examine the notes, then cross-checking with the timings. 'But we can't jump to conclusions. Not yet.'

'Of course not,' Lyn agreed, her gaze firm.

The kitchen grew dimmer as the sun began its slow descent, casting the schoolhouse in hues of amber and fading blue. Their conversation had a rhythm as they talked about theories and then moved on until the room itself seemed to vibrate with their intense focus.

'Look at this,' Ant pointed out, holding up a statement. 'If we cross-reference the times...'

'Then there's no way Mrs. Fairfield could have seen the suspect from her kitchen window – and we know she lied about being in the house on Sunday evening,' Lyn finished, a spark of excitement in her voice.

They leaned back, taking a moment to survey the fruits of their labour. Pages marked with pins and strings creating a web of connections only they could decipher. Yet, despite the progress, an undercurrent of unease remained; the killer was still out there, moving unseen among them.

'Getting nearer,' Lyn whispered, more to herself than to Ant. But he heard her, nodding in soundless agreement.

'Yup,' he said, glancing towards the window where the shadows lengthened. 'Minute by minute.'

The grandfather clock struck eleven-o-clock, its chimes echoing through the old schoolhouse as Ant rose from his chair. With a methodical calmness that belied the anxiety within, he moved from window to window, his fingers working to secure each latch. The last vestiges of daylight danced on the glass before succumbing to the encroaching night.

'Can't be too careful,' he murmured, double-checking the locks on the doors—front and back. His eyes scanned the perimeter, searching for anything out of place among the creeping ivy and the trimmed hedges that skirted the property. The village seemed to slumber under the watchful gaze of the silver moon, but Ant knew better than to trust appearances. Somewhere out there, danger was lurking.

Lyn watched him, her arms wrapped around herself.

She admired his quiet resolve, the way he took charge without fanfare, ensuring their safety with the same attentiveness he gave every task. 'Everything's secure then?' she asked, her voice steady despite the finger of fear tracing her spine.

'Like Fort Knox,' Ant replied, offering her a reassuring smile that reached his warm hazel eyes. He crossed the room to where she stood and unfolded her arms, taking her hands in his. 'You'll be alright,' he assured her, though they both knew guarantees were as thin as mist in these uncertain times.

'Thank you for looking after me,' Lyn said, her gratitude sincere. She leaned into Ant's embrace, the familiar scent of his cologne comforting.

'Always,' Ant whispered, pressing a kiss to her forehead. They stood like that for a time, drawing strength from one another, two hearts beating in the face of an unseen adversary. Their love was a reminder that even amid fear and uncertainty, there was something unbreakable binding them together.

Lyn stood on the doorstep, the cool night air nipping at her cheeks as she waved Ant off. His silhouette receded as he walked towards the Morgan sports car. She watched until the shadows swallowed him whole, a pang of loneliness tightening her chest.

'Take care,' she murmured to the night, though he was already too far to hear.

Turning back into the house, she slid the deadbolt into place with a resolute click and fastened the chain. The sound of the heavy door closing was a minor comfort against the uneasiness that had taken up residence in the pit of her stomach.

In the lounge, Lyn's fingers brushed against the velvet

fabric of the curtains as she drew them together, blocking out the night's prying eyes. The room dimmed to a cozy twilight, the familiar furniture casting long, benign shadows across the patterned carpet.

As she made her rounds through the substantial building, turning off lights and tidying away the day's clutter, each click of a switch deepened the silence that enveloped her. It was in this hush that a movement just beyond the window caught her eye. A fleeting shadow that danced away as soon as she tried to focus on it.

'Ridiculous,' Lyn chided herself, heart thudding in an erratic rhythm. 'It's just a fox, or Mrs. Banwell's cat on the prowl. Nothing sinister.'

With a steadying breath, she continued her evening ritual, moving from room to room. Her thoughts wandered to Ant, to the earl and countess, to the twisted puzzle that had cast a pall over their idyllic surroundings. But she pushed those worries aside, intent on preparing for bed and the promise of rest.

In the kitchen, she reached for the last light switch, the soft amber glow from the hall spilling in to hold back the darkness. Lyn paused, a sense of unease prickling at her nape. Her gaze fell upon the brass doorknob of the back door, its polished surface gleaming.

And then it turned.

Her breath hitched in her throat, the sound of metal against metal slicing through the stillness like a warning bell. Someone was there—someone who should not be.

'Ant, is that you?' she called out, using his name as both question and plea, even as logic told her it was impossible. He would not have returned so soon, not without knocking, without calling out to her.

A chill swept through her as the doorknob continued its

slow, deliberate rotation, the boundaries of her haven breached by an unseen hand. And as the night held its breath, Lyn's heart raced with the realisation that she was no longer alone.

Chapter Twelve

TIME FOR REFLECTION

THE MORNING MIST still hung over Horsey Windpump, with its new sails standing still against the brightening sky. Lyn arrived with a heart still fluttering like a trapped sparrow, her mind replaying the ominous turn of the kitchen doorknob the previous night. It was only the young undercover bobby. His cheeks flushed with apology when he realised his blunder.

'I'm sorry, Miss Blackthorn,' he'd stammered. 'I'm still getting my sea legs doing this plain clothes malarky. Could you—would you mind not mentioning it to the inspector?'

Lyn had seen enough earnestness in his wide eyes to keep his secret. 'Of course I won't. Perhaps we both learned something last night. You know, not jumping to conclusions?'

'Oh, er, yes. I see what you mean, Miss Blackthorn.'

The worried young officer made off when Lyn called him back. 'Listen, please call me Lyn. Everyone does. By the way, have you been on duty all night?'

'Well, yes, I have. And your name. I can't call you that.

Inspector Riley would have my guts for garters if he heard me calling you by your first name.'

Lyn smiled at the nervous bobby. 'I tell you what, why don't we keep it a secret just between me and you? Let's have a pact. If either of us catches sight of Peter…er, I mean Inspector Riley, we'll give the other one the nod, so he'll never know. How's that for a plan?'

The newly promoted undercover bobby gave the hint of a smile. 'That sounds good, but are you sure?'

'Oh, our plan is watertight, so let's say no more about it. Now, if you've been watching my house all night, the least I can do is cook your breakfast. A full English? Just one thing,' Lyn said with a smile. What do I call you and don't say constable? You must have a name, yes?'

The policeman's eyes veered between Lyn and the sausage and bacon resting on two separate plates next to the cooker. 'My real name is Roger, but everyone calls me "Dodge".'

'Ah, as in Roger the Dodger. I see. Well, Dodge, sit yourself down and I'll rustle you up some nice grub and a mug of tea…or do you prefer coffee?'

Dodger blushed, 'Er, coffee, if you don't mind; one sugar, and milk, if that's not too much trouble, er, Lyn?'

The poor lad, he's so embarrassed, Lyn thought.

In the ten minutes it took Lyn to cook breakfast, the pair talked about a variety of topics as Dodge began to relax and trust Lyn. In a trice, the food landed before Dodge, and he tucked in as if it were his first meal in a week. The young man's presence lifted Lyn's spirits and helped her overcome her worries. The young man served as a breath of fresh air in what had been a torrid time for her.

As Dodge left to catch up with some well-earned sleep, Lyn checked her mobile and noted she had a message. She scolded herself for not turning off the silent mode on her phone, which she always activated before going to sleep. She called up the message and heard Ant inviting her to join him and Peter at Horsey Windpump.

Lyn checked the time of the message against the current time. She reasoned they'd be awhile yet, so sat down to finish a second coffee before getting ready for the day.

As she approached Ant and Peter, already seated outside the small snack bar at the foot of the Horsey Windpump, she managed a smile. They welcomed her with hot coffee and a delicious cake.

'Morning, Lyn,' Ant said, his own eyes clouded with concern. 'Did you sleep well?'

'Fitfully,' she admitted, accepting the coffee.

'And how did the lad do?' Peter said.

'I didn't know he was there until he knocked about an hour ago. He said everything was quiet. I hope you don't mind, but I made him a coffee before he toddled off for some sleep.'

'Coffee?' Peter joked, 'Don't you go spoiling my young officers, they must learn the hard way, just as I did. It makes you a better copper.'

'Do they really?' Lyn responded, playfully pointing a finger at the detective.

Peter returned Lyn's playful smile before taking a sip of his coffee he and Ant had bought from the snack bar. Let's get down to brass tacks,' he suggested, opening his worn leather notebook. Page after page filled with names, dates, and question marks—so many loose ends.

'Any word on the second victim?' Lyn asked, hoping for a sliver of news.

Peter shook his head gravely. 'No change. It's not looking good, I'm afraid.' His words seemed to pull the warmth from the sunshine that bathed the tall, elegant Windpump.

They fell into a gloomy silence, the weight of their stalled investigation pressing down on them. To clear their heads, they took a stroll along the small staithe, where generations past loaded and unloaded goods for transport. The trio then turned left to walk towards Horsey Mere. The mill, standing proudly against the flat Norfolk landscape, represented resilience untouched by time. It was a stark contrast to the current mood, which hung heavy like the overcast skies of autumn.

When they arrived at their destination, the wide expanse of water surrounded by trees momentarily took their minds off things. A pair of Great Crested Grebes glided across the mere, their elegant necks arched like bows. Overhead, a marsh harrier circled, its keen eyes searching the reeds below, undisturbed by human troubles.

'Nature carries on, doesn't it?' Lyn remarked softly, as if speaking too loudly might shatter the surrounding tranquillity.

'Indeed,' Ant agreed, watching the birds with a distant expression. 'If only our case were as straightforward as their instincts.'

Their leisurely pace and the surrounding wildlife couldn't dispel the sense of helplessness that had settled over the trio. They were investigators adrift, lacking the compass of solid leads or the wind of progress to carry them forward.

'Why don't we head to the boat repairers? I assume they've collected her from her resting place,' Peter suggested with a sigh. 'Maybe there's something we've missed, some piece of the puzzle hiding in plain sight.'

Ant nodded. 'It wasn't an easy lift, but they managed it

in the end. Field Surfer looked deeply sorry for herself, let me tell you.'

As they turned away from the serene scene and made their way back to the realities of their investigation, each felt the nagging doubt. The solution to this mystery was as elusive as the muted whispers of the Norfolk Broads.

The scent of sawdust and marine varnish was thick in the air as Lyn, Ant, and Peter approached the bustling boat-yard. A rhythmic hammering of mallets against wood and the sharp whine of saws cutting through planks formed a lively symphony of industry. The workers moved purpose-fully, their hands and aprons showing the signs of their dedi-cated craftsmanship.

'Mind your step around here,' the yard manager cautioned, his voice barely carrying over the clamour. 'And I'd be much obliged if you take care aboard. She's not fully supported in her cradle yet. Anyway, why do you want to look, the other lot, the ones in white overalls? They've only just left?'

Lyn thanked the man but didn't answer his question. She watched the workers as they moved around unfinished boats and tangled ropes. She stayed landside, watching as Ant and Peter made their way towards the ill-fated vessel.

Ant grimaced, feeling the effects of his recent injuries as he climbed aboard the charred skeleton of the once proud wherry. The smell of smoke still clung to the damp timbers, mingling with the musty odour of waterlogged wood. Burnt edges blackened the deck, and the interior held the desolate aspect of a ruin long forsaken.

'Looks like she'll never sail again," Peter observed, his voice tinged with regret. He ran a hand along a scorched beam, the soot smudging his fingers.

'Nor reveal her secrets, it seems,' Ant added ruefully,

bending awkwardly to peer into nooks and crannies where evidence might have lurked. But their search yielded nothing but shadows and the creak of settling wood beneath their weight.

'Forensics might have found something we've missed,' Peter offered, though his tone suggested he didn't hope.

Back on solid ground, Lyn watched as the men returned, their shoulders slumped in disappointment. The three of them stood for a moment, absorbing the discord between the vitality of the boatyard and the stagnation of their investigation.

'Sometimes I wonder,' Ant began, his eyes scanning the horizon where the greenery met the sky, 'if all this effort is worth it.'

'You might be right,' Lyn murmured, 'But we can't stop now. Not while there's still a chance for justice.'

Peter agreed, though the weariness in his eyes spoke louder than his words. 'Come on, then. We've got a long day ahead.'

The mid-day sun flooded the boatyard in its comforting rays, painting everything in hues of gold and amber. Yet, as they left the boatyard, the trio carried with them a shadow that no light could dispel. A mystery unsolved and a darkness encroaching upon the idyllic landscape of Stanton Parva.

A thought occurred to Lyn. 'Why don't you call in on Gavin Holloway again, see if he's any more forthcoming than the last time?'

Ant looked at Peter. 'I don't suppose it can do any harm?'

Back in Stanton Parva, Lyn climbed out of her MINI. Ant pulled up behind her, allowing Peter to lift his tall frame from the tiny Morgan and have a stretch.

'I can't ignore the school any longer,' she said, her voice tinged with guilt. 'My deputy's patience is wearing thin.'

'Understood,' Ant replied, offering a supportive nod. 'We'll fill you in later.'

With a last wave, Lyn departed on foot, leaving Peter to navigate his stiff body into the sports car. In seconds, the car roared off to navigate the winding country lanes. The drive was hushed at first, save for the occasional sputter from the Morgan's engine, like an old man muttering in his sleep.

Ant wondered if Holloway would be more cooperative today, breaking the silence as they crossed an old stone bridge over a small stream.

'Hard to say,' Peter sighed, staring out across the fields. 'Men like him can be fools to their pride.'

They arrived at Holloway's farmhouse to find Gavin knee-deep in purple blooms, a frown creasing his brow as he surveyed the lavender crop. His displeasure at their arrival was palpable, like the thickening clouds overhead promising rain.

'Checking on the harvest?' Ant ventured, adopting a casual tone.

'You're a farmer. What does it look like? I'm looking for lost sheep?'

'Ah, you've heard,' Ant replied without making further comment.

'It's ready for cutting in a day or two if the weather holds,' Gavin said begrudgingly.

'Who do you sell it to?' Peter asked, getting straight to the point.

Gavin's frown deepened. 'Middleman,' he spat the word as if it had left a sour taste. 'Ask Whitaker about that. Anyway, I've got no time to stand around yappin' all day.'

Before they could press further, he turned on his heel

and marched off, his silhouette growing smaller against the sea of lavender.

'Interesting fellow,' Ant remarked, watching Gavin's retreating into the distance.

'Let's hope Whitaker sheds more light on the matter,' Peter said, steering them towards their next destination.

Thomas Whitaker greeted them with a hearty laugh, clad in plus-fours and tweed as though plucked from a hunting scene in a bygone era.

'Off to shoot pheasants, Thomas?' Ant teased, struggling to suppress a chuckle.

'Alas, it's not the season, as you well know, young Anthony,' Whitaker said while treating his guests to a twirl. 'But one must always be prepared!'

'Indeed, you look dapper,' Peter said with a straight face.

'Thank you, gentlemen.' Whitaker's smile was as smooth as the aged scotch he favoured. 'Now, what brings you to my doorstep?'

Peter got straight down to matters. 'This business with Gavin Holloway and the lavender—'

'Ah, his complaints have reached your ears too?' Whitaker's wry smile suggested he'd trod this path many times before. 'The man believes the world's conspiring against him.'

'Is it true you act as a middleman for, well, whoever buys it next?' Peter pressed.

Whitaker nodded. 'And I give him over the odds. Sometimes at a loss to myself. But loyalty between landowner and tenant isn't measured in coin alone. Your father and you know what I mean, eh, Anthony? You see, Inspector, we protect our own. The problem is, Gavin doesn't know that most years I subsidise him. That chip on his shoulder will be his undoing. Mark my words.'

Ant and Peter left Whitaker behind, leaving more questions than answers in their wake. Whitaker's laughter lingered like the sound of a faraway hunting horn.

As Ant and Peter waved goodbye to Thomas Whitaker, a shared silence enveloped them as they processed the meeting.

'He seems a genuine sort, doesn't he?" Peter finally said, breaking the quiet as he slipped into the passenger seat.

'He's of a kind. Perhaps like my family," Ant mused, starting the engine. The car hummed to life, a comforting sound amid their uncertainty. 'But if Whitaker is telling the truth, and he has nothing to gain from these crimes. It looks like we're at yet another dead end.'

'We're only finding dead ends lately,' Peter remarked with frustration, gazing out the window at passing hedgerows.

The Victorian facade of the police station came into view, its brickwork standing firm against the test of time. The desk sergeant, with a weary expression, leafed through a record book as they approached, greeted by the smell of aged paper and furniture polish.

'Anything interesting, Sergeant?' Peter enquired, leaning against the counter with hopeful anticipation.

'Nothing of note, I'm afraid, Guv,' the sergeant replied without looking up. 'A young chap confirming his vehicle documents, a missing cat, and Phyllis complaining about our front step being a death trap.'

'Phyllis and her escapades,' Ant chuckled softly.

'Pipe clay. She says it needs.' The sergeant finally looked up, his eyes reflecting a time gone by. 'Used to whiten steps. My grandmother swore by the stuff. Heaven help the soul who dared sully her pristine work after she'd finished. Every day until the night she died, she did that.'

'Pipe clay, eh?' Peter echoed, more to himself than anyone else, a furrow forming between his brows as he pondered over the day's earlier conversations.

'Indeed.' The sergeant closed the record book with a soft thud. 'A relic from another era, much like some of our villagers, it seems.'

The two men retreated to Peter's office, a room filled with the evidence of many cases won and lost. As they sat across from each other, the tension was palpable; both knew they were missing something vital, something as clear as the whitened steps of yesteryear, yet as elusive as the slightest smudge upon them.

'Where do we go from here, Peter?' Ant asked, his hands clasped together in thought.

The detective leaned back in his chair; the leather creaking under his weight. 'We keep digging, Ant. We look at what's in front of us until we see what's been hiding in plain sight.'

The wall clock ticked away, marking the passage of time and the urgency of their task. They needed a breakthrough, and they needed it soon. The stillness of the room was thick with the unsaid; the next move they made could very well be the turning point of their entire investigation.

A sudden knock on the door interrupted the silence, bringing the possibility of a new lead. Lyn slipped into the room, her presence a ripple of fresh energy amid the stagnant air of frustration. Ant's eyes brightened as she arrived and sat next to him.

'Any news?' she asked, the hopeful lilt in her voice already bracing for disappointment.

'Whitaker's out of the picture,' Peter said with a shrug, his grey eyes reflecting the bleak outlook of their investigation. 'And Gavin? Well, he's just Gavin.'

Just as they were about to continue talking, the desk sergeant entered with a tray of comfort, but no answers. 'I thought you could use some cheering up,' he said, placing the tray down.

'Thank you, Sergeant.' Lyn's smile was genuine. Each took a steaming mug and a ginger-nut biscuit, the humble offerings momentarily softening the hard edges of their predicament.

It was as Lyn wrapped her hands around the warmth of her mug, the steam curling like whispered secrets, that an idea sparked within her. 'What if Kevin Spindler is into something dodgy? Land speculation or a sour deal, perhaps?'

Peter, ever the pragmatic one, tempered her enthusiasm. 'Let's not chase shadows, Lyn. We've no evidence of a land dispute leading to the violence we've seen.'

The deflation in Lyn's posture spoke volumes; it was as if the steam from her tea carried away her fleeting hope.

'Then what's the point?' Her voice cracked with exasperation. 'We're running in circles, chasing our own tails!'

'Because we have to, Lyn.' Peter's tone was gentle but firm. 'At least I must, but Ant and you? You've given more than enough. Maybe it's time for a breather. Think of the school, of the Earl.'

A heavy silence settled over them, broken only by the occasional crackle of biscuit. Ant rubbed his chin, his dark eyes clouded with guilt. 'I...I know you're right. It's hard to let go.'

'Sleep on it,' Peter suggested, standing up to signal the end of the meeting. 'No pressure, remember? Do what's best for you.'

They walked down the corridor, shadows from the

fading light stretching, lost in thoughts about their sleuthing future in Stanton Parva.

Ant forked through the remnants of his shepherd's pie, the clink of cutlery punctuating the quiet that enveloped the kitchen. Lyn pushed a pea back and forth on her plate, the vibrant green a stark contrast to the muted tones of their mealtime silence.

'Bit of a tough day, eh?' Ant finally ventured, leaning back in his chair with a soft creak of aged wood.

Lyn looked up from her plate, the lines beneath her eyes a telltale sign of the weight on her mind. 'Peter certainly gave us plenty to ponder,' she replied, her voice carrying the strain of their long afternoon.

'He did,' Ant agreed, his hand absently stroking the grain of the table. 'I can't shake the feeling that we've been playing at detectives, lost in the chase's thrill.'

She nodded, a small smile flickering across her lips at the shared sentiment. 'It's been an adventure, but reality is knocking, isn't it?'

'Responsibilities,' Ant mused. 'They do have a habit of creeping up on you.' He paused, considering their future. 'Once we're married, life will only get busier.'

'True,' Lyn conceded. 'And we can't let our hobby interfere with what really matters. Our jobs, the children at school, your father's estate.'

'Perhaps it's time we stepped aside,' Ant suggested, his voice laced with reluctance. 'Let the police manage the grittier side of Stanton Parva.'

'Sounds like we agree, then.' Lyn's relief was palpable. 'A final decision over breakfast, eh?

'Stanton Broad Cafe?' Ant proposed, a hint of lightness returned to his tone.

'Perfect. We'll have clear heads after a night's rest.' Lyn

rose from the table, stacking the dishes with a newfound lightness.

'Tomorrow it is, then,' Ant said, standing to help her clear away the remnants of their quiet dinner.

As Lyn waved Ant off in a repeat performance of the previous night, she glimpsed a familiar figure in the darkness. It was Dodge.

The young policeman acknowledges his charge's wave, then vanished into the night.

Lyn stayed a while at the front door. She watched as the moon cast its silver glow over Stanton Parva, the lingering mystery tucked away in the shadows, waiting for dawn's light.

Chapter Thirteen

DECISION TIME

ANT NERVOUSLY TAPPED his fingers on the chequered tablecloth at Stanton Broad Cafe, their secret meeting spot. Lyn arrived, her blonde hair catching the early morning sun as it streamed through the lace curtains.

'Morning,' she greeted, slipping into the seat opposite him.

'Morning,' Ant replied, his smile not reaching his eyes. The waiter brought over two steaming mugs of coffee and a plate of buttered crumpets. The scent of breakfast filled the air, cozy and comforting, yet Ant's next words hung heavy between them.

'About last night,' he began, 'I've been turning it over in my mind. We need to think about what's at stake here.'

Lyn shuffled the sugar packets on the table, aligning them in a neat row as she often did when her thoughts were churning. The Stanton Broad Cafe, usually a comforting place, now felt like an inquisition.

'Ant,' she whispered, 'Are we forgetting what truly

matters?' Doubt filled her eyes, usually brimming with determination.

Ant leaned back, his chair creaking under the shift of weight. He studied Lyn's face, searching for the familiar spark of adventure they shared, but found only the shadow of concern. 'It's crossed my mind too,' he admitted, running a hand through his dark hair. 'The thrill of the chase has a price, doesn't it?'

'Exactly,' Lyn murmured, her gaze fixed on the window where a robin perched briefly before darting away. 'We started this together because it was something we both cared about. But the nearer we get to our wedding, the more I wonder if it's taking too much of a toll on us.'

'Us, or you?' Ant asked gently, reaching across the table to still her fidgeting hands with his own.

'Both, I suppose,' she confessed. Her shoulders slumped as she let out a sigh. She was always the pillar for the children at school, the one with answers. Yet here she was, riddled with questions about their future.

They sat in silence for a moment, the cafe's usual hum of chatter and clinking cutlery enveloping them like a comforting blanket. Then Ant spoke, his voice barely above a whisper. 'I fear, Lyn, that the path we're on might harm those we love.'

'Or worse,' Lyn added, her voice trembling slightly. She thought about the village, a tapestry of lives woven together, and how a single frayed thread could unravel it all.

'Every time the phone rings or there's a knock at the door, I hold my breath,' Ant said, his warm smile replaced by a serious furrow of his brow. 'I keep thinking, what if it's news we can't bear?'

'Ant,' Lyn paused, weighing her next words. 'I never

wanted our commitment to be overshadowed by...this.' She vaguely gestured towards their detective work.

'Nor I,' he agreed solemnly. 'There's pressure, isn't there? To see this through, to protect this place we call home. But not at the expense of our happiness. Our life together should be about more than helping Peter to solve cases.'

'Shouldn't it?' Lyn echoed, seeking affirmation. There was a pause, thick with unspoken fears, before Ant reached over and squeezed her hand reassuringly.

'Whatever decision we make,' he said, offering a tender smile, 'it's ours to make. And whatever the future holds, we'll face it—' He paused, leaving the sentence to hang between them.

'Together,' Lyn finished for him, a small smile tugging at the corners of her mouth.

The waiter interrupted the conversation as he approached to clear their plates, his presence pulling them back to the present. With a shared nod, they acknowledged the unvoiced agreement settling around them, to confront their doubts head-on.

Just then, Ant's pocket emitted a subtle buzz. He pulled out his phone, and as his eyebrows knitted into a frown, Lyn's heart leapt into her throat. They peered at the screen, where a message blinked back at them – a clue, perhaps, that demanded their attention.

'Looks like we've got work to do. Or do we tell Peter that we're packing it in?' Ant asked.

'Let me have a look,' Lyn said as she took the mobile. She studied the text for a few seconds. 'We can't ignore this, can we?'

Ant shook his head as he retrieved his mobile and slid it back into his jacket pocket. 'Peter asked us to think about what we want to do. What about we tell him we'll finish the case and then call it a day?'

As the pair walked through the familiar entrance doors of the police station, a booming voice drowned their senses. 'He's ready for you, and said to send you straight in. Keep him busy today, will you? Take him anywhere you want, so I can have a quiet shift.' The desk sergeant winked as Ant and Lyn breezed past the smiling bobby and into Peter's office.

'What's happened?' Ant asked, as he closed the half-glazed office door behind them.

Riley sat forward in his chair; his voice tinged with concern. 'We found something.' He paused, glancing between them before continuing. 'Another letter. It was lying on a pew at the church. And it's addressed to you two.'

Lyn's face drained of colour. 'I don't like the sound of that, given what's been going on this last week or so.'

'Addressed to us?' Ant echoed, disbelief. 'But why? We've been careful.'

'Very careful,' Lyn added, her voice betraying a note of concern.

'Apparently not careful enough,' Riley said grimly. He slid a plastic evidence bag across the table. A folded cream paper had bold black handwriting, visible through its translucent material.

'Have you read it?' Lyn asked, reaching for the bag but stopping short, reluctant to touch it.

'Only enough to confirm it's meant for you,' Riley said. 'Whatever game this person is playing; they want your attention—and now they have it.'

Ant finally took the bag, turning it over. His thumb brushed against the seal, a simple circle with no discernible mark or crest. His mind raced, piecing together what this meant. Their investigation had stirred more than whispers.

'Any idea who could have left it?' Lyn queried; her gaze fixed on the sealed letter.

'None. It's as if it appeared out of thin air,' Riley admitted. 'Phyllis was the one who found it, said she heard a rustle when she was doing her usual nosing about.'

'Trust Phyllis to be involved somehow,' Ant muttered, a half-hearted attempt at humour amid rising tension.

They shared a look, the kind that spoke volumes without a single word. A look that acknowledged the setback this letter represented, the potential danger it spelled out in voiceless, unseen ink.

'Open it,' Lyn said softly, her voice steady despite the uncertainty that shadowed her features.

With careful movements, Ant slipped the letter from the bag and unfolded it. The script was neat, deliberate, each letter crafted with purpose.

The truth often lies beneath layers of silence, Ant read aloud:

'Consider this your final warning. Stop meddling or prepare to face consequences far beyond your comprehension.'

A heavy silence followed, broken only by the faint ticking of the grandfather clock by the door. The message was obvious: their pursuit of honesty and resolution had led them into treacherous waters.

'Final warning...' Lyn whispered, her resolve flickering like the candlelight on the table.

'Consequences,' Ant echoed, his protective instincts flaring.

'Looks like our mystery has deepened,' Riley concluded, his gaze sharpening. 'And we'd best tread carefully from here on in. Have you thought anymore about what I put to you both yesterday? This note brings the matter into sharp focus, doesn't it?'

Ant and Lyn exchanged earnest glances. 'We've done more than that, Peter. We've talked and talked about the pros and cons of helping the police. In the end, it came down to what we wanted for our future,' Ant said.

'As, of course, it should. Things will get busy for you over the coming months. Once you're married, well, it'll be a whole new ballgame.'

Lyn shifted uncomfortably in her chair. 'And it's for that reason we've—' She looked at Ant for support. 'We've made the decision that this case will be our last.'

The room fell quiet as three close friends each pondered the implication of their discussion. Peter was the first to speak.

'I agree with your thinking, not as a police officer, but as, I hope, a close friend. But don't you want to get out now? Just look at that letter. It's evil stuff.'

Ant shook his head. 'It's exactly for that reason we'll finish the case. It's personal now. I won't be threatened. Don't think for a moment that Phyllis didn't read that note. It'll be all over the village by now. Oh, nothing will be said to either of us, but they'll be watching to see what we do.'

Peter frowned at his friend. 'Doesn't that speak to pride, rather than common sense?'

'Just the opposite, Peter. It'll show the village it must stand together when we are threatened. Otherwise, what's the point?'

Ant and Lyn exchanged another glance, this one tinged with determination. Despite the uncertainty, they remained dedicated to the truth, to each other, and to Stanton Parva.

'You'll need to be careful, you two,' Riley warned. 'You're playing with fire now.'

'Then we'll just have to be flameproof,' Lyn replied, a brave smile touching her lips.

Riley nodded; his expression was unreadable.

'You're right, Lyn. We'll be flameproof,' Ant echoed, his voice firm with resolve. He folded the ominous letter back into the evidence bag, an unspoken promise to confront the looming threat head-on.

As they left Riley's office, the weight of their decision pressed upon them like the heavy fog that often rolled in from the nearby marshes. The familiar streets of Stanton Parva seemed different now, tinged with an undercurrent of danger and suspicion.

Phyllis was already waiting outside the police station, her eyes wide with faux concern that couldn't hide her excitement. 'Oh, my. I heard about the letter! Be careful now. You never know what dark forces you might be up against,' she trilled, her words dripping with insincerity.

Ant gave her a tight-lipped smile, masking his true feelings towards the village gossip. 'Thank you, Phyllis. We'll keep that in mind,' he replied, guiding Lyn.

Ant's vintage Morgan spluttered to life as they embarked on the drive back to Stanton Estate. The roof leaked a little, a familiar quirk that usually elicited a chuckle from Lyn, but today it went unnoticed. Their conversation was sparse, each lost in contemplation.

Stanton Estate looked stunning, as usual. But this afternoon, even its protective walls seemed inadequate against the unseen threat that lurked.

Entering the study, Earl Stanton looked up from his book, his silver hair catching the soft glow from the desk lamp. 'You both look troubled. What's happened?' His voice held concern as he assessed their expressions.

Ant hesitated for a moment before speaking up.

'We received a warning today, Dad,' Ant began, his tone serious. 'Someone is trying to intimidate us into backing off from the investigation.'

The Earl's brows furrowed as he listened intently. 'I see. And what do you intend to do about it?'

Ant shared a determined look with Lyn before responding, 'We've decided that despite the risks, we cannot simply step back now. The threat only strengthens our resolve to see this through. We won't be bullied into silence.'

A flicker of pride shone in Earl Stanton's eyes as he regarded his son and future daughter-in-law. 'I admire your courage and sense of duty. Just remember, you have the support of your family and the village behind you.'

Countess Stanton entered the room at that moment, her graceful presence bringing a sense of calm with her. 'What's this I hear about a warning?' she enquired; her expression concerned but unwavering.

Ant met her gaze and repeated their encounter with the ominous letter, watching as a range of emotions flitted across his mother's face. When he finished, she smiled, a mixture of pride and determination in her eyes.

'It seems you have inherited your father's sense of justice and your grandmother's fearlessness,' the countess said, her voice soft but firm. 'Do not let this warning deter you from seeking the truth. We must always stand against those who wish to silence honesty and integrity.'

Ant felt grateful for his mother's support, emphasising how Stanton Parva stays strong when faced with adversity.

With renewed determination, Ant turned to Lyn, their unspoken bond reinforcing their shared resolve. 'We won't give in to fear or intimidation. We owe it to this village and to ourselves to see this through to the end.'

Lyn nodded, her blue eyes reflecting steely determination.

As the evening came to Stanton Estate, Ant, and Lyn sat in the study, going over the evidence they had collected. The weight of the warning letter lingered in the air, a reminder of the sinister forces at play in their once peaceful village.

'I can't shake off the feeling that we're missing a crucial piece of the puzzle,' Lyn murmured, her brow furrowed in concentration.

Ant glanced at her; his gaze filled with admiration for her sharp mind. 'I agree. There's something we haven't uncovered yet, something that ties all these events together.'

Just then, a soft knock echoed through the study, and the door creaked open to reveal Peter Riley standing on the threshold, his eyes wide with anticipation. 'Found anything new?'

Ant and Lyn exchanged a quizzical look before greeting their visitor. 'Come in, Peter. We were just discussing our next steps,' Ant said, gesturing for the detective to join them.

Riley stepped further into the study, his presence adding a sense of official gravity to the room. 'I can see you two are not ones to back down easily,' he remarked, a hint of admiration in his voice. 'But remember, we're in this together. I want to help you see this through while keeping you safe.'

Ant nodded appreciatively. 'We value your guidance and support, Peter. And we won't hesitate to reach out if we need help or if any fresh developments arise.'

Lyn looked at the evidence board they had carefully created, linking ideas and clues with strings and notes. 'Do you think there's a pattern we might have missed, Peter? Something that could lead us to uncovering the truth?'

Riley studied the board intently before turning back to them with a thoughtful expression. 'There might be,' he began slowly, his eyes scanning the evidence board. 'Where might a key most often be used? Let's make a list, then I'll tell you what I'm thinking.'

Ant and Lyn exchanged a determined look, ready to delve deeper into the investigation alongside Riley. The trio spent time meticulously listing down locations where a key could hold significance in their case. As they brainstormed and shared insights, a pattern started emerging from the maze of evidence before them. Ant's precision, Lyn's instinct, and Riley's knowledge all combined flawlessly, each playing a vital role.

After deliberation and the rearranging of sticky notes on the board, Riley pointed at a cluster of locations with a thoughtful expression. 'These places here', he began, tapping on key areas around Stanton Parva. 'They all have one thing in common - accessibility and relevance to our primary suspects. This might be more than just a coincidence.'

Ant's eyes narrowed as he studied the marked spots. 'You think the key is not just a physical object but a symbolic link between these locations?' he hypothesised, his mind racing with possibilities. Ant's heart raced as they realised they might have made a crucial breakthrough in the case, a discovery that could solve the mystery of Stanton Parva.

Lyn's gaze lit up with excitement, her intuitive nature homing in on the links. 'If we follow this trail, we might uncover a hidden connection that ties everything together,' she suggested.

Riley nodded in agreement; his sharp gaze fixed on the evidence board. 'It's worth exploring further. These locations could be the key to understanding the motives behind the threats. Also to tie them to our suspects,' he asserted, his confidence bolstering their resolve.

'Where do we start?' Lyn asked.

Riley took a moment to ponder before responding, the weight of their discovery settling in the room like a thick fog. 'Let's begin by focusing on the location that has the most connections to our suspects,' he suggested. One way or another, everyone is connected to the land. Either owning it, or growing crops on it.'

'That's a clever thought,' Lyn said. 'Even Nancy falls within your definition via her allotment.'

'I wonder if that's the answer to the puzzle our perpetrator laid for us. You know, the key thing...they're saying the land is the key that unlocks the reason behind all this?' Ant suggested.

The trio scanned the map of Stanton Parva and its surroundings, trying to prove Peter's theory. Who stood to gain the most? And why attack those two people in particular?'

'Have you found any link between the murdered man and the woman found at Mrs Henderson's property?' Lyn asked the detective.

'That was the first thing we went after. The problem is, without names or address details, we've little to go on. We ran the dead man's DNA through the national database, and it came back blank. He seems to have popped up out of nowhere. As for the woman, well, until she regains consciousness and can speak for herself, we don't have permission.'

'And the man she sat with at the Wherry Arms?' Ant asked.

'Vanished,' Peter replied.

Just then, Peter's mobile rang. He excused himself while he took the call. A few minutes later, the detective re-entered the lavish room.

'From the smile on your face, that must have been a good call. I don't suppose it was about our case?'

'It's more than that. A solid lead at last.'

The room hushed with anticipation.

'Well, are you going to tell us, or keep us hanging for what's left of the evening?' Ant said.

Peter sauntered back over to where the other two were. 'Constable Jones has only gone and found the Jaguar.'

The trio erupted into a spontaneous group hug, more out of relief than joy.

'And it gets better. Guess where he found the car?' Peter said, grinning.

'Don't make us wait. It's too cruel!' Lyn exclaimed.

'Acre Mill.'

Ant and Lyn shared a knowing look, remembering the rumours surrounding the abandoned building.

'Acre Mill? It's all but a wreck, but I get the link with our case,' began Lyn. 'As kids, we used to play there and tell each other ghost stories about the place. It got so bad we used to dare one another to go in alone. Wasn't there an old outbuilding next to it?' asked Lyn as she looked to Ant.

He thought for a few seconds. 'I remember a rugged old stone conical building without its top. The doors to the outbuilding had an enormous padlock on them, didn't they?'

'Yes, and I remember we all tried to break in, but never managed it?'

The two spent the next few minutes lost in recollections of happy times exploring the wonders of an unspoilt Norfolk landscape.

'Er...if you don't mind, we have an investigation to get on with,' Peter chided.

Ant and Lyn soon left their childhood days behind as

the detective's timely reminder dragged them back to the present.

'But how did PC Jones come across the car. I thought he was supposed to be keeping an eye on me... or rather, my home?'

'A good point. One which I asked him about when he called me just now. He followed up a lead from none other than Phyllis. It seems she almost clobbered him with her shopping bag for loitering around the Old School house. To make things worse. He was in his civvies and couldn't tell the woman why he was there.'

'Poor Jones,' Lyn said.

'All part of that learning curve I mentioned the other day. He'll have learned a lesson from the encounter, if only to stay out of range from anything that can cause harm-and that includes flying shopping bags.' Peter chuckled.

The light moment soon passed as Lyn pressed Peter for more information. 'You've still not told us what she said to young Jones.'

'What, apart from accusing him of being a thieving layabout?' Peter said, as he held back a strangled giggle. Eventually, the detective regained control of himself and revealed how Jones ended up at Acre Mill. 'Once he'd shown her his warrant card, she told him the postman had seen someone lurking about the place. He took particular notice because it was so early in the morning. The postie was on his way to collect the mail from the sorting office around five this morning.'

'And he only just rang you?' Ant said.

'Be fair on the lad. He'd just finished his night shift when Phyllis all but attacked him. He didn't think too much about what she told him until he woke up late this afternoon. Give him his due. He thought more about her remarks and took a run out to the mill in his own time. The place was deserted, but he noticed fresh tyre tracks leading to the outbuilding.'

'Wouldn't he need a search warrant to enter the outbuilding?' Ant asked.

The detective nodded. 'Usually, yes, but the door was slightly ajar. Just enough for him to make out the car. He thought it might be the one we're looking for, hence his call to me.'

The news galvanised the trio to plot their next move.

'One thing is for sure; I don't want us going in mob-handed,' Peter began. 'We don't want to scare our suspect away.'

'But if we're right about him or her giving us the clues in the first place, won't they be watching?' Lyn asked.

'I'm banking on it,' Peter replied. 'Now, here's what we should do...'

Chapter Fourteen

MILLING ABOUT

ACRE MILL MADE A STRIKING SIGHT, with its silhouette contrasting against the sky, surrounded by chestnut and oak trees. Detective Inspector Peter Riley observed his officers from a nearby barn hidden from the road by trees. The mill, once a hive of activity, now stood as a witness to untold secrets.

'Right,' Riley said crisply, breaking the hush of concentration that had settled over them. 'We'll keep the place under close watch. I don't want so much as a mouse to scurry by without us knowing about it.' His eyes swept over the assembled officers, who nodded in grim understanding. 'But remember, keep your distance, and stay out of sight. The last thing we want is the suspect getting wind of what we're up to.'

One brave young copper spoke up. 'Sir...do we know who we're looking for?'

'If anyone gets close to the outbuilding, don't intervene. Keep watch from your position, take a full description and give me a ring. Understood?'

A collective nod spread across the officers.

'Right, take up your assigned positions- and keep your radio volume down. I don't want police chit-chat ringing out over these fields. Now, off you go, and remember, keep your eyes open. I want no slacking on this one.'

Ant leaned against a gnarled tree just outside the barn, his dark hair ruffled by the breeze, watching the officers vanish from view. The chill in the air was more than just the onset of a wind blowing off the North Sea, which, even in high summer, could be bone-chilling; it was anticipation, electrified and tingling down his spine.

'Peter,' Ant called out, waiting to catch the detective's attention. 'I've been thinking...maybe we should go through the evidence again?' His warm smile was absent now, replaced by a furrow of concentration.

'What, again?' Riley arched an eyebrow. 'You think we've missed something?'

'Dunno, there's just something nagging at me,' Ant replied, pushing off from the tree. His Morgan may have been unreliable in the rain, but his instincts seldom were, and for the moment they were tugging at him relentlessly. 'A fresh set of eyes, a new perspective – it might give us the lead we need.'

Riley considered his suggestion, the gears turning behind his stern façade. 'Alright,' he conceded. 'I guess we can't do much until we see if the surveillance on Acre mill pays off. One more time. But let's be thorough. We need to stop jumping around from clue to clue or we'll never make sense of what's gone on.'

Together, they returned to the impromptu incident room Peter had set up in the barn, where the evidence lay spread across two tables. Each piece was a fragment of the larger enigma, and they pored over them anew, seeking the clue that would unlock the entire sordid affair.

As the examination drew on, the atmosphere thickened with the sort of tension that precedes a storm. It was Lyn who first sensed the shift, her sharp intellect always attuned to the subtleties of their investigations. She picked up a single document, her expression morphing from interest to incredulity.

'Ant, Peter, look at this,' she whispered, yet there was a tremor of revelation in her voice.

Their heads turned, eyes locking onto the paper in her hands. As recognition dawned, the room seemed to contract, the walls pressing in with the gravity of what lay before them.

'Blimey,' Ant murmured, the implications striking him like a physical blow. 'I can't believe we overlooked this before. It changes everything.'

'Are you certain?' Riley's question demanded an answer.

'Positive,' came the collective response, heavy with the weight of new found suspicion.

'Then we've got our work cut out,' Riley stated, his tone brooked no argument. 'Our prime suspect…it's someone we never thought to question deeply enough.'

The three of them exchanged a look that spoke volumes. They had been so sure, so confident in their previous assessments, and yet here they were, presented with a possibility that defied their earlier logic.

'Revisit everything,' Riley instructed, his resolve steeling. 'Alibis, interactions with the victim, everything.'

'Should we confront them?' Lyn asked, a trace of concern lining her features.

'Patience,' Ant counselled, aware of the risks. 'Let's not rush this. If we're right about this…we need to be sure.'

'Agreed,' Riley nodded. 'For now, we observe and gather more evidence. No sudden moves.'

The rain clouds contrasted with their revived enthusiasm for the case. Somewhere in the distance, a Bittern announced its presence with the loud call it had a well-earned reputation for. It was as if it were signalling the cloak-and-dagger dance that was about to unfold. The person they had discounted was now central to unravelling the mystery in Stanton Parva.

In the quiet of the barn, Detective Inspector Peter Riley leaned over the scuffed wooden table, its surface a mosaic of photos, documents, and assorted paraphernalia. His keen eyes darted from one item to the next, each an unspeaking bystander in the murky tale of Stanton Parva's most recent troubles. Beside him, Ant methodically shuffled through some papers, while Lyn hovered close by, her own scrutiny as sharp as ever.

'Have we got everything here from the Acre Mill search?' Peter asked, not lifting his gaze from a map strewn with notes and markers.

'Every nook and cranny,' Lyn confirmed, holding up the warrant that had granted them access to the dusty shadows of the old structure. 'Though it feels like we're missing something…it's staring us right in the face.'

'Could be,' murmured Ant, thumbing through a stack of photographs. 'But let's trust the process. Fresh eyes on old clues.'

'Right.' Peter pulled a photo close. It was of the sleek Jaguar. Fitch had confirmed the tire tracks matched those at the Lavender field layby. The car was a voiceless player in their drama, but it was what Fitch had found beneath its front seat that now held Peter's attention.

Lyn reached for an evidence bag, her fingers brushing

against the plastic with the faintest of rustles. 'The note...' she began, withdrawing the sheet of paper they'd set aside amid more pressing concerns. The handwriting was elegant, looping across the page with an air of intimacy that made one feel almost intrusive reading it.

Peter took the neatly folded paper, scanning the words. A meeting, yes, but more than that—a promise, a secret shared between the two people. The name signed at the bottom sent a ripple through him. Not a stranger, but a familiar face—one they'd seen in passing — exchanged pleasantries with, never suspecting the depth of their involvement.

'Could this be the link we've been searching for?' Lyn's voice held a mix of hope and trepidation.

'Maybe,' Peter replied, his mind racing with possibilities. 'Fitch?'

'Confirmed,' came the reply from the corner where the garage owner stood. 'Same tyre treads. Same mud traces. The car in that outhouse is the same one as I recovered from the A47.'

'Hmm,' Peter mused, tapping the letter lightly against his other hand. The ink mocked them, the loops and curls a taunting dance around the truth. The suspect's identity was plausible, but it couldn't be that simple, could it? And who was Don? Was it a real name, or something else? A pang of caution tightened in his chest. Too early for conclusions—they needed more.

'Let's keep clear heads,' he advised, feeling the tension in the air. 'We can't afford mistakes. Not now, not with so much at stake.'

'Agreed,' Ant said. 'We keep digging.'

'Spot on,' Peter affirmed. The final revelation was just

out of reach for Lyn, reminiscent of an Agatha Christie twist.

As the clock on the wall ticked away the seconds the trio worked on, the spectre of suspicion cast long shadows across the room. Just when the pieces of the puzzle seemed to align, a question arose, sending them back into the labyrinth of their case.

'Are we ready to face what we find?' Lyn's voice broke the silence, a whisper almost lost amid the scratching of pens and shuffling of papers.

'Ready as we'll ever be,' Peter replied, his voice firm despite the uncertainty that lay ahead.

They stood together against the creeping doubts, the weight of evidence heavy in their hands. The letter, a mere piece of paper, yet potent enough to shift the direction of their investigation.

And then a sudden realisation struck, icy and sharp—a detail so small yet so significant it threatened to unravel all they thought they knew. Peter's head snapped up, his eyes meeting Ant's in unspoken acknowledgement.

'Heavens,' he whispered, the implications dawning on him. 'It was there, right there, all along.'

Ant absentmindedly ran a hand through his dark hair, conveying more than words as the letter's name shimmered in the barn's dim light. The note paper continued to intimidate, its neatly curled script spelling out a suspect they had never truly considered.

'Barbara Hensley?' Lyn's voice wavered with incredulity. Her scepticism was almost palpable. 'But she's the last person I'd suspect. The woman comes into school a couple of time a year to show my older pupils the art of calligraphy. She's a real whizz at that sort of thing. '

'Just like the person who wrote the note.' Ant offered. 'When I called back at school the other day, all the staff were talking about events. Barbara was in school that day. She seemed as baffled as everyone else. I still find it hard to believe she could be involved in anything like this.'

Peter handed her the letter. 'It's no run-of-the-mill letter, is it, Lyn?'

She scanned the words again. 'I suppose being in love with someone can make you do things that—'

'That neither the person themselves, or others who know them, think they are capable of?' Peter said. 'I've seen it before. When two strangers who connect on a certain level meet, they can do horrible things that they may have only imagined doing alone.'

The profoundness of Peter's statement left the others speechless. After a while, the detective continued. 'While Barbara Hensley may appear a victim of the mysterious Don, we shouldn't assume too much. What if it was the other way around?'

A chill shot down Lyn's spine. 'To think that woman's had free rein in my school. It's horrible and goes to show all the background checks in the world won't stop a determined individual.'

Ant took the letter from Lyn's hands, scrutinising the looping handwriting once again. 'I can't believe we over-looked this before. It changes everything.' His eyes lifted, seeking agreement in their faces. 'We thought her above suspicion, but it seems our perpetrators play by their own rules.'

'Now it's our turn,' Peter replied, his tone hardening with resolve. 'The question is, how did we miss it?'

'Perhaps because we weren't looking for it,' Lyn

suggested, her gaze returning to the Jaguar's evidence bag. 'We were so convinced it was someone else.'

'Confirmation bias,' Ant mused aloud. 'We saw what we expected to see. But this,' He waved the letter lightly, 'Suggests something else entirely, and that they were working alone.'

'Exactly,' Peter agreed, his eyes narrowing. 'And if Barbara Hensley met the victim that night, whatever alibi she concocted is as flimsy as this piece of paper.'

'Are you saying she's been lying to us from the start?' Lyn asked.

'My officers have interviewed everyone in the village. Her statement seemed as unremarkable as everyone else's.'

'Perhaps there's more to her story than we're seeing?' Ant said.

'Either way, we've got a new prime suspect on our hands,' Peter declared. 'One we nearly let slip through our fingers.'

Lyn cautioned her colleagues. 'If Barbara's involved, confronting her without solid evidence could send her into hiding or worse…'

'Agreed,' said Peter. 'We'll keep this under wraps until we've firmed up our case.'

'Let's not forget Fitch's confirmation about the tyre tracks,' Ant added, tapping the report that linked the Jaguar to the scene. 'This is no coincidence.'

'Right,' Lyn said with growing excitement.

'Indeed,' said Peter, casting a last glance at the letter. 'We can place a car in the lavender field layby and found a love letter in the Jaguar signed by a villager to a man named Don. Now, unless something remarkable pops up, we've identified our main line of enquiry. Well, done, everybody.'

Despite previous letdowns, the group was excited as they ventured into new, unexplored territory where even unexpected people seemed relevant to cracking the case.

'We now need to delve into Barbara Hensley's background,' began Peter. 'Lyn, I need you to tell me everything you know about her. I'll then ring the Station with her details so we can check if she's known to us. We'll also begin the other checks we do when we have a person of interest in our sights.'

For the next twenty minutes, Lyn scoured her brain to brief Peter about their new suspect. Where she lived, how long she'd visited the school, any associates Lyn had seen her with. By the end of the session, Lyn felt drained by the experience—and sad that a trusted school volunteer may have deceived the whole school community with such a barbaric secret.

'You're exhausted,' Ant said as he gave his fiance a hug. 'Is there anything else we can do here until your officers report back, and you've checked Barbara Hensley out, Peter?'

'Being pragmatic, no. I don't think there is. Why don't we call it a day for now. We can meet up later back at the station, or the Wherry Arms if you like, to catch up?'

'I'll never turn down a pint of Fen Bodger,' Ant replied with a weary smile. 'Give us a ring when you're ready and we'll meet you there.'

As they drifted out of the barn, the weight of their discovery hung heavy in the air. They left behind the letter, a mass of evidence, and an eerie sense of foreboding waiting for them at the Acre mill.

'Authorised officers only to go in there, OK?' Peter said to a bobby stationed outside.

THE EARLY EVENING sun fought its way through the opaque glass of the Wherry Arms, as the trio reconvened to the backdrop of the pub's regulars playing dominos and darts. Ant fidgeted with his mobile while Peter leafed through his leather-bound notebook. Fitch had earlier tended his apologies to attend to matters at the garage, leaving his three friends to continue their work.

'Barbara Hensley's alibi,' Lyn said, her voice calm yet tinged with disbelief. 'We took it at face value. But now we need to comb through her past.'

Ant nodded, his mind visibly churning. 'Don't be too hard on yourself, Neither Peter, you, nor I spoke to her. She was one of dozens interviewed by a police officer. Let's forget that and concentrate on the present, OK? If she met with the victim that night, why? What's the connection we're missing?'

'Ant's correct, Lyn. You can't take responsibility just because the woman visits your school,' said Peter, before setting down his papers. 'Her motive is the missing piece of this puzzle. Except we can't be certain she knew our victims. Remember, the mysterious Don was probably the driving force. We need a search warrant for her house to see if there's any evidence, he ever wrote back to her. If we find nothing, it's almost certain he was the prime mover.'

The more they speculated, the more theories intertwined, forming a complex puzzle of motives and secrets.

'Could this all be about money?' Ant said.

'Money has a way of stirring up trouble,' Peter agreed. A seasoned detective, he knew all too well how greed could warp even the most upright citizen.

'And we can't ignore the emotional angles. Jealousy, revenge, fear…they're powerful motivators,' Lyn responded.

'True,' Ant said, his analytical gaze reflecting a deep understanding of people's motivations. 'But let's not forget, this is a community where everyone knows everyone's business. If she's hiding something, it'll surface.'

'Then it's settled.' Peter stood, signalling the meeting's end with an air of quiet authority. 'I'll get a search warrant. Meanwhile, you two keep a discreet look out,'

'Understood,' Lyn replied, her voice unshakable despite the undercurrent of concern that tugged at her. She trusted Ant and Peter implicitly, but she did not overlook the gravity of their investigation. 'But won't you showing up alert her and send her scurrying to—.

'To Don? Wouldn't that be delicious?' replied Peter with a twinkle in his eyes.

With their course of action decided, the trio shared a look of unvoiced camaraderie. The truth was out there, shrouded in the genteel facade of their English village, and they were determined to uncover it. As the trio paused to reflect on events, they felt the weight of the upcoming confrontation and its significance for their investigation.

'How soon can you get the warrant?' Lyn asked.

'If I'm quick, I stand a chance of getting it before the courts close for the day. That way, we can pay Henderson a visit early tomorrow morning. You might call it a wake-up call without the tea or biscuits.'

'Let's sleep on it,' Ant suggested, his tone betraying the reluctance of a man who loathed inaction. 'Let's see what the police turn up at Barbara Hensley's place. In the meantime, let's get you home.'

'I guess so,' Lyn replied, though the flutter in her stomach belied her calm demeanour. As she stood, pushing her chair back, she caught Ant's eye and held his gaze. In it, she saw her own worry reflected at her, tempered with a resolve that was uniquely his.

The pair left the pub when Lyn noticed the fading light play tricks on her vision, transforming the village into something ominous.

'Don't worry, everything will be fine,' Ant said as he watched Lyn open the door to her home, then turn on the threshold to face him.

'Watch your back, Ant,' Lyn called out, her silhouette framed by the warm glow of the interior light.

'Always do,' he replied with a wry grin that belied the gravity of their situation.

But as he drove away, the comforting familiarity of Stanton Parva morphed into a labyrinth of suspicion and doubt. In the distance, the silhouette of the old mill loomed, a sentinel keeping watch over the village's darkest secrets.

As he drove past the field in which the mill stood, his continued his struggle to make sense of their investigation. Suddenly, something caught his eye, a figure emerged from the shadows, their identity obscured by the failing light. Ant immediately slowed down and turned his car lights off. He pulled the Morgan onto a grass verge and cut the growling throb of the sports car's engine. His intuition told him this was no mere coincidence. The figure paused, seeming to sense his gaze, before melting back into the darkness whence it came.

Ant's heart pounded as he realised the game had gathered pace. He knew he had to tell Peter, though if the detective's planning held firm, his staff may already have alerted him to the movement. He rang the familiar number. No answer. Ant reasoned his friend was already liaising with his officers and communicating his orders.

He judged this was no time to impede police matters. Except a doubt crept in. What if Peter didn't know about movement at Acre mill? What if he left for home knowing someone was there? He might cause the investigation to come to a halt if the man bolted.

As he sat in the Morgan, the cool breeze seemed to speak to him. He knew what he had to do.

Chapter Fifteen

LETTER OF INTENT

DETECTIVE INSPECTOR PETER RILEY sat in his office, the early morning light casting long shadows across the paperwork strewn about his desk. With a steaming cup of tea cooling beside him, he poured over the background checks on Barbara Hensley. He ran a finger across his forehead as he read the reports that painted her as the epitome of respectability. No marriage, no scandals, just an unassuming volunteer at the local school who preferred her own company.

'Too clean,' Peter murmured to himself, 'There's got to be more to it.'

A sense of urgency gnawed at him; time was slipping through his fingers like grains of sand. He couldn't risk canvassing the villagers for information; Stanton Parva was a close-knit community where gossip travelled faster than a hare at a dog track. The mysterious 'Don' remained a shadowy figure, and without hard evidence from Barbara's home or a confession, he was nothing more than a ghost in their investigation.

With a decisive tap on his desk, Peter decided. It was Sunday, a day for church bells and roast dinners, not police raids, but duty called. He summoned Dodger, his young undercover officer, whose keen wit belied his inexperience.

'Ready for a field trip?' Peter asked as Dodger appeared, his youthful face eager.

'Just say the word, Guv.'

Barbara Hensley's house stood alone on the edge of the village, its garden blooming in tune with high summer. Its isolation was a blessing for Peter's desire to keep this search discreet. The detective gave the front door two sharp raps with his knuckles. No reply. After a second attempt, they walked around the back of the detached property and approached the kitchen door, finding it invitingly unlocked. Peter shook his head with a wry smile.

'Trust is a beautiful thing, but leaving doors open is asking for trouble,' he said as they slipped inside.

The house was hushed, a still life of domesticity. They donned protective shoe covers and gloves with practiced efficiency, ensuring no trace of their presence remained. Room by room, they searched, yet found nothing out of place in the tidy home. It was as if the house itself was determined to keep its secrets.

As frustration set in, Dodger piped up, 'My gran always hid her valuables in a tin up the chimney. Reckon it's worth a look?'

'Ever go up in flames?' Peter quipped, despite being intrigued by the suggestion.

'Never. She had central heating,' Dodger chuckled, then quickly added, 'Sorry, Guv.'

'Let's have a look then,' Peter conceded, eyeing the unused hearth.

Dodger removed his jacket and rolled up his sleeves,

revealing arms toned from weekends playing rugby for the village team. He stretched into the chimney, his face contorting with effort as he reached higher. Suddenly, his expression shifted to triumph, and he withdrew, cradling a small, square tin.

'Bring it to the kitchen,' Peter instructed.

They stood side by side at the countertop, with paper kitchen roll laid out to protect against any stray fingerprints. Anticipation hung between them like a charged current.

'Open it, Dodger. Your find,' Peter encouraged.

Inside, a stack of letters tied with a pink ribbon awaited them. Peter untied the delicate bow and withdrew an envelope, sliding out the single sheet of paper. As his eyes scanned the contents, they widened in shock. Dodger leaned in; curiosity etched across his face.

'Anything good, Guv?'

Peter's lips curled into a rare, knowing smile. 'Read it for yourself.'

Dodger took the paper, his gaze darting over the words before fixating on one detail. 'An address. The bloke's put his actual address on the letter.'

Both men shared a look of shared understanding. This was it – the break they desperately needed. And somewhere, in the quiet English countryside, the game was changing.

Peter glanced around the kitchen once more, ensuring no trace of their presence remained. The tin retrieved from the chimney now sat secure in an evidence bag, its contents potentially the key to unravelling the mystery that had gripped Stanton Parva.

'Dodger,' he said, his voice a low murmur, 'make sure the hearth is as it was. We can't have Barbara suspecting a soul's been here.'

'Right away, sir.' Dodger, still flushed with the success of his find, diligently swept the soot back into the shadows of the fireplace, his movements meticulous and measured. Once satisfied, he surveyed the lounge with a practiced eye, adjusting a cushion here, straightening a magazine there, until the room whispered nothing but undisturbed tranquillity.

Meanwhile, Peter busied himself in the kitchen, erasing their intrusion. With deliberate care, he folded the used kitchen roll, tucking it into his pocket.

'Let's go, quietly,' Peter instructed, his gaze fixed on Dodger. Together, they slipped through the back door, leaving it as they had found it: carelessly unlocked—a local habit that the villager hung onto as if living in another age.

On the drive back to the station, the tension became palpable, each lost in thoughts of what lay ahead.

Upon their arrival, Peter didn't waste a moment. He pulled out his mobile and dialled Ant's number. The call connected, and he was met with a cacophony of background chatter.

'Ant, it's Peter. Can you hear me?' he raised his voice above the din.

'Peter?' Ant's response were strained, his words battling to rise over the hum of conversation and laughter. 'I'm here with Lyn—we've just left the church.'

'Listen closely,' Peter began, detailing the morning's findings with concise urgency. 'We need you at the station—now.'

'Understood,' Ant replied, the gravity of the situation apparent even through the surrounding din. 'Sunday Roast will have to wait, Lyn. Duty calls at the police station.'

Lyn's eyes mirrored her confusion, but she nodded, trusting Ant's judgement. They exchanged quick farewells with their fellow villagers, their steps hastening as they descended the gentle slope towards the heart of Stanton Parva and its police station.

As Peter ended the call, he allowed himself a moment of satisfaction. The pieces were falling into place, though the full picture remained obscured. But soon, with Ant and Lyn's help, he would bring clarity to the chaos. Soon, Stanton Parva would know peace again.

Peter was practically shaking in his chair as Ant and Lyn hurried into his office. He had the look of a boy on Christmas morning, eager to reveal the secret behind the magician's trick. The room was spartan, save for the usual clutter of police work, and in the centre of Peter's desk lay an envelope—the kind that promised intrigue.

'Ah, there you are,' Peter said, barely containing his excitement. He slid two sets of protective gloves across the desk towards them. 'We need to preserve any prints.'

Ant picked up the gloves with a raised an eyebrow while Lyn donned hers with practiced ease, her head slightly tilted in curiosity.

'Go on, Lyn,' urged Peter, nodding towards the envelope.

She reached out and plucked the envelope from its solitary position on the polished wood. Her fingers danced with precision, carefully prying the paper apart to reveal its contents.

'Heavens,' she exclaimed, eyes scanning the text. 'An address.' She shook her head in disbelief, then added with a wry smile, 'We saw Barbara at church chatting away with the vicar as if butter wouldn't melt.'

'Really?' Peter's eyes twinkled with irony. 'Well, then, she's quite the actress.'

Lyn passed the paper to Ant, who read it with widening

eyes. 'This is solid gold,' he murmured. 'How do we play it, Peter?'

'We're going to pick them up simultaneously, but isolated from one another,' Peter detailed his plan with a tactical precision that spoke of years on the force. 'No contact, no communication. They won't even know the other has been arrested.'

'Smart,' Ant nodded, impressed. 'Keep 'em guessing, eh?'

The anticipation in the room was palpable, a tangible thing that could be sliced through with the proverbial knife. It was clear they were on the cusp of something big—just one more step in the dance of deduction.

'Right, I've got to get things moving.' Peter stood, the adrenaline of the chase infusing his movements with urgency. 'You two can stay here, but this might take a while.'

'Thanks,' Lyn said, peeling off her gloves. 'We'll be here waiting. Let us know the moment you have news.'

'Wouldn't dream of leaving you out of the loop,' Peter assured them with a grin.

Time seemed to stretch and bend in the confines of Peter's office as Ant and Lyn sat quietly, each lost in their own thoughts about the day's revelations. The soft ticking of the clock on an otherwise bare, cream painted wall, served as a reminder that with each passing second, Barbara Hensley's pristine image was being dismantled, piece by piece.

'Barbara, of all people,' Lyn murmured, shaking her head in disbelief. 'Always the first to volunteer for the school fete, and now...' Her voice trailed off as she came to terms with the woman's involvement in such dark dealings.

Ant leaned back in his chair, the creak of the leather unusually loud in the hushed atmosphere. 'It's always the ones you least expect, isn't it? Quiet, unassuming—then wham! They're caught up in something nefarious.' His fingers tapped a rhythmless beat on the armrest.'

'I'm just wondering what I'll say to my staff and the children,' Lyn mused.

The door swung open, and the desk sergeant's cheery face appeared, a tray with steaming mugs and a plate of digestive biscuits in hand. 'Here we go, tea to keep your spirits up. The waiting's the hardest part, isn't it?'

'Thanks,' Ant said, taking a mug and nodding towards the plate. 'Any word on our suspects?'

'Word just came in,' he replied with a grin, setting the tray down. 'Both picked up, nice and easy like. On their way here, ten minutes apart. They'll be none the wiser.'

Lyn reached for a biscuit, her mind still churning. 'To think—Barbara. It's too much to take in.'

'Life's full of surprises,' the sergeant chuckled before excusing himself, leaving the couple to their contemplations.

The room seemed to shrink as the gravity of the situation settled upon them until finally, the door opened again, admitting a sombre Peter.

'Quiet as lambs, both of them,' he reported, his eyes searching Ant's and Lyn's faces for a reaction. 'No questions asked. That's when you know—they understand the game is up.'

'Did they resist?' Lyn asked, a hint of concern colouring her tone.

'Nothing of the sort,' Peter assured her. 'Straight into the cars without so much as a peep. Now they're cooling their heels in the cells, incommunicado.'

'Good,' Ant said with a nod. 'What's your next move?'

'Let them stew for an hour,' Peter replied, a strategic gleam in his eye. 'A bit of food, a drink. Then I'll start with Barbara. Question them separately.'

'Are you planning to play them off against each other?' Ant enquired, leaning forward with interest.

'Perhaps not as dramatically as in your intelligence days,' Peter contemplated, a half-smile tugging at his lips. 'Subtlety has its merits. Remember, Barbara has no idea we've been in her house. She doesn't know we've got Don, or the letters.'

'Understated yet effective,' Lyn commented, her respect for Peter's methods clear.

'Exactly,' Peter agreed, his focus sharpening. 'Now, off with you two. This could take hours, and there's nothing more to be done here.'

'Keep us informed?' Lyn asked as she stood, her expression earnest.

'Without question,' Peter promised, ushering them once more towards the door, leaving them in suspense for the next chapter of the tangled mystery.

Ant and Lyn ambled out of the police station, exchanging a glance that conveyed mutual understanding. Peter's parting words hung in the air like the aroma of fresh coffee, a delicious sense of something worthwhile in the offing.

'Let's grab a bite at the Wherry Arms,' Ant suggested, his voice betraying a touch of fatigue mingled with an appetite for normalcy after the morning's events.

'Good idea,' Lyn agreed, her thoughts drifting to Barbara and the shockwaves her arrest would send through the village.

Upon entering the bustling pub, they were greeted by the familiar nod of Jed, the owner, who had pre-emptively reserved their favourite alcove in the far corner—a snug haven away from the cacophony of Sunday patrons. They settled into their seats, the worn upholstery wrapping its comforting embrace around them.

'Two Sunday roasts and a pint of Fen Bodger Pale Ale for me,' Ant said, barely audible over the din. 'And a glass of your lemonade for Lyn, please.'

'Coming right up,' Jed replied with a knowing smile, disappearing back into the throng.

As they waited, Lyn's gaze idly swept across the room until it rested on a figure whose profile piqued her interest— the man from her birthday party at the pub, the same one who had been with the girl found at Mrs Henderson's cottage.

'Ant,' she murmured, nudging him discreetly under the table.

'What's up?' he asked, following her eyes.

'Over there. Doesn't that look like—'

'Yes, it does,' Ant whispered, craning his neck subtly. The man was a solitary island amid the sea of chatter, nursing his pint with a faraway look.

'Be careful,' Lyn cautioned as Ant rose, his chair scraping gently against the stone floor.

'Always am,' Ant said with a wink and made his way to the bar.

'Another round when you're ready, Jed,' Ant called out casually, positioning himself next to the taciturn stranger. He ordered their drinks and then leaned against the bar, mustering his most congenial smile. 'Lovely day, isn't it?'

The man gave a noncommittal grunt, eyes fixed on some distant point beyond the bar.

'Strange happenings lately,' Ant continued, keeping the conversation light. 'Like about that poor girl.' He let the thought hang in the air, a baited hook.

It worked. The man stiffened, his grip tightening around a pint glass. His eyes flickered with recognition—or was it fear? Without a word, he stiffened his gate, jostling the crowd and sloshing beer onto the jumper of an unsuspecting patron.

'Oi!' the drenched villager protested as the man elbowed his way out of the pub, leaving a trail of apologies in his wake.

Ant watched him go; the door swinging shut behind the retreating figure. He returned to Lyn, his expression grave.

'Got a reaction at the mention of the girl,' he reported, sliding back into his seat just as their meals arrived.

'Looks like we've got more layers to unravel in this little saga,' Lyn mused, cutting into her roast as the aroma of gravy wafted up enticingly.

'We have,' Ant agreed, taking a hearty swig of his pint. 'This gets more complicated all the time, doesn't it?'

Their lunch continued amid the pub's cheerful clamour, but a new thread had woven itself into the fabric of their quiet village life—one that promised further complications to present themselves.

———

ANT TURNED THE KEY, and the Morgan's engine fell silent. The sun high in the sky cast a gentle warmth over the Norfolk landscape, a picturesque tableau of mid-summer vitality. With the roof down, they had driven past fields where golden wheat swayed, punctuated by the occasional scarecrow standing sentinel. Birds traced patterns in the clear blue expanse above them, their calls a soundtrack to the serenity.

The Broads were alive with activity; graceful sailboats danced upon the water as families and friends enjoyed the tranquillity of Sunday leisure. Roe deer, like shy phantoms, skipped across narrow country roads before vanishing into the thickets that bordered the fields.

'Ant, why have you stopped here?' Lyn asked, her voice tinged with confusion as he settled the sports car into the layby at the bottom of the lavender field.

'I don't know,' Ant admitted, an unconscious thought seeming to have guided the wheel. They sat in silence, the distant birds breaking the peacefulness that enveloped them.

'Look, Gavin has cut the lavender, it's all gone,' Lyn observed, her gaze sweeping over a landscape where once purple blossoms perfumed the air.

Ant stepped out of the car, his eyes surveying the field. The lavender had been sheared back just above the old growth, leaving much more of the ground visible than before. Without explanation, he began walking towards the spot where they'd found the body.

'Ant, what are you looking for?' Lyn asked as she followed him, her footsteps hesitating in the rich soil.

'Nothing,' he replied, his voice distant. 'It's just... this is where it all started.'

Lyn placed a comforting hand on his arm. 'Let's go home. Have some quiet time before Peter calls.'

As they turned to leave, Ant's gaze caught sight of some-thing—an anomaly amid the precise rows of pruned plants. A black object lay in the distance, stark against the earthy hue.

'What's up?' Lyn's voice carried a note of concern as she observed his fixed attention.

'Wait here,' he said, heading towards the object. But Lyn couldn't resist; curiosity drew her forward until she stood just behind him, struggling to take in the discovery.

'What have you found?' Lyn asked, curious to catch sight of the object of Ant's attention.

'Proof,' Ant murmured, his voice barely above a whisper. 'That the man and woman in custody are innocent of the murder and attack.'

'Are you sure?' Lyn's voice wavered with disbelief.

He stepped over his find and turned to face Lyn. 'Look.' He gestured to the object, then retrieved a white handkerchief from his pocket. Gently, he wrapped the item, cocooning it within the linen.

'We need to get this to Peter,' he said, urgency tightening his features.

They drove back to the police station, the countryside passing in a blur. No words passed between them; the gravity of their find filled the space between them. Lyn cradled the shrouded object in her lap, ensuring it remained safe beneath the fabric.

Tension hung in the air like the stillness before a storm as they arrived at their destination. The station was a hive of activity, but their purpose was singular and clear. With the precious evidence secure in Lyn's careful grasp, they sprang through the doors, each step bringing them nearer to unravelling the twisted threads of mystery that had ensnared Stanton Parva.

Their shoes clipped against the linoleum with an urgency that matched the pounding of their pulses. Peter, just rounding the corner, halted at the sight of them, his eyes alight with a similar fervour.

'Peter,' Lyn gasped, her breath catching from the sprint.

'Ant, Lyn,' he acknowledged, his voice barely concealing the excitement. 'This way.'

They followed him into the sanctuary of his office. Lyn's hands trembled as she placed the enigmatic bundle in the centre of Peter's stark work desk, the surface otherwise unadorned save for a case file lying open, its contents a jigsaw awaiting completion.

Ant watched Peter's face as he carefully undid the handkerchief, revealing the ominous object beneath. For a moment, Peter was still, absorbing the implications of the find. Then, lifting his gaze to meet theirs, a resolute nod cemented the weight of the evidence.

'Between what you've brought me, and what the two prisoners told me,' Peter said, his words methodical and certain, 'I know exactly who committed the murder. The same person who almost killed for a second time. Tonight, we collect a debt on behalf of the victims.'

The room seemed to shrink around them, the gravity of Peter's declaration pressing in. Ant felt a chill despite the warm glow of the desk lamp. They were on the cusp of untangling a web woven with deception and malice—a web that had ensnared innocent lives and cast shadows across the idyllic village they all cherished.

'Tonight,' Ant echoed, determination etching his features. The game was afoot, and justice awaited its due.

Chapter Sixteen

END GAME

MONDAY MORNING USHERED in a tapestry of light and shadow across the verdant landscape surrounding Stanton Parva. The sun suffused Horsey Windpump in a warm glow. Its sails, freshly painted and repaired, cut through the air with a gentle whoosh, the rhythm akin to a calm heartbeat echoing through the stillness of the day.

Peter, his shoulders squared but demeanour softened by the tranquil scene, joined Ant and Lyn on a rustic wooden bench beside the Staithe. The water glistened like diamonds as ducks glided through, leaving a gentle ripple behind them.

'An idyllic setting for such a dark discussion,' Peter mused.

'Certainly, a contrast,' Ant replied, his voice carrying the gravity of their task.

Lyn nodded. With her hands folded neatly in her lap, she said, 'So we're agreed. We'll send out the invitations today then. Personalised and discreet, to ensure everyone shows up tonight without suspicion.'

'Exactly,' Peter confirmed. 'I'll speak to Barbara and Don myself. We don't want them rattled before the curtain rises on our little drama.' His eyes held a spark of determination, the same spark that had seen many a criminal brought to justice under his watch.

As they ironed out the finer details, the trio spoke in hushed tones, knowing the gravity of the evening's upcoming performance. The barn, once a hub of rustic activity, would transform into a stage where truth and deceit would dance under the scrutiny of their investigation.

'Officers will be tucked away, out of sight, until I give the word,' Peter explained. He checked his watch, a simple but reliable timepiece that had been his companion through countless cases. 'Six-thirty pm sharp. We'll orchestrate the gathering to play out precisely as Agatha Christie would have penned—each suspect will feel the heat of guilt, to face either exoneration or exposure.'

'Everyone will be there,' Lyn affirmed, her mind already running through the list of suspects. She pictured each face, each set of eyes that might flicker with fear or indignity when accused. They discussed how to lead each one down the precarious path of suspicion, to weave a narrative where each character bore the mark of potential guilt.

'Remember,' Ant added, his tone softening the edges of the plan, 'it's not just about unmasking the perpetrator but understanding why the innocent might have appeared guilty. We must tread carefully.'

'Of course,' Peter agreed, standing up from the bench, his silhouette momentarily casting a long shadow across the path. 'Each person has their part to play in this little theatre of ours, willingly or not. Tonight, we bring down the final curtain.'

Ant and Lyn exchanged a glance, both acknowledging

the weight of what was to come, yet hopeful of the resolution it promised. As they parted ways, the sails of the Wind-pump continued their steadfast rotation against the skyline —a reassuring sign that life in Stanton Parva would carry on, undisturbed by the shadows lurking within.

As the sun climbed higher, the village remained blissfully unaware of the denouement that would unfold in the barn that evening.

The barn, usually a place of pastoral repose, now buzzed with a nervous energy. Its rustic timbers were lit by the soft glow of lanterns as shadows danced across the faces of Stanton Parva's most colourful characters. Detective Inspector Peter Riley stood at the centre, his gaze sweeping over the assembled villagers like a lighthouse beam cutting through fog.

'Phyllis, Betty,' he began, his tone stern but kind, 'your penchant for... creative storytelling has caused a stir.'

Phyllis, all five-foot-nothing of her, perched on the edge of a hay bale, her hat casting a curious shadow. 'Well, Peter,' she retorted, the corners of her eyes crinkling in mirth, 'if people didn't do such interesting things, I wouldn't have to talk about them, would I?'

A chuckle rippled through the tense atmosphere, and even Peter's lips twitched in reluctant amusement. He cleared his throat, regaining his composure. 'Regardless, your... observations have been, surprisingly, of help. So, thank you.'

Phyllis beamed, nudging Betty beside her, who merely nodded, her chance to speak once again spirited away by her indomitable friend.

'Next, Bert,' Peter turned to address the robust man leaning against a wooden pillar. The scent of motor oil seemed to emanate from him, a reminder of his workshop where bacon sizzled each morning.

'Your knowledge of that Jaguar,' Peter paused, eyeing Bert with a detective's scrutiny, 'and the secluded nature of your premises had us wondering. But after thorough investigation...'

'Let me guess, I'm in the clear?' Bert interjected; his gruff voice tinged with mock indignation. 'After all the teas I've brewed for your lot. You might've at least pretended to enjoy them.'

'Rest assured,' Peter replied, his tone warm but firm, 'We never doubted the quality of your hospitality.'

Bert crossed his arms, the ghost of a smile tugging at his weather-beaten face. 'Just don't go making a habit of this, eh? A man's got a reputation to consider.'

Laughter filtered through the barn, easing some of the tension, as the villagers exchanged knowing glances. In Stanton Parva, everyone's business was fair game for speculation.

As the last echo of mirth faded, Peter's expression sobered. The joviality of the moment gave way to the gravity of their purpose. The villagers leaned forward, anticipation crackling in the air like static before a storm.

Each person sat ensnared in their own web of thoughts and fears, awaiting the last act of the night's drama. And in the wings, justice itself waited patiently to take the stage.

Peter Riley stood at the head of the barn, his silhouette etched against the setting sun that peeked through the wooden slats. The golden light draped over Nancy Fairfield, who sat with her back rigid, her fingers fidgeting with the frayed edges of her floral shawl.

'Mrs. Fairfield,' Peter began, his voice cutting through

the hushed murmurs of the attendees like a scythe through wheat. 'You've been less than forthcoming.'

Nancy's face tightened, the lines around her mouth deepening. 'I don't know what you mean, Detective Inspector.'

'Your little fibs,' he pressed on, 'led us down garden paths that were more wild goose chase than investigation.' He paced before her, his footsteps balanced and deliberate.

'Protecting your reputation, were you? While we wasted precious time, that could've been better spent pursuing the real culprit.' Peter's tone was hard, yet there was a glint in his eye that suggested he enjoyed this theatrical denouement as much as any sleuth might.

'Reputation is everything in the gardening club,' Nancy retorted, her voice quivering slightly. 'But I never meant—'

'Information, Mrs. Fairfield,' Peter interrupted, 'fed to rival clubs is hardly the concern of the law. But lying to police officers during a murder investigation is.'

The other villagers shifted uncomfortably in their seats, casting wary glances towards the cornered woman. Yet, amid the tension, there lay a thin thread of anticipation, for they knew the play was far from over.

Before another word filled the barn, Kevin Spindler rose from his chair, the wood creaking under the sudden absence of his weight. 'This is preposterous!' he bellowed, his face reddening. 'My family has tilled this land since before the Stanton's laid claim to a single acre!'

'Yet here you are, Mr. Spindler,' Peter said, turning his focus on the irate man. 'Accused of deceit just to get your hands on more of it.'

Kevin's chest puffed out, indignation coursing through him. 'You dare accuse me of such pettiness? After I've sweated blood for this soil?' His voice thundered through the barn, echoing off the rafters. 'I'll have your badge for this, Riley! I'll see you in court!'

A ripple of anxiety passed through the crowd, the drama reaching its crescendo. But then, a smile crept across Peter's lips—a knowing, confident curl of the mouth that seemed to say he held all the cards.

'Mr Spindler,' Peter said, his voice now a velvet threat. 'There's no need for lawsuits. Our investigations have cleared your name of the crimes in question.'

'Then why am I here being dragged through the mud?' Kevin demanded; fists clenched at his sides.

'Patience,' Peter replied, his smile unfaltering. 'All will be revealed soon.'

The room fell into an uneasy silence; the villagers suspended in a state of collective expectation, their eyes flickering between the disgruntled gardener and the accused landowner, wondering who would be next in the detective's line of fire.

Amid it all, Ant and Lyn exchanged a glance that spoke volumes—of trust, of partnership

As the tension in the air grew almost tangible, Peter's opening salvo ended, leaving everyone teetering on the edge of an answer that dangled just out of reach. The promise of revelations hanging thickly in the musty air of the barn.

Detective Inspector Peter Riley leaned back against the weathered wood of the barn; his arms folded as he surveyed the assembly with keen grey eyes. The hushed murmurs ceased when he stepped forward, clearing his throat—the signal that he was about to begin.

'Barbara,' he began, his voice unwavering and commanding as he addressed the woman, who sat with her hands clasped tightly in her lap. 'Your antics have brought nothing but disarray to this investigation. Your clandestine meetings, the secrets you've been keeping—they caused a search warrant for your house.' There was a collective intake of breath from the villagers gathered in the makeshift incident room.

'Privacy is not a privilege when it obstructs justice,' Peter continued, the disappointment etched into the lines of his face. Barbara's cheeks flushed a deep crimson, her usually poised demeanour crumbling under the weight of public scrutiny.

Turning his attention to Don, Peter's gaze intensified. 'And you, Don,' he said, the tone of reprimand unmistakable. 'Your little escapade on the A47, abandoning your vehicle like it was hot to the touch—what were you thinking?'

Don shifted uncomfortably, his fingers unconsciously twisting into the end of his ponytail. His eyes darted around the room, avoiding the piercing stare of the detective. 'It was... I panicked,' he mumbled, his voice barely audible.

'Panicked?' Peter echoed sharply. 'All because of a past you thought you'd buried. You came clean to Barbara, and yes, she forgave you for your history of fraud. But consider the cost! Your furtive behaviour almost led to innocent villagers being accused of murder.' His words sliced through the air; each syllable heavy with censure.

A look of shame crept over Don's features, his shoulders drooping as he bowed his head. The silence in the barn was palpable, broken only by the occasional shuffling of feet or the restless flutter of a collared dove in the rafters.

In a gentle gesture that belied the tension of the moment, Barbara reached out and laid her hand on top of Don's, offering taciturn support. Her eyes met his, conveying forgiveness and solidarity even in the face of public admonishment.

The villagers watched the scene unfold, their expressions a blend of empathy and curiosity, wondering how the strands of this tangled web would be unpicked. Ant and Lyn stood side by side, their presence proof of their role in bringing the truth to light.

As Peter prepared to continue, the atmosphere brimmed with anticipation. The story was far from over. Each word from the detective's mouth spun the narrative closer to its unforeseen conclusion.

Gavin Holloway sat with his arms folded, a defiant scowl etching deep lines into his rugged face. Detective Inspector Peter Riley paced before him, words cutting through the dusty air of the barn like a scythe through over-ripe barley.

'Mr. Holloway,' Peter began, his voice cool and unyielding, 'your reputation precedes you. A man quick to raise his fists at the slightest provocation.'

A murmur rippled through the assembled villagers. Gavin's eyes, hard as flint, never wavered from the detective's gaze.

'Let's consider the facts, shall we?' Peter continued. 'You had the means, the opportunity, and heaven knows you're not short on motive.' He paused, allowing the weight of his words to settle.

'Anyone trespassing on your land might well find themselves on the receiving end of your temper. But...' Here, Peter paused again, his expression shifting ever so slightly.

'Despite your robust approach to trespassers, you didn't commit these heinous acts, did you?'

The silence in the barn was suffocating. All eyes turned to Gavin, who now looked less certain, the beginnings of confusion clouding his previously indignant features.

'You did, didn't you, Thomas Whitaker?' Peter suddenly

spun on his heel, directing the question at the impeccably dressed gentleman seated at the back, his surprise guest.

Whitaker, with an air of nonchalance that only money can buy, twirled his handlebar moustache with an almost theatrical flourish. 'Ridiculous,' he scoffed, waving away the accusation with a well-manicured hand.

'Come now, Detective,' Whitaker drawled, standing to address the room with that practiced charm that dripped from his every syllable. 'You cannot seriously entertain such folly.'

But Peter was relentless, his voice a sharp contrast to Whitaker's velvety tones. 'Oh, but I can, Mr. Whitaker.' He stepped forward, his gaze unwavering. 'You had us fooled, playing the benevolent landlord, "subsidising" young Gavin here for his lavender crop.'

A few heads nodded, recalling the supposed generosity of Whitaker towards his tenant. Yet Peter's tone suggested a different story, one rife with deceit.

'In truth, you've been squeezing every penny from him,' Peter declared, his eyes locked onto Whitaker's. 'The Stanton archives don't lie, unlike some. A dispute over land stretching back generations, a grudge nursed like a fine wine.'

'Qui possidet prosperat,' Peter intoned, mimicking the grandeur of the Whitaker family crest. "He who owns prospers". But at what cost? Lives hang in the balance because of your greed and duplicity.'

Whispers broke out among the villagers as they absorbed Peter's words, their gazes darting between the hotheaded Gavin and the suave Thomas Whitaker. The air crackled with tension.

'Your actions have endangered lives, Mr. Whitaker,' Peter said, his voice rising with the gravity of his accusation.

'One life already lost, and another that hangs precariously by a thread.'

Gasps punctuated the heavy atmosphere as the implications of Peter's statement sank in. The villagers' expressions were a mixture of shock and morbid fascination, the unfolding drama more gripping than any theatre production.

As the sun dipped below the horizon, casting elongated shadows across the barn, the truth loomed large and undeniable. The day's pretence had fallen away, leaving raw reality in its wake. It was a moment ripe with possibility, the end of one chapter heralding the dawn of another, as Ant and Lyn exchanged a glance that spoke volumes.

The stage set, the players in place, and the ultimate act of this rural mystery was about to unfold.

'Perhaps we should reconsider Gavin's movements, and his rather volatile temperament,' Whitaker suggested with an air of distraction, twirling his moustache as if the entire assembly were engaged in nothing more pressing than afternoon tea. 'Why? because he came to my house at precisely 1.00 pm on that dreadful day and accosted me at my residence, demanding money with such vehemence that I feared for my safety.'

Gavin's face looked a picture of righteous indignation. 'He's talking rubbish! I did no such thing!'

'Curious,' Detective Inspector Peter Riley interjected, his tone even but his eyes sharp as flint. 'An odd time to recall such an event, Mr. Whitaker, especially when a note in the victim's pocket pointed to a meeting at four o'clock, hours after you claim this confrontation took place, and feeble attempt to frame your tenant for murder. The crime had yet to occur, assuming Gavin ever made such a visit, which I conclude he didn't.'

Before Whitaker could muster a defence, Lyn quietly approached, her arms cradling an object draped in white linen. She placed it gently on the table amid the barn's rustic adornments, the gathered suspects forming a cautious circle around the object.

'Thank you, Lyn,' Peter said, peeling back the cloth to reveal a revolver that gleamed ominously in the dim light. A chorus of gasps rippled through the crowd.

'Recognise this, do you?' Peter asked, eyes locked onto Whitaker's suddenly pallid face.

'Never seen it before in my life,' Whitaker blurted, but his voice lacked conviction.

'Ah,' Peter smiled thinly. 'Yet how curious that your family's coat of arms is etched upon it.'

'Stolen!' Whitaker protested, his earlier composure cracking like thin ice beneath winter boots. 'The local constabulary has failed to address a string of thefts recently!'

'Is that so?' Peter mused. 'But didn't you tell Lyn and Anthony about sending several guns off for cleaning? Yet Anthony noticed a missing revolver from your collection.'

Whitaker faltered. 'Nonsense?'

'Not so,' Ant replied. 'You keep your guns on a shadow-board. The silhouette from the missing revolver was easy enough for me to recognise with my military background.'

Peter took up the conversation. 'That gun was not out for servicing. You used it to murder. We've matched the bullet from the dead man to this revolver, and my officers are currently turning your home inside out. Should they find evidence of your supposed repair order, I'll eat my hat, but we both know they won't.'

'You're talking rubbish!' Whitaker spat, his usual charm evaporating into visceral anger. 'I wore gloves!'

Silence descended — a thick cloak smothering the

room. Whitaker's face slackened with the realisation of his damning slip.

'Did you?' Peter's voice was soft but carried the weight of iron. 'That's a heck of an admission, Mr. Whitaker.'

Defeated, Whitaker sank into his chair. 'I told you, he'd been swindling me for years, and when I found out, I demanded what he owed. The wretch laughed at me. At me! He had to pay. And he did.'

Peter's eyes bore into his target. 'Do you realise that not once have you called your victim by name? Does he not merit a name in your eyes? He had a family, you know. A wife and two teenage children. Does that not bother you?'

Whitaker sniffed nonchalantly. 'He should have been more careful who he crossed.'

'There you go again. You can't bring yourself to call the man by his name, can you? Well, I will. It was Leonard Ingham. We traced him through a DNA sample after his wife reported her husband missing. Talking of his wife, her name is Janet, by the way. She called him Les. To his children he was simply, Dad. Nothing special, some might say. But you took that away from them. Didn't you?'

Whitaker's shoulders dropped. It was if mention of his victim's name, and details of his family forced the killer to confront his crime.

'You compound your heartlessness by inflicting a wound so dreadful on your niece. She remains at considerable risk of succumbing to her injuries. What have you to say for yourself?'

'She was going to marry that commoner. The silly girl called him her "betrothed". I ask you. I saw them coming out of the Wherry arms together more than once,' he hissed venomously, glaring at Ant, who averted his gaze.

'Quite the medieval mindset. That "commoner", as you

put it also has a name. It's Jack Archer. He fled for his life because he thinks his fiance is dead. Can you imagine what that must feel like? ' Peter quipped. 'Did she deserve what you did to her?'

Whitaker crumbled. Head in his hands, his voice broken. 'She…she ran from me,' Whitaker confessed. 'Down the path of that house. Through the gate, into the shadows of the garden. I couldn't see her, then I—'

'Attacked her,' Peter said, cutting through Whitaker's stammering attempt to justify his actions. The words hung in the air, heavy and final.

'I… I—' Whitaker began, his voice filled with emotion.

'Didn't mean to do it?' Peter finished for him, his tone now soft, yet resolute.

'Still, you refuse to name the people you do harm to. I'll help you, shall I? The young lady's name is Wendy. Can you not bring yourself to call her by her name?' Peter said, finding it hard to control his emotions.

The fight drained from Whitaker like water from a sieve. 'I just wanted her…Wendy, to listen…to return to her family. She screamed at me. I thought someone might hear her. I tried to grab her but…she fell…and then—' His voice trailed off into a whisper, 'She just lay there.'

Peter leaned forward, his gaze never waning. 'Fortunately for you, she is not dead, at least as of now, although there is no certainty she'll ever regain consciousness. And the keys? What was their purpose?'

A moment of muted contemplation passed before Whitaker spoke. 'In my panic, I thought to mislead you. Found them in my pocket—they were for a new property. I thought it might suggest a connection with the man… Archer, I mean.'

'Ah, you used his name. At least that's something. But brand-new keys?' Peter arched an eyebrow.

'I had several made for the new house,' Whitaker muttered. 'I'd forgot they were there.'

The room fell quiet once more. Villagers exchanged uneasy glances as the gravity of Whitaker's sins sank in. The man who had held himself above all others now sat exposed by his own hubris, his legacy tarnished by greed and violence.

Ant was the first to break the silence. 'Do I get an apology for kidnapping me and wrecking my father's Wherry, and almost toasting me in the process? By the way, nice touch converting that pub into a going concern for one night, before turning it back into a wreck within twelve-hours. That almost threw us off the trail.'

'And another for the nasty note you left in the church for us to find. Not least, by pure chance, you almost got an innocent lady charged with murder. It was in the same hand as the one found on the body. You got slap dash there, didn't you?' Lyn said with a wry smile.

Whitaker looked over to Lyn and smirked. 'Congratulations on matching the notes. I wanted to keep you on your toes. As for you,' Whitaker said, turning to Ant. 'Thank you for the compliment. I only had to take the shutters off the front, and make the bar look lived in. It's amazing what blokes will do for fifty-quid, cash-in-hand. As for the rest of it, the Stanton's are not without low cunning either, are they? You set yourselves up as paragons of probity and charity. In fact, you're no better than I. Our sort has what it has by taking from others. Oh, most of your family's shenanigans took place centuries ago, but like me, you hang on to what's yours like the devil. Well, you poked your nose in where it wasn't wanted, so I decided to teach you, and your father, a lesson.'

'Did you, really,' began Ant. 'Well, it didn't work out too well for you, did it?'

Whitaker grimaced as he sniffed the air again.

'OK, think we've heard enough,' Peter said in a tone that brought the conversation to a prompt end. He reached into his tweed jacket, the fabric slightly worn at the elbows, and produced his police radio with a practiced ease. The muted crackle of static filled the barn before he spoke. 'All units, move in.' His voice, though soft, carried the weight of authority that defined his career.

The barn doors swung open, uniformed officers entering with solemn purpose. They approached Whitaker, who seemed to shrink under their gaze, the magnitude of his downfall reflected in the steely glint of their stare. With a firm hand on his shoulder, Peter recited the cautionary words with a restrained empathy, 'Thomas Whitaker, I am arresting you for the murder of...'

'Enough,' Whitaker cut him off, his voice a mere whisper as he rose to his feet, unassisted but defeated. The villagers watched in stunned silence as two police officers led him away, the click of handcuffs reverberating like the final verdict of justice served.

Once the echo faded, Peter turned to face the remaining attendees, his expression softening. 'I must extend my apologies for the unpleasantness of this evening,' he began, addressing the room with an earnest sincerity. 'It was imperative to confront Mr. Whitaker in such a manner as to prevent any suspicion that could've led to his flight.'

Nods and murmurs of understanding rippled through the gathered crowd. Despite the discomfort, there was an unspoken respect for the necessity of the ruse. With a last nod of gratitude, the villagers dispersed, leaving behind the lingering scent of hay and the residue of the day's revelations.

As the last of them filed out, Ant gazed at Lyn. Their glance held a conversation of its own—a shared relief that Stanton Parva could breathe again, freed from the choking grip of fear and suspicion.

Lyn's eyes sparkled in the fading light; her hands clasped in front of her as if holding onto the moment. Ant's lips curved into a smile that reached all the way to his warm, dark eyes, reflecting a partnership strengthened by adversity.

Together, they stepped outside, the cool evening air washing over them with the promise of peace. Acre mill stood soundless in the background, a sign of continuity and the enduring spirit of the village they both loved.

'Some adventure,' Ant murmured, his voice tinged with the fatigue of a long day.

'Yup,' Lyn replied, her tone matching his.

They shared a quiet embrace. 'We did it, together.' And as the sun dipped below the horizon, casting a golden glow over the fields of Stanton Parva.

As the last of the squad cars vanished into the dusky embrace of Stanton Parva's narrow lanes, Ant took Lyn's hand and led her away from the barn. The gravel crunched underfoot, a soothing melody to their frayed nerves. In the distance, the village settled into its evening routine, lights twinkling in chocolate-box cottages while the scent of wood smoke whispered promises of hearth and home.

'Imagine,' Ant said with an air of whimsy, 'just a few days ago, we were planning floral arrangements and canape selections for our wedding.'

Lyn chuckled; the sound as clear as the stream that

meandered through the landscape. 'And now? We're wrapping up murder investigations. Talk about a detour.'

'Ah, but think of the stories we'll tell our children and their kids,' he mused.

'Grandchildren?' Lyn raised an eyebrow playfully. 'That's presumptuous, Viscount Stanton. We haven't even got ourselves down the aisle yet.'

'True,' Ant conceded, his thumb tracing circles on the back of her hand. 'But after all this, I'd say we make a great team, don't you?'

'Indubitably,' she agreed, borrowing a term from their favourite detective novels.

They paused beneath a mature oak, its branches stretching protectively above them. The sky, a canvas splashed with hues of orange and purple, framed their moment, a calming balm to the end of a tumultuous investigation.

Epilogue

ANT AND LYN spent the late evening with his parents at Stanton Hall. After a delicious dinner, Ant looked at his father. 'You know, the only thing that's puzzling me about the case is that chap, Simon Broadbent. That's if it's his real name. He's the one I told you about who gate-crashed our table in the Wherry Arms on Lyn's birthday. And call me paranoid, but he had tabs on us throughout this case. You know, sort of watching from a distance.'

'And that worries you?' the earl responded.

Ant looked at Lyn. 'It's just that Whitaker mentioned nothing about following us. He had plenty to say about other things, but not that. The thing is, he knew a lot about Lyn and me. Spooky, really.'

He caught a furtive glance that passed between his parents. 'Is there something you're not telling me?'

'Don't be silly,' Lyn said as she attempted to divert her fiance.

A second glance shot between his parents. His mother gave the earl an imperceptible nod.

'What is it, Dad?' Ant asked.

The earl hesitated for several seconds, dabbing his mouth with a napkin as if buying time.

'Simon Broadbent is Lieutenant Colonel Sir Simon Broadbent of the Army Intelligence Corps.'

Ant looked stunned, while Lyn gave the earl a confused glance.

'I don't understand,' Lyn said.

'I do,' Ant began. 'They want me back, don't they? Let me guess, he came to see you two, or you wouldn't have known what I was talking about. Why didn't you tell me, Dad?'

Once again, his parents exchanged glances.

'I told your father to tell you. Instead, he worried the news might trigger your PTSD. You've guessed correctly that they want you back. Something about a mission few intelligence officers have the skills for. However, you are one of them.'

Ant's demeanour hardened. 'I get it. They wanted to see how I handled myself. But how did they know about the ca...oh, I get it? The eyes and ears they have on the ground told them. If only the public knew they'd be—'

'Terrified,' the earl said, cutting across his son.

'Oh, I get it?' Lyn began. 'So, Mr Broadbent was the one who almost ran us over?'

Ant reached over to hold her hand. 'Now that I know what I know, Broadbent was having a bit of fun at our expense. He'll have been trying to spook me. You know, building up my stress levels to see how I'd react over the following days.'

The room fell into an awkward silence. Eventually, the countess spoke.

'I told Broadbent to get stuffed.'

The earl spat his coffee out. David, the butler, almost tripped up as he cleared the table, while Ant and Lyn broke out into spontaneous laughter.

'Mother,' started Ant. 'I've never heard you use that term before!'

'Me neither,' the earl added as he dabbed coffee stains off his dinner jacket.

'Bravo,' offered Lyn.

The countess smiled like a Cheshire cat. 'I told him to leave you alone since you'd left all that behind you and were about to marry. I added that if he didn't like it, I'd take the matter up with the Prime Minister. That shut him up.'

'You know the PM?' Lyn asked.

'Well, I know the family. His mother and I are old friends, and that boy always does what his mother tells him to do.'

Lyn shook her head in disbelief before all four broke out in raucous laughter.

'Talking about marriage, it's about time you settled on a date, isn't it?' Ant's mother quipped.

Without hesitation Lyn quipped, 'Late summer.'

'Goodness,' the earl commented. 'You don't muck about, do you?' His features lit up at the prospect of finally seeing his only son married to a woman they'd known and loved forever.

'Well,' Lyn began. 'It'll take some doing to get everything organised, but we can do it if we get a move on.

'Do I get any say on the matter?' Ant protested in a half-hearted fashion.

'No, not really,' Lyn replied with a bewitching smile.

'What about a date then?' the countess asked, a hint of eagerness in her tone.

Lyn called up the calendar on her mobile and swiped the screen until it rested on September.

'The 6th will do nicely. That's the first Saturday of the month, so the weather should be kind to us, if we're lucky.'

'Let's do it,' Ant replied. That's if Fitch ever finishes tuning the engine on my Morgan.'

'Dream on, Anthony Stanton. If you think I'm going to get into that leaky shoebox in my wedding dress, you can think again. Oh, by the way, talking of things falling to bits. I've arranged a dentist appointment for you next Wednesday.'

'What?'

'I told you the other day that if you didn't, I would. So I have. You've been pulling faces and holding your jaw since we found that poor man in the field.'

Ant's parents looked on with an amused smile as their son gave Lyn a begrudging nod of acceptance.

That settled, and with their hands entwined, they looked at Ant's parents with tenderness. All four took a stroll in the night air to drink in the joyful news, each couple hand in hand.

And as the night drew its curtain around them, the stars seemed to glow with approval, winking down at two people who'd weathered many storms together, ready now to embark on life's greatest adventure.

vinci-books.com/murderrsvp

A sinister wedding day threat: "Murder, RSVP." Will the bride and groom survive their vows?

Ant and Lyn's wedding plans are shattered by a chilling message: "Murder, RSVP." Racing against time, they must uncover the truth behind the threat before their special day ends in tragedy.

Turn the page for a free preview…

Murder RSVP: Chapter One

AN INVITATION

Wednesday, 3rd September: 10.00 am

Amid the sweet scent of peonies, Lyn Blackthorn's laughter floated through the air. She delighted in tying another pastel ribbon around the oak banisters of Stanton Hall, the ancestral home of her husband to be, Anthony Stanton. Lyn effortlessly moved around ladders and tables filled with wedding items, her shoulder-length blond hair tied back in a messy bun.

'Ant, do you think we've got enough bunting?' Lyn called out, her voice bright with excitement. She stood on tiptoes to adjust a stubborn floral arrangement, her 5' 6' frame stretched to its limit.

'Enough to wrap around Stanton Hall twice over,' Ant replied with an affectionate chuckle, his hands occupied with a tangle of fairy lights. The anticipation for their big day shone in his eyes like the mid-morning sun glinting off the nearby broad.

Just then, the grand doors of the Great Hall creaked

open, and in sauntered the Earl and Countess Stanton like a gentle summer breeze. The Earl, tall and erect at 6'1', despite the ravages of age and ailments, shared a warm, easy-going smile with the couple.

'Dad, you look the bee's knees!' Ant said, noticing the crisp lines of his father's morning suit, a blend of timeless tradition and modern style.

'Only trying to match the splendour of what's being created here,' the earl said. He gestured to the festoons of decorations and transforming the enormous room.

The countess approached Lyn gracefully and with a warm smile. 'My dear, everything looks positively enchanting,' she said, her sharp mind already noting every detail laid out before her.

'Aw, thank you. It wouldn't have been possible without your guidance,' Lyn replied. Her laid back nature blended seamlessly with her surroundings. She knew that the support from Ant's parents was unwavering, as it was loving.

'Now, dear Lyn. Don't you think it's time you called me mum?' Her tone carried the wisdom of her years mixed with genuine affection.

'Then it must be dad for me,' the earl chimed in. He placed a hand on Ant's shoulder, conveying a father's pride and a sense of deep love to the young couple.

'Mum, Dad,' Lyn corrected herself, her cheeks tinged with colour.

As they turned to admire a display of wedding favours, the wind outside picked up, playfully tossing leaves against the windows. It seemed to serve as a reminder of the ever-present dance between change and the steadfast nature of tradition. Inside Stanton Hall, the promise of new beginnings filled the air, mingling with the laughter and chatter of the wedding preparations.

'Can you believe it?' Ant mused, his arm slipping around Lyn's waist. 'On Saturday, all this will come alive with friends and family.'

'As you say,' the earl agreed, his gaze drifting nostalgically around the ancient hall. 'And our little slice of history welcoming your future together.'

'Here's to the bride and groom,' the countess raised an imaginary glass, her eyes twinkling, 'And to traditions that stand the test of time.'

They immersed themselves once more in the joyous task at hand, unaware of the danger that would soon cast itself over their idyllic preparations.

———

Wednesday, 3rd September: 2.00 pm

The amber glow of the Wherry Arms pub enveloped Ant, Lyn, and their longtime friend, Fitch. As usual, they occupied their favourite corner of the village hostelry. Outside, the breeze toyed with the thatched roof, a playful whisper against the sturdy walls of the centuries-old establishment.

'Ah, nothing like a drink with mates after a day of wedding madness,' Lyn sighed contentedly, her blond hair catching the dim lighting in soft waves.

'I agree,' Ant replied, his eyes alight with mirth as he watched the popular pub fill with locals. 'Imagine, in four days' time, you'll officially become a Lady of the Manor.'

Fitch chuckled, raising his pint in a toast. 'To Viscount Anthony and Viscountess Stanton. May your reign be long and filled with fewer surprises than your sleuthing days brought you.'

Lyn laughed, her temperament shining through even as

she pondered their future. 'I'll settle for a quiet first week before we dive into our roles. The last thing we need is the village thinking we're bringing a whirlwind of change on our very first day. As for the sleuthing, those days are behind us now.'

'Change is good,' Ant countered gently, his gaze fond as he considered his bride-to-be. 'Besides, if anyone can win over the village, it's you. Headteacher and now Lady of the Hall; you've got quite the fan club.'

'Speaking of change,' Fitch interjected, 'have you given any more thought to those renovations at the hall you mentioned a couple of months ago?'

'Slowly but surely,' Ant nodded. 'We want to respect the past, yet there's no denying the allure of central heating on a frosty morning.'

'Or reliable Wi-Fi,' Lyn added with a smile. 'Imagine your dad trying to stream his favourite historical documentaries with the current setup. It'd be easier to summon the spirits of his ancestors for a live reenactment.'

They shared a chuckle, the trio all too aware of the earl's endearing struggles with technology.

'Still,' Ant mused, the humour fading from his voice as a shadow of concern crossed his features, 'We have to tread carefully. The Hall is grade two listed, so we can't so much as knock a nail in without council approval.'

'Ah, but that's where you excel, my friend,' Fitch said reassuringly. 'You'll navigate those choppy waters with the grace of an old sea captain.'

'I'm more focused on not tripping over my dress on Saturday than the intricacies of listed building planning permissions,' Lyn added with a giggle.

'Here's to not tripping, then,' Fitch raised his glass again, an impish twinkle in his eye.'

'Cheers to that,' Ant echoed, clinking his glass against the others. 'Now, let's enjoy this calm before the storm of festivities on Saturday, shall we?'

'Agreed,' Lyn smiled.'

As the playful banter between lifelong friends continued, Jed, the landlord, picked his way through a crowded bar towards the merry trio. He carried twin envelopes of creamy vellum. The Wherry Arms, a haven of oak beams and laughter, had seen its share of mysteries, but none so curious as the missives now carried across its worn stone flagstones.

'Ant, Lyn,' Jed called out, 'Seems you've got mail.'

Lyn's eyes lifted from her half-finished pint of lemonade, curiosity piquing her lips into a tentative smile. Ant turned, a spark of intrigue lighting the depths of his ocean-blue eyes.

'Post?' Lyn quipped; head tilted. 'Who'd be sending us letters here, I wonder?'

'I didn't get a proper look at the lad,' Jed replied, setting the envelopes on the small, round table. His voice, usually a jovial bellow, dipped into a hushed tone, as though the paper demanded reverence. 'He left them on the bar then scarpered before I could say boo.'

Ant reached for the envelopes, fingers brushing against the thick paper. A seal pressed into the wax caught his eye— a symbol unrecognisable, neither family crest nor familiar motif. He exchanged a glance with Lyn, their shared excitement tinged with uncertainty.

'Odd, isn't it?' Lyn said, her easy-going nature wrestling with the wariness that crept up her spine. 'To receive invitations, isn't it? And without a face to attach them to.'

'Invitations or otherwise,' Ant said, thumbing the edge of one envelope, 'it's the timing that has me puzzled. Four days before our wedding, and here we are, about to open two curious invitations.'

'Perhaps they're just late in replying,' Fitch chimed in, ever the beacon of optimism. 'A straggler hoping for a seat at the feast?'

'Or a late gift, wrapped in secrecy,' said Lyn confidently, yet her hand hesitated to break the seal.

'Either way, it seems we're to be the stars in our own little English mystery.' Ant's attempt at humour didn't quite mask the undercurrent of tension. The wind outside picked up, rattling the windows as if to underscore the drama within.

'Then let's not keep our audience waiting.' Lyn drew a deep breath, her decision made, her gaze meeting Ant's with resolute clarity. With careful fingers, she pried open the first envelope, the sound of tearing paper echoing like a muted prelude to the unknown.

'Steady on,' Ant murmured, a protective edge to his voice as he echoed Lyn's actions with the second envelope. His former service in the military had attuned him to danger.

They opened the envelope together, their faces showing a mix of curiosity and nervousness.

'Let's see what secrets these whispers carry,' Lyn said bravely. Her pulse quickened, the anticipation building a suspenseful pause in the cozy haven of the pub.

Lyn's fingers paused as she unfolded the parchment. The ancient wisp of paper that seemed at odds with the jovial clinking of pint glasses and the low murmur of conversation around them. Ant watched, his own invitation lying flat against the dark wood of the table, a silent spectre amidst the warm glow of the pub.

'Heavens,' Lyn exclaimed, her voice a ghostly thread in

the suddenly still air. The invitation carried no festive news, no joyful summons to friends and family. Instead, a ghastly depiction of Stanton Hall, etched in ink so black it leeched warmth from the room.

'Read it aloud,' Ant urged, though the unease in his voice betrayed his military calm.

'At the stroke of twelve, on the day of your wedded bliss, expect not a kiss... but the icy embrace of the abyss,' Lyn recited. Her words fell heavily in the silence. An involuntary shudder coursed through her body.

Ant lifted his gaze from his own card, mirroring Lyn's shock. He depicted the same haunting scene, but the message was different, yet equally menacing. "When the bells toll for thee, let the village be witness to what cannot be."

A cold draught filled the pub as if on cue, sending a chill through the hostelry. It was as though the very elements conspired to underscore the dread of the moment.

'Who would send such a horrible thing?' Lyn's sharp brain wrestled with the puzzle, even as her heart raced with foreboding. Her eyes, usually so full of resolve, now flickered with the flame of concern.

'Someone with a taste for the dramatic, or...' Ant's words trailed off, his thoughts unspoken yet hanging heavy between them. The easy-going laughter and banter of the Wherry Arms felt worlds away, replaced by a tangible concern that pressed in upon their shoulders.

'Or someone who means to do us harm,' Lyn finished for him, the gravity of the situation settling upon her like a mantle. The Earl and Countess Stanton had been nothing but supportive, enveloping them in the fabric of tradition and community. Yet here they were, the future Lord and

Lady Stanton, targets of a threat that seemed ripped from the pages of a gothic novel.

'Let's not jump to conclusions.' Ant attempted to rally, though the effort seemed Herculean, as he tucked the invitation back into its envelope. 'We'll figure this out.'

'I hope so.' Lyn's voice was steely now, her determination clear. The envelope crinkled in her grip as if echoing her resolve.

Ant and Lyn sat in shock, regularly glancing at the poison post. The mystery that had landed in their laps promised a path that would lead them through imagined and real dangers in the coming days.

'Peter, we need you,' Lyn's voice was firm as she dialled their police friend's number, the urgency clear in her tone. Ant nodded his support from across the table.

'Trouble at t'mill?' came Peter Riley's joking response, a throwback to old detective serials they all enjoyed. But his levity quickly faded under the gravity of Lyn's voice.

'More like trouble with a capital 'T',' Lyn said. 'We've received an unsettling invitation...'

'Alright, give me half an hour.' There was the sound of rustling, a testament to Peter's readiness to leap into action, even after hours. 'I'll be with you soon.'

'Thank you, Peter.' Lyn ended the call, but her eyes stayed on the phone, as if willing it to bring them immediate answers.

Ant tried to chuckle; a hollow sound that got lost in the pub's hubbub. 'That man could find a needle in a haystack even if the haystack was on fire.'

'Something tells me he'll need to be on form to sort this out for us,' Lyn replied, reaching out to squeeze Ant's hand. The touch meant to comfort, but Ant flinched, an involuntary reaction that didn't go unnoticed by Lyn.

'Hey, you, okay?' Her concern etched in the lines around her eyes.

'Fine,' Ant lied, trying to staple a smile onto his face. His gaze drifted to the window, where the wind played a mournful tune as it whirled around ancient structures. This was a tune he understood.

'Ant...' Lyn started, but he stood abruptly, the legs of the chair scraping against the stone floor like a distress signal.

'I need some air,' he murmured and pushed his way past the other patrons, their curious eyes tracking his retreat.

Outside, the clean Norfolk air hit his lungs, but it did little to ease the tightness in his chest. He leaned against the pub's red brick wall, the rough texture grounding him to the present. Somewhere in the mid-distance, a dog barked, a mundane sound that should have been reassuring.

'Damn it,' Ant whispered, pressing his palms against his eyelids. Memories he'd fought hard to contain chose this moment to surge forward—a cacophony of sounds and sights from days he wished remained forgotten.

'Deep breaths,' he coached himself, the words a mantra against the encroaching panic. 'In and out, just like Dr Thorndike taught you.'

'Talking to oneself now, are we?' The earl's voice, deep and steady, emerged from the shadows. Ant hadn't noticed his approach, but there he stood, a figure of unwavering support.

'Old habits,' Ant joked weakly, meeting his father's parental gaze.

'Let's walk a bit,' the earl suggested, offering his arm in a gesture that was both respectful and protective. Together, they paced slowly along the cobblestone path of High Street, the rhythm of their steps a gentle counterpoint to Ant's racing heart.

'What's up?' the Earl asked, his voice carrying his experience. 'Come on, get it off your chest. You know what happens when you keep things bottled up.'

Ant briefed his father on recent events, then made a heartfelt admission. 'I wish people didn't assume I'm the strong one,' Ant admitted, his humour failing to mask the truth of his words.

'Strength isn't about never falling down, Anthony,' the earl replied sagely. 'It's about who's there to help you up when you do.'

'Speaking of help, didn't you say the inspector will arrive soon? A good man, that one,' the earl said. 'And don't you worry, we'll sort this mess out before you can say 'wedding cake."

'Here's hoping,' Ant responded, allowing a genuine smile to cross his features for the first time since opening the envelope.

'Come on, let's head back inside,' the earl urged gently. 'We can't have the groom catching a chill before the big day.'

'Nor the bride thinking I've bolted,' Ant added, finding humour despite the darkness that loomed over the wedding.

They returned to the pub, ready to confront whatever challenges lay ahead.

Ant's hand was a tremor as he fumbled with his pint of Fen Bodger Pale Ale. The glass had a life of its own, mirroring the ghosts of doubt that had taken residence in his mind since the envelopes arrived.

'Potential suspects?' Lyn mused aloud; her tone was deceptively casual as she leaned back in her chair. 'It could be anyone harbouring a grudge. Or someone who simply thrives on causing chaos.'

'Or perhaps someone with a vendetta against the Stanton's?' Ant suggested, his voice low. 'The wedding is the talk of the village.'

The earl, who had been quietly observing from his chair, gave a slow nod. 'We can't rule out the possibility that this is an attack on what the family represents. Loyalty to the village, to each other—'

'Exactly, Dad.' Ant's eyes were steely now, the initial shock giving way to resolve. 'We ought to find out who's behind this before they try to do more than just scare us.'

'Peter will have his work cut out,' Lyn added.

'Speaking of which—' The earl fell silent as the pub door opened, allowing a breeze to slip through the bar, carrying whispers of encroaching autumn.

Detective Inspector Peter Riley stepped into the pub, the understated authority in his stride belying the urgency of his visit. He cast a quick glance at the foursome before speaking. 'I got here as soon as I could. Let's see these invitations, then.'

'They're grim,' Lyn warned, passing the envelope with a steady hand.

Peter's eyes scanned the contents, his expression unreadable. 'We'll need to move quickly. Someone wants to throw a spanner into your plans, and we can't let them succeed.' His words carried a promise to solve the case.

'Thanks, Peter,' Ant said, gratitude warming his voice. 'We're counting on you.'

'It could be an insider,' mused Fitch, the village garage owner, his thickset frame making for a powerful presence.

'Or someone who feeds off old rivalries,' Lyn responded, her teacher's mind categorising and assessing. 'Someone who never forgave or forgot.'

'Let's not jump to conclusions,' Peter cautioned. 'We'll consider every angle. Just remember, conjecture won't solve this. Evidence will.'

'Time is of the essence, though,' the earl said, a touch of steel beneath his calm exterior. 'We must act swiftly to ensure the safety of these two, or indeed, anyone who might impede this obnoxious individual.'

'Agreed,' Peter affirmed. 'We have until the wedding to unravel this lot. My gut feeling is this is more than mischief. It carries all the hallmarks of malice.'

As the afternoon wore on, the small gathering felt the menace of an unseen adversary. Yet amidst the brewing storm, their unity was as unyielding as the ancient walls that sheltered them—walls that had withstood countless trials.

Ant drummed his fingers on the wooden table as a rhythmic counterpoint to Lyn's reassuring pat on his hand. 'We won't let some cowardly letters push us around,' she declared with a chin-up defiance that could rally an army— or at least a roomful of concerned villagers.

'Quite right,' Ant's father chimed in, his voice steady. 'The Stanton blood isn't known for cowering. We face storms head-on.'

'Speaking of which,' Peter Riley said, flashing a smile that was equal parts reassurance and mischief. 'We'll crack this before you can say 'I do.' Though I'd prefer not to have any unscheduled 'adventures' interrupting the nuptials.'

'Adventures?' Lyn quirked an eyebrow. 'Is that what we're calling threats these days?'

'Only the ones that come with RSVPs,' Peter replied, winking at her.

'Goodness, no sense in letting the blighters think they've got us rattled,' the earl said. 'Besides, Lyn would have my hide should my darling boy show up looking anything less than dapper on his wedding day.'

'True,' Lyn agreed, a playful glint in her eye. 'Can't have the groom outshone by the flower arrangements.'

'Or by Fitch's top hat,' the earl added dryly, eliciting chuckles all around.

'Let's not forget, there's more to this than bravado,' Peter interjected, leaning forward. 'This isn't just about being stoical; it's about keeping you two safe and catching whoever is behind this.'

'Which means we need a solid plan,' Lyn said, her voice taking on the commanding tone she used when organising school events. 'Peter, you'll chase down leads. Ant, you'll focus on keeping Stanton Hall running, so there are no hiccups for the wedding. And I'll make sure the community doesn't panic.'

'Teamwork,' Ant nodded.

'Right, then.' Peter stood, the transition from banter to action seamless. 'I'll have a chat with Jed. I'll get him to go over things again. It's amazing what people remember once they put their mind to it.'

Amidst pub chatter and howling wind, they echoed—a reminder of unwavering bonds.

Ant gave the heavy parchment of the invitation another look, the gold-embossed lettering mocking him with its twisted elegance. He attempted to chuckle, but it turned into a strangled gasp.

'Who'd have thought getting married would drop us into a plot thick enough for Agatha Christie herself?' Lyn jested.

'Modern-day England, where you expect rain on your wedding day, not... this.' Ant flicked the corner of the paper as if it would somehow make the words less ominous. 'An 'exclusive' event, they call it.'

'Exclusive as in 'by invitation only' rarely implies a threat,' Lyn replied dryly, her usual buoyant spirit dimmed by the unwanted invitation.

'Perhaps it's someone's idea of a sick joke?' Ant suggested. Lyn's demeanour illustrated she was far from convinced.

'Jokes are funny. This has the chill of the Phantom Coach of Potter Heigham,' she said, struggling against the tide of concern.

'Right. Ghosts, misty threats, and all we're missing is a hound baying,' Ant remarked, trying to lighten the mood. His attempt at humour seemed to dissipate like breath in the frigid air outside the Wherry Arms pub.

'Let's not borrow trouble from tomorrow,' Lyn responded. 'We've got Peter on it, and he's worth his weight in gold, or should that be in detective novels?'

'True. Though I wish some things stayed within the pages of books,' Ant conceded, stroking his chin thoughtfully. 'I'd rather deal with a bad-tempered flock of sheep any day.'

'Or unruly schoolchildren,' Lyn added, her mouth twitching upward. 'They're far less cryptic than whatever game this is.'

'Game or not, we won't let it spoil our day,' Ant said, the resolve in his voice steadier now. 'Dad's right about tradition and resilience.'

Ant glanced at the time on his mobile home screen, then stood. 'Let's head back to yours for an hour to do some thinking,' Ant suggested to Lyn. 'Then we'll have to get back to the Hall, because it won't prepare itself for our wedding.'

'Nor fend off mystery invitations,' Lyn quipped, rising to join him. They walked arm in arm, finding comfort in their shared experiences.

As they stepped outside, the wind howled around them with renewed vigour. It was as if nature itself was whispering of changes on the horizon, of ancient traditions and new vows entwined with questions that begged answers.

Murder RSVP: Chapter Two

TEA AND QUESTIONS

Wednesday, 3rd September: 4.00 pm

Ant and Lyn sat opposite each other at the worn pine kitchen table of the Old Schoolhouse, a bastion of stability in an otherwise uncertain afternoon. The air was still, and the dim light struggled to fully illuminate the puzzling scene before them. Two cream-coloured envelopes, each bearing their names in an elegant, sweeping script, spread out like a bad hand in a game of poker.

'Curious,' Lyn murmured, her normally light-hearted tone edged with unease. Her fingers hovered over the invitations but refrained from touching them, as though they might bite.

Ant reached for the invitation addressed to him. His hands betrayed a faint tremble that belied his calm facade. The manifestation did not escape Lyn's observant gaze.

'Ant, darling,' she said softly, concern etching her brow, 'Are you alright?'

'Of course,' Ant replied, though the tremor in his voice

suggested otherwise. He chuckled, but it was hollow, nothing like his usual warm baritone. 'Just the weather playing tricks on my nerves,' he lied, nodding towards the window where the leaves outside barely stirred.

'Antony Stanton, I know windblown leaves when I see them, and I know you.' Lyn's eyes locked onto his, her expression firm, yet filled with empathy. 'PTSD flaring up?'

'Perhaps a touch,' he admitted, setting the invitation down as if it weighed far more than paper should. 'But I'll manage, Lyn. I always do.'

'Managing isn't living,' she countered gently, reaching across to still his restless hands with her own. 'You don't have to go back to your military doctor if you're uncomfortable with him. What about Dr Thorndike? He was brilliant with you last time.'

'Dr Thorndike,' Ant repeated pensively, as if tasting the idea. 'Yes, I suppose I could... I'll think about it.'

'Don't just think, Ant,' Lyn said, squeezing his hands reassuringly. 'Promise me you won't just smile and soldier on.'

'Smile and carry on,' he mused, a ghost of his usual humour flickering in his eyes. 'Isn't that the English way?'

'Perhaps,' Lyn conceded, a playful glint in her own eye. 'But sometimes even the English must admit when it's time to ask for help.'

'Very well,' Ant replied. 'I promise I'll contact the doc.'

'Thank you,' Lyn said, her smile genuine as she released his hands. 'Now, let's figure out who sent these blasted invitations before whoever sent them gets too close. I'm having no one ruin my wedding day.'

Doggedly renewing their spirits, Ant, and Lyn leaned in, heads together, ready to face the tempest ahead.

Lyn's laughter was a gentle breeze through the tension

that hung in the kitchen, dispersing it like autumn leaves. 'Once we sort all this unpleasantness,' she said with a twinkle in her eye, 'We'll have our wedding, and then New Zealand awaits.'

'New Zealand?' Ant quirked an eyebrow, momentarily distracted from the ominous invitations. 'With its serene lakes and those towering mountains?'

'Exactly,' Lyn nodded, leaning back in her chair, her blond hair catching the late afternoon light. 'We can leave all this behind us. Remember, we're retiring from our amateur sleuthing, so when we get back, a new life lies ahead for us.'

'Retiring?' Ant snorted, picking at the edge of the invitation as if trying to peel away the mystery. 'Except for this last hurrah where some bonkers bloke is trying to see us off before we can cut the cake.'

'Stress-free, isn't it?' she chuckled, shaking her head.

A firm knock on the front door punctuated their shared moment of levity. They exchanged a glance, the warmth of their mirth replaced by uncertainty. Who could that be?

'Stay here,' Lyn murmured, a protective edge to her voice as she stood up, but Ant was already on his feet.

'Four fists are better than two if it's our mystery bloke,' he replied, his tone light but resolute. Together, they navigated the narrow hallway toward answers that awaited them beyond the heavy wooden door.

Ant's hand brushed Lyn's as he reached for the Yale lock, a silent pulse of understanding passing between them. The door swung open to reveal Detective Inspector Peter Riley, his familiar face creased with ill-disguised concern.

'Peter!' Lyn exclaimed; her voice threaded with palpable relief. 'Thank goodness it's you.'

'Come in, come in,' Ant said, stepping aside, an

unspoken understanding warming his eyes as they met Peter's.

'Sorry to drop by unannounced,' Peter began, his tone apologetic, but the urgency in his movements belied any genuine regret as he crossed the threshold. He slipped off his coat, hanging it on the aged brass hook by the door—a minor act that echoed countless visits before.

'Unannounced is the least of our worries,' Lyn replied, leading the way to the kitchen.

Their steps were brisk, a counterpoint to the drone of the kettle beginning its chorus anew. The kitchen, usually a bastion of hearty meals and laughter, now held a taut silence, the air charged with a sense of foreboding.

Peter entered the kitchen, taking in the scene—the invitations on the table, Ant's trembling hands, inviting him to join their council.

'Looks like I've stumbled into a tempest,' Peter said, settling into the seat with the ease of a seasoned officer.

'More like a hurricane,' Ant quipped, attempting to slice through the tension with a hint of humour. 'But not the kind you can track on a weather map.'

'Indeed,' Peter acknowledged, his deep-set eyes reflecting a well of determination. 'Let's see if we can't make sense of this latest gust.'

In the cosy confines of Lyn's kitchen, with the wind whispering secrets to the windowpanes and the steadfast presence of their trusted friend, Ant, and Lyn felt the flicker of hope. Together, they would withstand this tempest.

'Peter, we've been over it a thousand times,' Lyn said, the skin around her eyes tightened with concern. 'It's as if our wedding guest list has sprouted fangs overnight.'

'Spot on,' Ant added, his voice steady but his fingers betraying a serious health problem as they rested unsteadily on the tabletop. 'Someone knows about Saturday, and they're not sending well-wishes.'

'Curious that they should choose now to strike,' Peter mused, steepling his fingers beneath his chin. 'A time of celebration turned into something... ominous.'

'Whoever it is,' Lyn pressed on, 'they've done their homework on us.'

'Quite the puzzle,' Peter conceded, his mouth tipping downward slightly. 'But I assure you both—'

He paused, locking eyes with them, his commitment tangible.

'—I'll do everything within my power to unravel the mystery. Protecting you is more than duty; it's a promise. Speaking of which,' he continued, leaning forward slightly, 'We've canvassed the area for that young lad Jed chanced upon. And the landlord's memory proved sharper than we thought. Gave us a few threads to pull at.'

'Jed's a sharp one,' Ant acknowledged with a smile, the lines of worry around his eyes softening. 'I've always said he'd make a better detective than half the blokes down at the station.'

Peter agreed, his lips twitching upwards. 'Let's hope those threads lead us somewhere less tangled than Phyllis's latest yarns about the earl's rose bushes.'

'Or her theories on global warming,' Lyn chimed in, the tension easing from her shoulders as she shared a conspiratorial grin with the two men.

Peter chuckled. 'Now, let's get started on untangling this knot before it tightens any further. Time and tide and all that.'

Ant's hand rested on his invitation, his fingers tracing the embossed lettering again, as if he could draw out the sender's identity through touch. Lyn reached across the table, her hand covering his—a silent sign of togetherness in their shared turmoil. Ant acknowledged his fiance's loving gesture. Then he turned his attention back to the envelope. 'I don't recognise the cypher. It doesn't belong to any of the families we know of. I spent hours in the archive room at the Hall. Nothing in Debrett's, or any of the other reference books I looked up. This must just be a made-up design that purports to represent...and forgive me for sounding pompous, a noble family.'

Peter inspected the coat of arms on the wax seal, broken in two, when Ant and Lyn opened the envelopes. 'I'm happy to believe what you say. You move around in these circles, I don't.'

Peter's comment didn't take a rise out of Ant. His comment was born of a well-established friendship with the pair.

'Peter,' Ant began, his voice steady with an undercurrent of emotion, 'we can't thank you enough. Having you—'

'With us,' Lyn concluded. Her gaze meeting Riley's with a depth of trust that was earned over countless investigations and social contact.

'Stop it, you'll have me blushing next,' Peter replied. 'You've got my word on it. I'm in this with you to the end.'

'Thank goodness,' Lyn said with a half-smile. 'We're rather fond of having you around, especially when there's a rogue element trying to spoil the happiest day of our lives.'

'Rogue element seems about right,' Ant mused, leaning back in his chair. 'But who? That's the million-pound question, isn't it?'

'Indeed.' Peter pulled out a small leather-bound notepad from his jacket pocket, flipping it open with a practised motion. 'Now, let's hash this out. Any ideas who could be behind this? Old grudges, perhaps? Or someone with a vendetta against you getting married?'

'Could be anyone with a bone to pick,' Lyn said, tapping a finger against her chin. 'Remember Ian Lister? The disgraced Police Commander? He's always had it in for us since we had him put away for trying to set someone else up for a crime he committed.'

'Desperation leads people to dramatic measures,' Peter pointed out, scribbling notes. 'When I worked for him in Kent, he could be incredibly kind to his staff. Then, without warning, he'd change into something resembling a tyrant. You remember how he treated me when he came here to take over the investigation I'd begun? He was determined to have his way. Ruthless, some might say.'

'Then there's Phyllis,' Lyn suggested, albeit hesitantly. 'I know, from the sublime to the ridiculous. She's been quite vocal about the 'decline of traditional village values.' Maybe she sees our modern take on the wedding as a step too far?'

'Phyllis?' Ant chuckled, despite the seriousness of the conversation. 'I doubt she'd go beyond tutting disapprovingly over her garden fence, while ordering her mate, Betty, to carry on digging the flower beds.'

'Still,' Peter interjected, 'no stone unturned, right? We'll investigate Lister and monitor Phyllis, just in case.'

'Speaking of stones,' Ant added, 'What about Roger Arbuthnot? He's been acting odd lately. Though I can't imagine him being involved in something so sordid.'

'He's harmless,' Lyn countered. 'And he adores you, Ant. He wouldn't jeopardise the wedding.'

'Hm...I suppose you're right. This sort of things makes you jump at shadows,' Ant conceded with a sigh. 'I guess we should also consider the possibility of an outsider, someone not tied to the village's way of doing things.'

Lyn giggled, 'What? You mean like murder?'

'You've been watching too much Midsomer Murder on the telly,' Ant replied, thankful for a moment of mirth.

'An interloper amidst our tight-knit community,' Peter said thoughtfully, closing his notepad with a snap. 'A modern-day marauder clashing with the old-world charm of our hamlet.'

'You've got it,' Lyn said, a determined glint in her eye. 'We find this person, and we ensure the wedding goes ahead without a hitch,' Lyn replied.

'Gotcha,' Ant replied.

'Then it's settled,' Peter concluded. First, we'll review Jed's statement, then check if Lister knows any of the people he's associated with. Finally, we'll monitor the activity in the village. Nothing escapes the collective gaze of our residents for long.'

'Let's hope not,' Lyn said, rising from her seat. 'Because come Saturday, rain, or shine, wind or calm, we're getting married.'

Grab your copy...

vinci-books.com/murderrsvp

About the Author

Keith lives in, and writes about, the evocative county of Norfolk, England.

"I've had an interesting working life, from selling ice cream to teaching management studies on cruise ships," says Keith.

Having started in the construction and furniture-making industries, Keith spent the final twenty years of his career lecturing in further and higher education, eventually becoming Assistant Principal in a large Norfolk college. Now happily retired, Keith spends his time writing mystery stories and making a nuisance of himself at home and with his grandchildren.

Acknowledgments

A special thank you to Peter R, Jo W, and Mike D, without who *The Lavender Killer* would not have made it to publication.